For Wally Ritchie

My hockey dad got it right

Orphans of Winter

Special Thanks to:

Maureen Whyte for believing in the story, George Down for tirelessly guiding the tale, S. Gale (Mack) Johnsen of the Toquaht First Nation, member of the Nuu Chah Nulth Tribal Council, for generously sharing Nuu Chah Nulth culture, to Robi Walters for his creative eye, Adrienne Weiss and Allan Briesmaster for their attention to detail, … and to Ande, Josh and Toby for their love and support.

Prologue

He was just ten years old that fateful winter morning, but for the rest of his life Harold Richard would tell anyone who would listen about the encounter. He would recount how he had been banished to the shed by the headmaster to serve yet another penance of piling firewood. He would claim the barn-board door (which he would have normally kicked open and then slammed shut as his last demonstration of rebellion) was already askew, a rather violent growling – which he recognised immediately as the Wolf – coming from inside.

He would be sure to mention how he had tiptoed closer, vainly trying to silence the crunch of an early snowfall beneath his feet. He had instinctively reached for a nearby tree and snapped off a low branch that might serve as a weapon should the creature suddenly bolt from the shadows. He would state that the animal must have sensed his arrival, for she suddenly emerged to stare him through with her cold blank eyes and then, just as suddenly, disappeared back into the dark confines of the shed, almost asking him to follow. He would describe how he had bravely edged over to the door, first just to glance inside the frame, then to tiptoe around the heap of split wood in the middle of the floor.

There on top of a mound of sawdust, he would forever maintain, he simply found them – a pair of leather-booted skates and a talisman carved

from a single piece of fir. It was long and narrow in the shaft, flat and wide
at the end.

~

Harold Richard played in only six games for the Port Alberni Senior
A men's hockey club. Yet in that short time – or perhaps because of it –
his prowess and success had grown legendary. Local talk held that he was
the best the town had ever seen; that he could skate like the wind; long
tireless shifts at full speed, rushing around the outside of defencemen at
will and then racing back just as fleet to his own end of the rink to shoulder an opponent out of the play. They say he played the game powerfully,
stealthily ... like a hunter.

Yet Harold Richard had never hunted a day in his life. He had left his
village when he was seven years old for the residential school in Gold
River. Visits back home were both infrequent and discouraged, as they
were likely to impede the process of "civilisation" by tempting the lad with
his primitive traditions and cumbersome native language. True, some at
the school had worried about the precedent of allowing such a tangible
reward as a pair of skates and a hockey stick to be the consequence of a
student's detention. But the headmaster was a student of hockey. He was
of the opinion that when played with proper discipline and codes of conduct, the sport – much like well-folded laundry, the symmetry of a well-
solved mathematical equation or a dorm full of well-made beds – carried
an implied redeeming Christian civility. Besides ... the game flowed out
of the boy like a birthright. Powerful, swift, and unstoppable by any opposition his own age in the local village, Harold was allowed to try out for a
peewee team in the town of Campbell River. When he turned seventeen he
was offered a chance to play for the Senior A team in Port Alberni.
Although he hadn't yet finished his schooling, he was lured from the headmaster's care by a sizeable donation from the team's sponsor and the pre-
tence that a job cording wood at one of the town's mills awaited him.

~

He had played six games and collected ten points when the news came. Mary Hudson, a fifteen-year-old student back at the Gold River school, was pregnant. After repeated interrogation from the headmaster and his cane, she had finally broken down and confessed the child was Harold's; that he had taken her to the woodshed and told her of the Wolf. Told her how, long ago, his ancestors were chiefs of their village, renowned for their great hunting and whaling skill; how young men in his family would go off to the forest ... alone. There they would seek the spirit of the Wolf and be purged and cleansed by bathing in the icy streams, and by rubbing roots and stone into their skin until it bled.

But the school officials and the representative from Indian Affairs were not interested. They only sought to know if she had gone to the shed on her own or whether he had lured her there. If Harold had held her down. If he had penetrated her by force. Mary Hudson defended her union with Harold to the end. Through weeps and sobs she tried to make them understand why she had to sleep with him. Once Harold's Spirit Quest began – once he left to skate his hockey far away in Port Alberni, he had told her – he would not be able to sleep with anyone. So she had lain with him there, with their coats spread out to protect against the rough sharp edges of wood chips and bark, on his last night at residential school.

To the officials her story made obvious Harold's lack of societal respect and indeed the prevalence of a residual savage pride – even after years of residential schooling. The Indian Affairs officer felt he had no choice but to see that the boy was punished fully under the law.

~

Harold Richard died at the hands of four RCMP officers after resisting arrest on a cold winter night outside the Port Alberni arena.

⌣

Since Mary Hudson's mother had passed away the year before, and since Mary herself was still a minor, it was decided the child would be placed in the care of its paternal grandparents. Harold's mother took special care to say all the right things when the board missionary assigned by Indian Affairs came to interview her. She spoke of raising the baby according to the *Good Book* that the man had brought with him. She was careful not to say "Father" to the man, because he was the type that wore the suits, not the robes, and she had heard they didn't take to one another's business. She promised not to expose the infant boy to drink, nor to slothful ways, though she wasn't too sure what that meant. She made pains to avoid anything that might offend … anything *Nootka*. It would have been so much simpler and easier, she thought many times throughout the encounter, if she could only have told the man how a feed of squirrel had been her son's undoing. How it had been given to him by an unsuspecting sister, when he was just a tiny boy crying for something to eat. How that sister herself grew up to be angry and full of drink. But she stayed her course and custody was granted right after that one and only visit … with the proviso that the boy would be sent to the Gold River Residential School on his seventh birthday as a matter of course. The contingence was made legal when the man returned two weeks later with two pages of writing at the bottom of which he had the woman mark an "x" in lieu of her name.

She called the baby James. It was the name by which the missionary had first introduced himself, and she quite liked the sound of it.

Part One

Chapter One

It was the dead of winter. They had come upon the sedan, inverted and crumpled in a snow bank just west of the turn-off for Deception Bay. Under the barrage of blowing snow and ice, the storm, not satisfied with the havoc it had wrought, had already begun to bury its carnage; drifts were filling in around the tires and undercarriage, up against the door panels.

The younger of the two constables jumped from the squad car and sprinted for the wreckage, yelling back theories to his partner as he went. It was the officer's first winter of duty in Keewatin. His first crash. The sedan must have been surprised by the upcoming bend in the road, he reasoned. It must have lost control on a patch of ice, the left side striking the edge of the rock face that cropped out near the curve and flipped the car right into the unforgiving Canadian Shield that lurked just beyond.

Content to leave the frantic pawing of snow and gravel and the up-close search for inverted organs and minced flesh to his stronger, more enthusiastic partner, the older officer stayed behind to radio for help. Twenty-four winters in northwestern Ontario ... twenty-four winters, each with at least one grizzly accident scene, had long since killed any fascination he had with confronting mortality. And if experience had offered him anything, it had proven that a wider vantage-point often yielded the clearer picture.

He found his eye drawn to the colour of the car rather than its contorted shape. It was a medium brown. It was the colour of Oxford shoes and brief-cases. It was similar to the officer's one and only suit ... the one his wife had bought for him on their thirtieth anniversary. It was the colour of duty and responsibility and family values, with nothing that suggested risk or foolhar-diness or high speeds on tight curves in the middle of a blizzard.

The officer's trance was broken by his partner's return. He was pale and clutched onto his rib-cage as he gasped for breath. There had been one occu-pant, the rookie panted. Male ... Caucasian ... possibly mid to late forties, though the state of his remains made it difficult to determine with any accu-racy. He was soaked in blood. Glass had shattered into his face and eyes, and his limbs were mangled more severely than the chassis around him. The head ... the head appeared to be ... partially severed. It was bad, the constable reported. As bad as you could imagine.

~

Within a few minutes, the older officer had ducked his head under the hood of his parka and strode back down the highway, wading through a cou-ple of snowdrifts that were quickly re-forming from where the nice brown sedan had smashed them down. He counted his strides as he went – keeping a rough running calculation of his distance from the fatality – all the way back to a ribbon of burnt rubber left on a bare patch of pavement kept shel-tered by the rock face on the north side of the road. He bent down to touch the tire deposits and was curious to find some warmth in them. He was now seventy yards back from where the remains of the car lay. Perhaps more. (He'd get his partner to measure precisely, once the lad regained his stomach.) Given the poor visibility and the whiteout conditions, the officer doubted the driver could have even made out the upcoming curve from that distance, let alone be surprised by it. And yet this was where he had slammed on his brakes.

The officer moved from the open pavement to a section of hardpacked snow and ice lying between drifts in the oncoming lane, scraping the sole of his boot along behind him to test for slippage. That's when the idea first struck him, accompanied by a mighty blast of wind and a shiver the length of his spine that had little to do with the cold. He squinted hard through the driving ice and snow – dropping his head now and again from the merciless sting of flying crystals – going over the distances again, from the skid mark to the wreckage; from the toes of his boots to where the road started to bend. Then with a quick shout to his partner, he sprinted for the squad car.

∼

As ranking officer on the scene, he surely didn't show much in the way of an example; abandoning the accident scene before help arrived … leaving his junior out in the middle of a squall to wait without a car or radio back-up. His report would later mention something about immediately discovering traces of a second colour of paint embedded into the accordion folds of the wrecked chassis. But at the time, as he drove away, with the questioning gestures of his partner shrinking in the rear view mirror, all he knew was that a possibility – indeed an instinct he never before realised he possessed – had entered his head so clearly, that in an instant he had no recourse but to believe it to be true.

∼

Stephen Gillis was not a man given to curiosity. He was an uninterested man. An unenthusiastic man. He was one without any reservoir of eager resolve for any pursuits save for those that came naturally, and as such was usually out of sorts with most any surroundings apart from the small and precise boundaries that made his life manageable. The chilled air of an arena. The dank and musty corridors that led from lobby to dressing room, from dressing room to ice. The open highways of Western Canada, their never-ending orange lines dissecting the night just ahead of the high beams on his trusted Ford Taurus. The open road that bound him from one arena to the next, yet still left him the freedom that comforted him the most. The freedom of being nowhere in particular.

Western regional scout for the Toronto Centennials was the job title on his business cards and up until that fateful March night it had accommodated his character beautifully. It afforded him the solitude for which he first and foremost lived. He was uninterested in career advancement, unenthused by the prospect of being moved up to scout the professional ranks themselves, in bigger arenas with brighter lighting, where those dank smells had long since been disinfected away. He did not dream of owning a big home, or a more expensive automobile. His Taurus had been with him since he first took the job, and it served him admirably, connecting the dots on the prairie map – getting him from game to game. (The only stress was a nagging little voice inside his head reminding of his complete lack of knowledge about things mechanical that always tempered his feelings of freedom for the open road with some scenario of a blown head-gasket – whatever that was – on some deserted highway in a blinding snowstorm.)

But more important than a sense of freedom was the fact that scouting – by definition – was a position that demanded nothing beyond a single-minded focus for observing the game itself – which was perfect since Stephen Gillis had no desire to translate the sport into any greater context. In fact, he had no will to explain or justify its importance at all. It needed not be "the business of hockey" as it would be so termed by his superiors – the board of directors, the president, Hellyer the general manager. Nor did it need to be an arena for collective bargaining agreements and equitable labour practices as it was for contract lawyers, union negotiators, and player reps.

For generations fans of the blue-and-white-clad Toronto Centennials had been living and dying by the exploits of the storied old franchise. The lawyer and the businessman together, jumping up as one just like the farmer and the trucker sitting beside them. The company man who scored complimentary tickets from his firm's client, right beside the poor soul who just blew two weeks pogey to scalp his way into the game. Men and women, old and young, all cheering with the sweet noise of agreement. But while those cheers could be seen as related to the work of a scout; while the players they root for may be in uniform solely because of the diligent effort of an associate in Western Canada, such passion was beyond the focus of Stephen Gillis. Because for Stephen Gillis, there was one other important thing that hockey was not. Hockey was not a game. And this had also served him just fine. No, to keep his boundaries safe all he needed to know was that hockey would continue to be all these other things to all these other people – a business, a sport, an industry, a passion. For with all these unquestionable certainties, his role and his solitude would always be ensured. He was a scout by necessity. And he had forged his livelihood from nothing more than a contentment to watch the sport played at more obscure levels – driving from town to town through bitter cold and blinding squalls – because, in a nutshell, that was all Stephen Gillis had ever dared to know.

～

It was quite strange then that he started talking to the old man at all, that blustery March night in Prince George, late in the season in a half-empty arena. Strange in that he didn't merely reach the point that he always reached whenever locals in the stands felt the need to instigate a conversation. The hometown team had only managed a dozen wins the entire year, and was mired in an oppressive eleven-game losing streak. But first-place Kamloops, led by the talented Bill Parkinson on defence, was in town that night and Stephen had made the trip to watch him perform. As usual he had shunned the option of a padded chair and positioned himself above the seats along the rails – the unofficial standing room section that formed a ring around the top of the bleachers. From there he was free to see the entire flow of the game relatively inconspicuously, hidden amongst the local old-timers and rink rats who regularly adorn every arena from St. John's to Whitehorse – a coffee in one hand, the other playing with the change in their pockets, feet shuffling as they discuss their own particular version of hockey's glory days to anyone who will listen.

The old man wore an old wrinkled overcoat, and a pair of blue rubber snow boots that provided neither warmth nor style. On his head a toque with the home team's crest shot straight up at attention, and in his arms he carried an old crumpled shopping bag – one hand on the string handles, the other cradled with a careful awkwardness under the bottom – like a father's first time holding his newborn.

"I'm not from these parts," he stated by way of introduction, though Stephen had been too preoccupied with his cell phone to take notice immediately. He had, after all, been caught at a weak moment, busy as he was summoning all the deference he could muster, while still imploring his GM's assistant to supply him with any sort of rationale that might justify the player trade Toronto had made earlier in the day; a trade that for the second year in a row gave away a minor league prospect that Stephen had himself scouted – this time a speedy right winger named Marois who was developing nicely in the team's farm system – for an aging veteran whose career had peaked four years ago with a modest twenty-three goal season.

"Nope. My dad ran a grocery store back east in Newfoundland. Ran it right up until the day he packed up mother and me. I was only ten years old at the time, so I really don't know what went into the decision. All he ever told me was that one day he heard the call. Said it happened while he was wrestling with a crate full of cabbages. 'We are stockpiling for the millennium,' he used to say. 'Lest we be put out of business on that glorious

Final Day!' Dad sure loved his produce analogies. Anyway, he settled on a seminary … out here in Edmonton. Apparently every other one he looked into suffered from watered-down theology. Too much navel-gazing at the expense of training the pastor for his role as witness to Christ as our personal Lord and Saviour."

Throughout his five years as a professional scout, Stephen Gillis had acutely honed his ability to ignore extraneous noise around him, often employing quick but effective head gestures to serve as hints to any observant bystander that he preferred silence to chatter while he was working.

"Pretty strange way for a fellow to introduce himself, I suppose," the old man continued as he placed the shopping bag gently to the floor and settled against the rail next to the scout. "But what the hell eh? My old man was also the first one to lace a pair of skates on me right? So tell me … who's catchin' your eye tonight? Smart money'd be on that big Number 7 on the blue line for Kamloops I guess."

When the possibility of silence seemed too remote, however – and his five years of experience had granted Stephen the ability to make that call relatively quickly – he defaulted to a different plan. It would be his standard speech reserved for those overly familiar old-timers observant enough to glean his profession from his actions, yet insufficiently sensitive to realize he had absolutely no desire to talk with them about it. It was a calculated speech delivered with his gaze fixed firmly on the ice, following the flow of the play without so much as a blink. It focused on how the fundamental difference between a scout and the casual fan could be found in the way the two watched a game unfold. How the fan would consider his favourite team's play only by judging each and every rush up the ice without thinking of the opposition as anything other than a constant. And in so doing, the fan would unwittingly reduce the ice surface to three sections: his own team's end where defence is a consideration; the neutral zone, where speed is gathered for the attack; and the opposition's end, where it's hoped all the action will occur. The scout, conversely, was required to make the ice a complete mirror, giving neither team nor any one particular player special weight. One team's line rush was to be considered only in the context of the other team's defensive strategy, for one's success or failure could not be judged without the other. Stephen Gillis would then typically use the ensuing pause as an opportunity to turn to the person and point out how the latter style of observation required a great deal of undivided concentration, and then quickly return his gaze to the game at hand, hoping the recipient was equal to the comment's implication.

"That's fascinating," the old man returned eagerly. "Because if I'm hearing you right, you're saying a scout, by definition, cannot be a fan of either team. And that's absolutely fascinating because my philosophy is exactly the opposite. For a scout to be of any use at all, I think he has to be a fan of both. I think he's gotta be part of the roar of the crowd, you know? Now I know the boys you work for just preach wins and losses, plain and simple. But I have to tell you, when you want proof that hockey really matters – proof that what you're doin' really matters – well it all comes back to the roar of the crowd doesn't it? I mean if that roar dulls, even the slightest bit, well then there's room for doubt … for player and fan alike. And once doubt creeps in, there's a lapse in effort. And I know, coaches are paid to get players over something like that. But a scout like yourself could make a coach's life a whole hell of a lot easier if he could just spot the kid who never doubts in the first place, couldn't he, Stephen?"

Stephen raised his eyes far enough from the game to find the old man's returning smile strangely disconcerting.

"Stephen Gillis," the old man stated with a flourish of the hand. "In the Big Leagues for all of three weeks. Well … eighteen days actually, but I prefer to round up. Seven games, one goal, an assist, three minor penalties – and as I recall, a considerable measure of spunk. Apart from that, a career minor leaguer. Muskegon for three years, Fort Wayne and Peoria for four each – then, at the age of thirty-three, retired to the world of scouting."

The smile widened and he extended his hand.

"Willie Skilliter," he said. "You could say I'm something of a scout myself."

Stephen stepped back and stared silently, inspecting his intruder. Apart from the colour clash of his piecemeal wardrobe, especially the man's gaudy knitted hat, he could have been a scout. He had certainly nailed the low key, "no one important" appearance – the veil that old-school scouting especially preferred. The theory was straightforward enough. If a scout were to undertake his job without such clever cloaking, before you knew it – old school would argue – you would be affecting the outcome; a mitigating factor instead of an objective observer, causing would-be snipers to shoot from every conceivable angle, playmakers to debut no-look backhand drop passes, enforcers to drop their gloves before the national anthem had finished echoing around the rafters.

Sure enough, those first few minutes of the game had proved, yet again, that the old school had merit. Prince George had started their second-string goalie, Olan Krutzweiser, a nineteen-year-old from Quesnel once highly touted out of midget hockey, but who had never panned out to the team's satisfaction. It was only his eighth start of the year. Yet there he had been all through the warm-up, with his eyes darting around the bleachers, peering methodically section by section, in a systematic search for a clipboard or a notebook tucked beneath a slightly more expensive coat. Knowing that as long as a blue chipper like Parkinson was the opposition someone would be there watching. And no doubt, his own performance – perhaps an unexpected forty-save night or, dare he dream, even a shutout – might redirect some of that attention. Sadly not two minutes into the game came the inevitable, just as Stephen had returned his attention to the play. Poor Olan made a meal of his first shot of the game; a soft wrister from just inside the blue line came at his right side, waist high. He snatched his glove out dramatically, but overplayed the puck which rolled up over his arm and trickled across the goal line.

The Kamloops player celebrated with just the right amount of indifference required for a fluke goal against a last-place team. Meanwhile the faithful few supporters who had ventured out through the weather united to voice their displeasure with a chorus of jeers and boos. Prince George's coach yelled to change the lines and his diminutive fourth-line centre skated back to Olan to give his goaltender a reassuring rub of the helmet.

"Gee Stephen, you think he knows you're up here?" Willie chuckled as he pulled a program from his overcoat and searched for the goalie's name.

"Just pressing too hard."

"Nice of that little centreman to come back and pick him up though," the old man returned. "Native kid, you know." He scanned the booklet for the current stats. "Where is he ... where is he? Oh, right here. 'Casey Bruford. 61 games, 7 goals, 9 assists for 16 points.' Only 12 minutes in penalties too. You should take a peek at this one, Stephen. Looks like a real team guy."

The scout pulled from the liner pocket of his coat a thick coiled pad full of printed ledgers and columns, and somewhat impatiently flipped all the way through to the back before reading. "Casey Bruford. 5'9" and 155 pounds. One powerplay goal, two shorthanded. Only a minus four on a bad team, but he doesn't see the ice that much. Fair speed. No size. No physical game. No shot to speak of."

He returned the ledger to his coat with a sigh.

"I suppose you got the lad's shoe size and favourite food in there too?"

"I cover them all. It's called staying competitive."

"Staying competitive, my eye," the old man scoffed. "That kind of analysis would've told you to stay away from some kid named Orr because his knees looked a little wonky. All this weighing and measuring and data-storing you fellahs do now. Hell I say, here's hoping progress balls up modern times like never before. Just might come to pass, too. Remember back at the turn of the century. We hit the big Two Thousand and everybody ran around so afraid it was gonna mess up all the computers, scared that none of them would be able to make sense of it all and they'd send us all back to year zero to try it all over again. Might not be a bad idea, come to think of it. Hell, my old man made a living off watching for signs of the end of the age and all that mayhem. He went a bit more for the fire-and-brimstone mind you, so I doubt he would've figured it would play out that way. A bunch of poor souls whose rent is due being informed by some database that their paycheque won't be in the mail for another two thousand years, it doesn't really capture the thunderbolts of Revelations, you know what I'm saying Stephen?"

"I know what you're saying. I have no idea what it means. Look … Willie is it? You're obviously talking to the wrong guy. The only thing the year 2000 meant to me is that players born in '82 were eligible for the draft."

"Well I suppose that's one way of looking at it. Just an arbitrary number. No inherent significance. Mind you, for me growing up, I couldn't very well suspend the very beliefs I was raised with. The end of the world, Armageddon, the ultimate battle between the forces of Light and Darkness. You know, the Revelations stuff. Shame too. Because the way I see it now? The apocalypse wouldn't be such a touchy proposition if a guy were just allowed the option of relaxing into the oblivion of it all. Like an endless nap on a big soft mattress with all these fluffed-up pillows where he could just think things over calmly for an eternity or two. Every now and again, I think that might be very nice. But then my father's voice intercedes from its permanent residence in my head, and I remember all those promises of painful and eternal damnation for anyone who doesn't take the religious high road. That was my old man's heaven and hell. No room for middle ground. Nowhere to just lie back and think about the big picture without all the stress. Kind of wears a person down, you know?"

"Nope. Like I said, the only Sunday morning religion I knew involved getting to the rink for 6 a.m. practice or heading out of town for a tournament."

"Then count yourself lucky my friend. You weren't weighed down in the prime of your youth with perpetual doom … scared to hell and back over the possibility of being passed over on the Almighty's Draft Day. I'm tellin' you, it was always there with me. No matter how well I rationalised my old man's fury, there was always a dark little corner of my mind that went along for the ride. I guess it's that crack of doubt again … that tiny sliver between your thoughts. Hard to slip into, but once you do, it's sheer hell trying to claw your way out. I mean I'd get in these states … just spiralling down deeper and deeper into the darkest of fears … picking up speed as I went, leaving behind more and more of everything I'd always counted on as constant. All too soon I couldn't be sure of anything at all. Everything seemed to get sucked through that crack and into this never-ending black hole. I'm tellin' ya Stephen, you get deep enough into that kind of horror and all you do is pray for something to come up and break the fall. Rock, concrete, earth … doesn't matter how hard it is, as long as it's solid."

"Your guy just missed a tip-in."

"ATTA BOY CASEY! KEEP PLUGGIN'! … But here's the rub Stephen. You know what always used to bring this on? Hockey. Yes sir, I'm telling you, the game of hockey was the trigger. Playing as a kid, watching on TV, hell just taking in a game at the local rink. For years I just assumed the association was strictly personal. But recently I believe I've come to a clearer understanding on the matter. You see, I've come to believe the connection between religion and sport runs far deeper than the mere particulars of my own upbringing. Just think about it. Consider how sports fanatics the world over can work themselves into a religious fervour … how masses of people will congregate, by the tens of thousands, screaming and yelling and losing control all as one. Surrendering their own hard-earned money for the privilege to do so. And with the cost of tickets these days, Stephen, it's not an insignificant tithe. The followers of false gods – that's how my old man would have judged each and every one of them – the unwitting followers of false gods."

"Not tonight. Can't be more than a couple of hundred in here."

"Ah but in my book, these ones aren't the idolaters, Stephen. They're the residue. They're the remains of whatever purity is still in the game. And why? Because they'll still risk icy roads and bone-chilling cold over the numbing comfort of a rec room and a television converter. You can't get this type of experience, sitting alone while some satellite dish pumps in a game from Phoenix or Tampa Bay, can you Stephen? … HAVE AN EYE FOR THE TRAILER, CASEY!"

"Franchise'll probably be in Boise by next fall."

"Kind of reminds me of what the old man always said about the Catholics. Now I know you said you weren't one for the religious stuff, but I'll try you anyhow. You see, according to father dearest, the priesthood, by its very design, robbed the masses of their right to a personal spiritual life. Not a big papal fan, my old man. He believed the priesthood had taken a person's relationship with the Almighty away and made it their own institutionalised possession. They decided who was the sinner and who was the saint. They interpreted the gospels instead of encouraging their parishioners to read for themselves. 'Self-appointed middlemen for the Almighty' my old man called them. 'Think of the danger, William,' he'd say. 'If one wished to bend the Lord's ear, one first had to get the priest to lobby the appropriate saint and then hope the message was passed along. Would one not soon begin to confuse the hierarchy? Would one not begin to confuse priest and saint and God Almighty as one and the same?' The irony is, dear old dad himself wasn't above coaching his flock himself. And I'm talking about a my-way-or-the-highway type of coaching that would've made both John Calvin and Mike Keenan proud. But try calling him on it and he'd just grin one of those grins that let you know how much clearer he believed he saw things. 'But William,' he'd say, 'I only speak God's Word. And God's Word cannot be denied.'"

He reached into his shopping bag and pulled out a weathered old scrapbook, its corners rolled up and tattered, pages overflowing with the stuffing of yellowed newspaper clippings, some taped or glued, some merely jammed inside.

"I should show you some of these," he said and proceeded to make something of a production of his own carefulness, as he gingerly removed a few of the articles from inside. "I collect 'em from time to time when something about them speaks to me particularly. Look … this one here for starters … about that outfielder in Cleveland … the one who used to throw baseballs at sports reporters whenever he got ticked off with 'em. And somewhere in here … yeah there they are … a whole bunch from the earthquake that hit during the World Series back in '89. See there? *A's and Giants Rocked as Candlestick is shaken moments before game time.*"

"I don't follow much baseball," Stephen returned, dodging the somewhat irritating flap of newsprint now being shaken under his face.

"OK … what else then," Willie continued unfazed. "How 'bout this one … about that Colombian soccer player gunned down in his hometown two days after he put the ball in his own net during a World Cup game. And this one's from the World Cricket Championships a few years back. The national team from India had to forfeit their final match because their own fans started a riot."

"Look, buddy …" Stephen interrupted, trapping the flailing articles with a slap of his palms and scrunching them back against the old man's chest. "I'm trying to be polite here. I don't want to know about your religion, or your father, or your take on baseball. And I sure as hell don't have the time for a chat about cricket!"

Willie knelt to the concrete floor to smooth out the clippings one by one, delicately returning each to its allotted space in the scrapbook.

"Well who does?" he chuckled as he worked away. "I mean really. A bunch of men standing around in knitted vests for hours on end, while one of them paddles a ball at will."

Suddenly he sprang to his feet with a litheness that seemed to defy his age.

"OK!" he chirped. "Let me just try a couple more out on you and if nothing grabs you, I promise I'll leave you be."

Stephen stood inert and silent, his unblinking eyes glued to centre ice even though the Kamloops squad had the play pinned far down in the Prince George end of the rink for several minutes.

"This first one I know you'll appreciate, because the gist of it is especially pertinent to scouting. I clipped part of it out from one of those sports pool magazines that rates every player a thousand ways from Sunday. The whole article went on for pages, chock full of charts and tables, comparing every single player stat known to man: goals and assists, plus/minus ratings, shooting percentages, average ice time per game … everything under the sun. Everything, that is, except their team's wins and losses! Now I have to confess to you, I pull this one out almost every day,

Stephen, because, well, I just don't know what to think. On one hand, I think wins and losses are the sole measure of a competitive team sport and all these other numbers have just become a smoke-screen – a diversion for players and fans who have given up on the dream of winning. And I know you'll probably argue they're a tool for determining a player's value, but what's the consequence of that value? Does it really necessarily mean he'll be an asset to his team? Or is it all just a bargaining tool when it comes to renegotiating that player's contract? So many points and so many body-checks translates into four million a season instead of just three and a half? I mean I can't really see a professional athlete's lifestyle suffering either way, so I'm left to believe the rising salaries are just smoke-screen too. Just one more diversion. One more stat. Something slightly more tangible to hang an ego on than, say, a goals-against average. But then, on the other hand, when I hear some lucky plug of a grinder being interviewed after he banked a game winner in off a team-mate's rear end saying how 'it wasn't pretty, but we had a job to do out there and we got the job done' … I can't help but wonder, well if there's no more joy in winning than that then why the hell does anybody bother?"

"They bother because hockey is big business," Stephen shrugged, venturing slightly from the comfort level of his scouting expertise. "And whether we like it or not that business is as much about concession stand revenues and licensing fees and player payrolls as it is about wins and losses."

"But that's just the thing. The average fan doesn't need to hear about all that. The average fan's got enough on his own plate. Rent or a mortgage, bills and taxes. He doesn't need to hear the game-winning scorer calling the game a 'job,' does he? Of course he doesn't. He needs the game to free him from all that. But when you start making excuses about the so-called business of hockey, and when you throw in skyrocketing ticket prices and a couple of players holding out for multi-million dollar contracts … then maybe a players' strike … well soon enough your so-called average fan is following the game with a big chip on his shoulder, demanding results for his dollar. Soon enough he's not even cheering any more."

He paused a moment to scan the play for himself. "Sorry to hear about the Marois trade, by the way. I have to tell you, I can't see the logic behind it at all."

And with that comment, he gave himself away, at least to Stephen's way of thinking at the time. This old man, this complete stranger walking up and assuming familiarity, feigning camaraderie – hell, even expertise – all in the hope of gleaning the inside dope on a player trade. Stephen failed to question how the man already knew of the Marois trade – which was odd, for the scout himself had only learned of the transaction by phone a few minutes earlier and news of it would not be released to the press until the following afternoon.

Perhaps he had been too fixated on the man's sheer gall. The idea that this stranger, strictly by having the nerve to walk up and start rambling on, expected some sort of private glimpse into the realm of professional hockey that he could take home and tell his friends and family. And for what? To get the scoop on how a respected employee of one of the most storied franchises in hockey drove four hours through a blizzard just to sit in an empty arena and evaluate an eighteen-year old defenceman?

"Ah what the hell, eh? The guy you got still might work out. He had a couple of good years a while back."

"So did Howie Morenz. And if he wasn't dead, I'm sure we'd send off another couple of prospects for him too."

"And all the work you put into finding these youngsters. Must make you want to pull your hair out some days –"

"What makes me want to pull my hair out is a total stranger walking up to me like some long-lost friend and bothering me for no apparent reason! Got it?"

Willie took the outburst with neither a wince nor blink, nor anything remotely apologetic.

"But I'm not here to bother you, Stephen," he leaned in and whispered. "I'm here to help you." And with his eyes firmly planted on the play, he pulled another article from the pages of his scrapbook, this one much older and frayed around the edges.

"Last one … as promised," he said, and still with eyes on the ice unfolded it across his palm and handed it to Stephen. "In fact, it's the very first one I ever clipped out."

ESTEVAN CLUB WINS THIRD ANNUAL
KINSMEN MIDGET TOURNEY

Led by captain Steve Gillis and his four-point explosion in the final period, the Estevan Home Hardware Midget squad overcame a three-goal deficit to defeat the home side Kenora Optimists last Sunday at the Coliseum.

"HOW DID YOU … HOW THE HELL DID YOU …"

"Like I said," the old man repeated, his eyes tracing the puck's path, the corners of his mouth now flattened into an expression of concern. "Whenever they speak to me."

Chapter Two

Willie's newspaper clipping failed to mention three crucial details about the events of that tournament over twenty years ago. The first occurred during the opening period of the final game, when Stephen Gillis, then a talented fifteen-year-old, 135-pound centreman, was dropped from his spot on the first line for what his coach deemed a completely lacklustre effort throughout the entire tourney. Young Stephen had never been sat down before and it had left him feeling intensely and utterly awkward. Such is the essence of the punishment, when it comes to being benched. A player is left to feel completely abandoned and yet utterly in the way; conspicuous by his absence on the ice, absolutely convinced that the entire arena has abandoned the game to observe how he is managing to endure this pathetic moment of his existence. He will sit in silence, head down, decked out unnecessarily in full equipment – in Stephen's case with the captain's "C" proudly embroidered on the chest of his jersey – to sit amongst those who are still prepared to do battle. He will sit and slide further down the bench with each player change only to move back to the other end when it's time for his former linemates to charge out the door.

The next detail occurred during the second intermission of that game just as the arena's Zamboni took to the ice to flood and smooth out the

ruts and the gashes the last period had inflicted. In a completely unprecedented move, Stephen Gillis's father – a man who had never missed so
much as a minute of his son's minor hockey career – gave up and walked
out the arena door. It happened shortly after Stephen had headed down
the corridor toward the dressing room, shortly after his father had
grabbed him by the shoulder pads and with a quivering rage that shook
the boy until his skates chattered on the cold cement floor, screamed with
an uncontrollable fury that could only be fuelled by family or foe. Now the
screaming itself was nothing out of the ordinary. Stephen's team-mates
had heard Mr. Gillis's wrath echo through most every arena from Ontario
to Alberta at one time or another, the barrage always ending with a slap of
the wall or a foot into the door – whichever surface his boy happened to
be pinned against at the time. And they would always keep their heads
down when their captain re-entered the dressing room afterwards, only
the most curious risking a quick glance to search for evidence of tears in
the boy's eyes. Tears they believed surely would result from such continual
hounding, yet strangely enough, tears that none of them could ever
remember seeing. The room would be silent for a good five minutes while
each player offered private and silent thanks to the hockey gods that their
own parents didn't take such an interest in the game, and that Old Man
Gillis never directed his wrath at the team as a whole. Meanwhile, the
coaches, for their part, would huddle outside the dressing room for yet
another inconclusive discussion regarding the behaviour of their star
player's father, weighing both the volume and the frequency of his outbursts against the weekly financial contributions he made to the team's
operating budget.

   But while the yelling that day may have been just routine, the venom
was anything but. No one – not the coaches or the players or even Stephen
himself – had ever seen the man so worked up. Swearing, sweating, red-
faced contortions and foot-stomping gyrations … the saliva that spewed
from the corners of his mouth and sprayed through the bars of his son's
face mask as he screamed over and over about the goddamn lead in his
son's legs, his goddamn hands of stone … and about the boy's Jesus-

mother-fucking-goddamn lack of goddamn-mother-shitting concern about it all. For Christ's sake, this was his fucking year of eligibility for getting drafted into Major Junior, and here he was, candy-assin' around, not giving one goddamn-mother-pissin'-flying fuck! The combination of anger and frustration finally proved too much, and in one last barrage, the father unleashed to exhaustion, his rage on his one and only son. (For years Stephen would focus mostly on the frustration aspect of the day, holding out for some sense of legitimacy in his father's actions. Such is the way with fathers and sons.)

"STOP WASTING MY GODDAMN TIME!" he screamed, leaving those last words to echo in young Stephen's head for all eternity, as he threw his son back against the dressing room door and stormed from the arena.

~

From the time he first ankle-burned around a half-rink full of toddlers, Stephen had always wished his father would cheer more like the other parents did. For while it was true many of them could be just as demanding with their kids, even lose their temper from time to time (more frequently, the higher Stephen rose through the levels of competitive minor hockey), there was still contained within their zeal at least the implication of happiness. When Harold Carmichael's dad yelled for his son to "Come on Harry! Keep on diggin' Harry," from the bench Stephen would see his team-mate's eager feet churn all the harder. And every time Sheldon Kawinski popped in a goal, the boy could immediately turn and pump his fist in the direction of his mom and dad, confident that both would also be jumping up and down, not standing impassively with arms folded and calling down for their son to "quit gawking up here and keep your head back in the game."

This was the stuff of Stephen Gillis's hockey fantasies. There were no dreams of scoring the winning goal to capture the Cup, lifting it high overhead and skating victorious to the approving roar of thousands. For

Stephen knew from an age too young to remember that, all other things being equal, if he ever realised his father's wish and made it to the Pros, indeed if he helped win a championship, his dad would merely demand two. That was his way. Goals and victories were expected results, not causes for celebration. Especially any goal or win which occurred solely because of an opponent's glaring error. "That'll never catch a scout's eye," he would often say during the mandatory post-game de-briefing when – even on road trips – instead of climbing aboard the team bus with sixteen other sweaty teenagers, Stephen would tumble into his father's sedan to have his successes qualified and his deficiencies hammered home. This was the perch from which he would be reminded that, above all, scouts would always be looking for a carefully bred aggression combined with well-honed technique; that such a mix had to be constantly maintained in young Stephen's game. They would, for example, want to see a takeout executed with the precision of four backward crossovers, a weight shift from the left leg up and through the right shoulder, and a harnessed release of hatred at the point of contact. "Hockey is an angry sport," his old man once heard Gordie Howe admit somewhere or other on the banquet circuit, from then on adopting it as his son's personal mantra. While in later years Stephen would question whether he was taught to play angry or whether it was the teaching itself that had pissed him off enough to make him effective, all he knew at the time was that on those occasions when he ploughed through a team on an end-to-end rush or when he put the opponent's captain into the boards – those were the only times he ever got a nod of approval. Or sometimes a hand on the back – more of a stiff momentary placement than an actual pat – on rare occasions accompanied by "that's more like it" or simply "better". No ... good play was not cause for celebration. Good play was expected as a matter of course. Like a farm kid doing his daily chores. Defeat was a failure to do what was expected, to live up to the type of son he was meant to be. Failure was maddening. Failure was an embarrassment. Failure brought well-deserved yelling and screaming. And no matter whether an arena was jammed with five hundred shouting fans or held a mere half-dozen disinterested rink rats, his father's was the only voice young Stephen ever heard out there on the ice.

~

In January of 1907 the Kenora Thistles Hockey Club defeated the Montreal Wanderers to capture Lord Stanley's Cup. A plaque on the wall in the Kenora arena's lobby still sits to commemorate the effort; below it is an old photograph of the team – seven players arranged in two rows with their names listed underneath. Young Stephen had stared at the old photo for a long time, his equipment slung over his shoulder, still drenched and heavy with sweat. He noted how flimsy their equipment appeared; their padding no more than an extra layer of stuffing under a heavy knit sweater. There were no helmets. No shoulder or elbow pads to speak of. He remembered how his father once told him about Johnny Bucyk. How he and his friends growing up "on the wrong side of the tracks" had resorted to frozen cow dung for a puck because the real thing was a luxury unheard of. To Stephen's eye, the players in the photo looked like they might well have done the same.

The third player from the left in the bottom row caught the boy's eye especially. His name was Silas Griffis and Stephen couldn't help thinking the man held his stick rather awkwardly. Perhaps it was nervousness in front of the camera, occasions for photography probably being quite rare back then. On the other hand, it was possible that such a grip was as far as hockey had evolved back in 1907. Perhaps Silas had been the first in his family even to give the game a try. Maybe *his* father had thought the whole idea of chasing a piece of rubber, or cow shit, or whatever around a frozen pond a completely ludicrous proposition. Because surely somewhere back in the darkened ages, before history and myth had turned the game into religion – his own father into a frenzied convert – the sport of hockey must have been new. An amusing experiment void of all the nostalgia since bestowed upon it.

Normally he would have already been outside, making a quick beeline for the familiar idle of his father's sedan, jumping in before the cold winter air had a chance to freeze his matted brown hair. But the car was nowhere to be seen and, uncertain whether to wait for its return or to make the unprecedented walk to the team bus, Stephen continued to loiter, gazing up at the old picture, stalling for time, hoping the correct decision would somehow make itself evident. His mind drifted back to the game just completed. How he had been freed by the coaches from his purgatory on the bench to start the third period. How the weightlessness of his skates had been immediate with his very first stride. How he scored his initial goal on an end-to-end rush that, for the first time in his life, he instigated without the drone of angry instruction from the stands. How he completed the play with a deft wrist shot high to the right-hand corner; exactly where he had aimed. And then, on his very next shift, setting up à la Gretzky behind the net, he feathered a pass over two defenders' sticks right onto the tape of his pinching defenceman who blasted it home. Estevan was shorthanded when Stephen scored again, intercepting a cross-ice pass at his own blue line and deking the Kenora goalie on a clear breakaway. He passed to an open winger for an empty-netter with a minute to go to record his fourth point of the period.

The ice had been so clear; every shot and every pass so true. It was as if the opposition had been moving in slow motion and so predictably that he knew instantly how to react. React? Hell, he had time to react and then wait for the play to evolve as he had predicted. He was a hare in a snail's game. He had owned the rink. He had played without the voice from the bleachers and had finally heard the roar of the crowd. And it felt good. Even an hour later, standing in the lobby before the Kenora Thistles roster, it still felt so very good. So good in fact, the boy didn't immediately notice the OPP constable step inside the doorway and shake the snow from the hood of his parka. Nor did he see the officer looking anxiously about as he conferred first with the arena manager and then with Stephen's coach.

It could be argued that the final detail missing from Willie's newspaper was not directly a sports-related matter. But Stephen would always know otherwise, for his own clipping – the one he kept in a shoebox somewhere in his apartment – he had snipped from the *Winnipeg Free Press* two days later; two days after the constable approached and with a tenderness so foreign to the boy it would haunt him forever, placed a gentle hand on Stephen's shoulder. That version was brief:

"Lawrence Gillis, 44, of Estevan Saskatchewan was killed when he lost control of his sedan while travelling westbound on Highway 17, ten miles west of Keewatin shortly after three o'clock Sunday afternoon. Mr. Gillis was pronounced dead at the scene. He is survived by a wife and one son."

Some sons are granted years to live out their rebellion against the dreams and expectations of their fathers. For Stephen Gillis, his lasted but twenty minutes ... *stop time.*

Chapter Three

Stephen spent the better part of the intermission pacing the length of the bleachers impatiently awaiting Willie's return from the concession stand. "You're riled right now Stephen," the old man had said shortly after tucking the article back into his scrapbook. "What we need is a coffee, good and hot to settle ourselves." And leaving the young scout stuttering and stumbling to demand an immediate explanation, he had sauntered off – to Stephen's eye looking distinctly pleased with himself.

"Here, give those fidgety hands of yours something to hang on to," he announced loudly, returning with two steaming styrofoam cups just as the teams filed back out from beneath the bleachers for the start of the second period.

"Don't expect much though. They don't brew much of a cup here. You want good coffee, you should try Melfort – best you'll find anywhere … and they're only Tier Two."

The young scout's eyes fell to an old weathered hockey stick that Willie was carrying pinned tightly alongside his cherished shopping bag under his arm. It was caked dirty white with gummed-up tape and the brand name was all but worn off, leading Stephen to suspect it had been out of use for quite some time.

"People throw out the damnedest things," Willie exclaimed. "Look, not a thing wrong with it. Hell, when I was a kid, a find like this would have been a gold strike."

He tapped the heel of the blade on the concrete and it produced a surprisingly healthy solid sound.

"Can you remember your first real hockey game Stephen? With actual referees and the score clock turned on? Mine's up here like it was yesterday. Seven years old I was. Same year I got my first pair of hand-me-down skates and shin guards. Ah but those were the days, weren't they Stephen. When it was all just about having fun. You know what else I remember? My tenth birthday, I got my first-ever helmet. One of those old round Coopers. You ever come across one? Little dome-shaped number with the front and back that looked practically the same. You know I think I got an old photo of me wearing it somewhere in here. Might even have the thing on backwards for all I knew—"

"It was never fun," Stephen interrupted softly, his voice cracking involuntarily.

"How's that Stephen?"

"Look, I don't know who you are or why you've got that newspaper article in your book there, but if you really knew anything about me, you'd know it was never about fun."

Stephen sent his still-full coffee cup splattering into a nearby trash can and stabbed his hands back inside his coat pockets. That was as much as he was prepared to say. If this guy wanted more out of him, then he'd have to say so directly. And if the old man actually had something to say himself, then he would have to open up and say it. Not hint around the matter with a series of pointless theories about religion and sports.

"You know what I think, Stephen?" Willie broke the silence cheerfully. "I think you work too hard. You ever take any time off? Maybe go out to the coast? Maybe do a bit of golfing? Might do a world of good."

He waggled the hockey stick as if it were a three-wood and unleashed a couple of practise swings, all the while staring down the length of the rails as if there were some massive fairway sprawled forth in front of him.

"Then again, " he sighed, "I tried taking up the game a few years back myself. Had a little heart problem so the doc suggested I find an activity to help relieve some stress. Stress? Hell, you want to talk about stress! First this puny little golf pro shakes my hand, and hits me up for ten lessons at thirty bucks a shot. Then he proceeds to instruct the stuffing right out of me, and all with this phoney little English accent the guy put on like a bad suit. 'Now remember William, a sport worth playing is worth playing correctly … head down … feet slightly apart. Ball forward in your stance William. Don't release your shoulders too quickly, William. Chin down. Eyes on the ball. Arms relaxed. Grip firm. Wrists loose. Fingers pointed …' Well, after seven or eight of these little contortion acts, I'm in the middle of a backswing that apparently is still too quick, with an elbow that's apparently still too bent … and the revelation hits me with the weight of one of my old man's cabbage crates! *THIS ISN'T FUN!* Hell, I'd never worked so hard at relaxing in all my life. I guess maybe that's the way it is for some people. Too much clothesline in us to ever make very good kite string. I'm thinkin' maybe that's how it is for you and hockey?"

He tossed the stick into a nearby trash barrel and planted his elbows back on top of the rail.

"The thing that really gets me," he continued, "is that nobody ever discusses strategy any more. Used to be the average fan loved to play armchair coach. How a particular centre should take a draw. How far a goalie should cut down a shooting angle. Line combinations and breakout patterns. The x's and o's that make the sport what it is. Nowadays, if a team loses two in a row, that same fan just cries for a trade. Or a new coach or general manager. Nobody has the patience for improvement any more, which is a damn shame for you I suppose, since spotting improvement is what scouting is all about! Hell, any dead weight can pick some hotshot out of the crowd and say, 'Gosh we should trade for that guy.' … COME ON PARKINSON, YOU'RE NOT DRAFTED YET! … See, this is just what I mean. Parkinson there should be taking that play right to the slot! When he grabs the puck in open ice like that and the other team just gives up the blue line, he should recognise they're playing him to pass and drive one right on net!"

"It's his wrist."

"His wrist, my ass. It's indifference! You may be content to merely weigh and measure players. See how many barbells they can lift before they fall over. Clock how fast it takes them to skate from blue line to blue line. But in my opinion, it only takes dead weight to carry a stopwatch. Get the guy with the widest shoulders, the longest stride and the biggest reach, then hope to hell that someday it will all translate into hockey sense. It's a travesty."

"Seventy-three points in 30 games before he broke that wrist. Parkinson's the real deal."

"And now look at him. Going through the motions of the 67th game in a 72-game season, knowing the hockey world has already pegged him for the first round. He's learning how to play out the string, Stephen. Do you really want a player who already knows how to do that at the tender age of nineteen? Little precocious for my taste if you ask me."

"I don't remember asking you," Stephen replied.

"Ah I tell you, it's a damned strange profession scouting, isn't it?" the old man raced on. "Perched up here overtop of the crowd. Just far enough away to feel a bit superior. Really kind of pompous in a way. I mean, in the end, there isn't one tangible thing a scout can point to that proves he's any more qualified at assessing talent than the next guy. No diplomas or university degrees for us to frame and put on the wall. At some point a scout just has to believe he knows what he's doing. That he deserves to lean up here in judgement and tempt these kids with the hope of deliverance to the pros."

"I'm sorry, where exactly did you say you were a scout?"

Willie leaned over the rails further until his chin rested comfortably on his mitts. His eyes squinted into the empty space above the ice surface, as if straining to spot a memory there. "Oh … it's quite a few years ago now," he chuckled. "Just dabbled a bit, you know." He chuckled again. "Once I managed to get proficient with a road map, that is. I couldn't tell you how many nights I spent holed up in my room, studying my old Oxford atlas. Looking up the towns and cities and highways. Plotting routes here and there. As for why I chose to while away the hours in such a way … well to be honest, I've never quite nailed that one down. I guess some people just have a need to be orderly. And I mean orderly right down to knowing where we're situated at any given moment. You'd do well to look for that quality in the players you select, Stephen. A player who wants to see how he fits into the entire map of a hockey game can be of great service. He may not turn out to be the flashiest, but at least he'll know why one particular play works when another one doesn't. That's all maps are in the end. Glorified x's and o's. Or as the intro to my old Oxford atlas puts it, *positioning in relation to a geometrical system of latitudinal parallels and longitudinal meridians."*

He lifted his head and looked about, for the first time appearing concerned about the sensibilities and reactions of any others within earshot. Then he leaned in closer to continue his talk in a rather hoarse whisper.

"So late one night I'm in my room. And I've pulled out my stack of maps because I have a notion to give the isolated roads of northwestern Manitoba some serious study. Well for some reason, all of a sudden, right out of nowhere, the old man's voice jumps into my head spewing fire and brimstone and eternal suffering for those who have wasted their ways. I don't know why it happened then. He did a lot of missions into some pretty remote areas, maybe that had something to do with it. Anyway I guess my imagination took quite a bite out of it, 'cause before I can catch myself, I'm slipping into the cracks. Free-falling right through the pit in my stomach and into oblivion. My own personal hell set up just like I left it. But then all of a sudden, out of nowhere another voice pops up in my head – totally unprecedented at the time – and just the very sound of it breaks my fall instantly. It was nothing like the old man's. Still kind of mysterious and haunting, but not an ounce of despair. And it says to me, 'So Willie, all this worrying about a Day of Judgement and look where it's got you.' Well like I was confiding to you earlier, Stephen, writhing around alone in the cosmos, questioning my very existence is where it got me. So it says to me,

'Maybe the problem isn't so much in the judgement. Maybe it's more a matter of boundaries.' And BAM! –"

He slapped his hands together with a smack that echoed the length of the arena's girders.

"– right at that instant … right at that very instant, I happen to glance back down at my maps. Only now they're different. Brighter to the eye and with a depth that I had never known existed. Every point, every dot on that map just sparkled. And there were lines, Stephen. Associations. Designs and dances bouncing between each and every point, just waiting for someone to come along and trace them. I'm tellin' you Stephen, it was a thing of beauty. Every speck and every marking was along for the ride. None of them prejudged. None of them left behind.

"You want another coffee Stephen? You look as if you could use –"

"I want to know what you want from me."

"Me? Not a thing really," Willie replied, curling up his chin as if slightly perplexed by the young man's assumption.

"Then why did you show me that article!"

"I told you. Because it spoke to –"

"ENOUGH OF THE BULLSHIT ALREADY!"

"OK, OK …" Willie relented with a sigh which suggested briefly to Stephen the faint hope that by enduring the man's rambling thus far, he had passed some sort of test, albeit marginally, and would now hear what the old man was really selling. And indeed Willie did clear his throat before proceeding, in a way that suggested everything he had spoken up to that point was by way of preamble.

"There exists today," he began, "a speculative field of study which searches for and plots out the very energies of Mother Earth herself."

"Oh for Christ's sake!"

"Stephen, please … listen to me. This is important." Willie tugged on the arm of the scout's trench coat to draw him back within whispering range. At the same time he stole a glimpse of the ice surface below, where the players were settling in for a faceoff in the Prince George end. Parkinson stood comfortably poised just inside the blue line.

"Stephen, even if you forget everything else we've discussed today, you must remember what I'm going to tell you next. Now, I'm going to assume you have never heard of the phenomenon known as *ley lines,* am I right?"

Stephen turned stone-faced and stared.

"Right ... well, let's start at the beginning then. A ley line – or 'ley' for short – occurs when a straight track drawn across a surface map connects a number of previously separate but nevertheless important historical sites. Churches, old hill forts, burial mounds, mottes ... that sort of thing. Some proponents of the phenomenon believe that such ancient sites have come to exist in these alignments because the currents of the earth have suggested them to the cosmic subconsciousness of civilisation itself."

Willie dove back into the shopping bag. With far less delicacy than before, he eagerly whipped open the pages of his scrapbook.

"Look ... there," he sputtered with a noticeable crescendo of urgency. "I found a big write-up a few years back about the St. Michael's line in southern England, probably the most impressive of all the known leys. You see, in this case, not only do a series of important sites all line up ... they actually all go by the name St. Michael's. Look at the map there in the article. St. Michael's churches in Glastonbury and Burrowbridge ... Stoke St. Michael's down in Somerset and St. Michael's Mount out in Cornwall."

"And this of course ... spoke to you?" Stephen rolled the words slowly out of his mouth as he gave the page barely a cursory glance.

"Why to the very scout in me, Stephen," Willie returned earnestly. "See, after Flin Flon I knew I had to figure out where this whole revelation was taking me. So I started boning up on my alternative spiritualisms and cosmologies, earth mysteries, eastern religions, philosophies, metaphysics, lots of New Age stuff of course."

"Of course."

"Hell, anything I could get my hands on really. Anyway, when I came across the idea of these ley lines ... well it just felt so right, I couldn't help but let it be my guide."

"So what? You started scouting players according to a road map?"

"It's not so out there, once you develop an eye for it, my friend."

"Christ, you're serious, aren't you!"

"Hey, scouts play hunches all the time. I'm just giving you the inside track on the basis for mine. Think of it as the ultimate search for chemistry – at least in the sense the hockey world throws around the term. Remember that line for the Montreal Juniors back in the seventies? The '3D' line, they were nicknamed. Denis Savard, Denis Cyr and Denis … whatever the third fellah's name was … never turned pro. Each one with the same first name. Each one born on the very same day of the same month in the same year. And as a line, they played like they'd lived inside each other's heads since birth. I mean they could dominate."

"They could dominate because they could all skate like the wind and handle the puck like it was tied to the blade of their sticks. The rest is just coincidence."

"Yeah, well … one man's coincidence is another man's chemistry." Willie's response was somewhat absent, as his eye caught the Bruford kid jumping over the boards for a rare shift. The smirk had also vanished from his face and his whisper had almost thinned to silence. His head began to shake back and forth slightly and he began to rub the palms of his mitts together with a rather restless vigour.

"You need to find that chemistry, Stephen," he mumbled. "You need to find it. It's so dark down there between the cracks. You have no idea how dark it gets."

Parkinson had been out on the ice more than a minute and a half when he finally flipped the puck out of his own end, in the general direction of a cross-ice winger up near centre, and then chugged for the bench. An alert Prince George defenceman read the play however, and gloved down the clearing attempt, hammering the puck back towards the Kamloops blue line. It ricocheted off the toe of an opponent's skate and came to rest fortuitously on the blade of Casey Bruford's stick. Dutifully, Parkinson doubled back and got into position in plenty of time to deal with the turnover, playing the angle on the diminutive centreman in textbook fashion. Given the situation – isolated by a defenceman and near the end of a long shift himself – the prudent player would normally try to draw that defenceman near him, and then dump the puck deep into the opponent's zone so a line change could be negotiated on the fly. But for some reason, Casey chose that moment to ignore such good sense and instead tempt fate, bracing himself to take on the behemoth rearguard. Whether it was fearlessness or stupidity or merely an awareness that a scout was watching over him from on high, he dropped his head, bent his knees as low he could and, with a sudden burst of speed, aimed to squirt both the puck and his body through a space between Parkinson's hip and the boards. "ATTA BOY CASEY," Willie screamed hoarsely from his perch just as the boy splattered against the glass and fell to the ice, the force of the collision causing the big defenceman to recoil and crash in a heap beside him.

"DID YOU SEE THAT!?" Willie yelled, jumping up and down. In his excitement, he grabbed a handful of the scout's trench coat as he repeatedly thrust a pointed finger at the undersized forward, who was first to his feet and hustling back towards his bench.

"Yeah ... pretty good hip-check for an indifferent defenceman, I'd say," Stephen quipped, as he turned his attention to the Kamloops winger who had swooped in to pick up the loose puck and start a dangerous-looking rush back down the ice.

"No! I'm talking about Casey. The way he dug right in. I mean he got right down there, with a good wide stance. He committed to that one-on-one. I mean totally committed! Dropped the inside shoulder as far as he could, shielded the puck with his free hand ... then just bore down and gave it all he had and –"

"And Parkinson obliterated him. Look pal, you can go on about this Bruford kid all you want, but a play like that doesn't turn him into a prospect. Truth is, it does a lot more to disqualify him."

"Disqualify him? My God man, can't you at least recognise the effort –"

"Effort that had no impact on the play whatso –"

He was halted by the piercing sound of the referee's whistle, sharp as a dart, blowing the play dead.

Parkinson was still down. He was writhing on the ice and holding his wrist tightly against his chest, his gloves tossed in agony back against the boards.

"Fuckin' little Indian shit!" the injured player screamed, his fury echoing up and down the length of the rafters, all the more amplified by the lack of a crowd in the building. It was the kind of fury that accompanies sudden pain. The kind that lashes out at the nearest target. The kind that shows up in the game from time to time.

Willie shook his head and tossed the remainder of his coffee into the garbage.

"No impact, you say?" he snorted, then buttoned up his coat, grabbed his shopping bag and started for the exit. "Better look after your superstar there."

~

Stephen did not stay for the final period. And he had no inkling of the contest's completely implausible finish until he awoke the next morning to the sound of the radio alarm and the voice of a local sports caster giddily reporting the outcome of the game.

"Led by the surprise four-point effort from seldom-used Casey Bruford, Prince George rallied from a two-goal deficit to record a 5–3 victory over first-place Kamloops. It was the team's first win over their BC rivals in three years and for Bruford, a team record for points in one period. As for Kamloops, well they're reeling from far more than just losing a hockey game. All-star defenceman Bill Parkinson – a player expected to be chosen high in the first round of next summer's draft – will miss the balance of the season after he re-injured his left wrist in a collision with Bruford, midway through the second period."

~

He had caught up to Willie in the lobby, grabbing him by the coat sleeve and swinging him around so hard the old man fell back up against the door.

"Hey pal, in case you haven't noticed ... I wasn't standing there listening to you because I'm interested in your hard-on for some part-time junior. You're gonna tell me why you saved that article ... Now!"

Gently but firmly Willie removed Stephen's grasp from his cuff one finger at a time. "Estevan, Saskatchewan. Your home town. Just north of 49 degrees latitude. Right?"

"What's that have to do –"

"Right?"

"If you say so. What about it?"

"Well the Bruford boy comes from the outer coast on Vancouver Island. A place called Estevan Point. Also just north of the 49th parallel. You can look it up yourself."

Willie gave one firm nod for emphasis, threw the hood of his parka up over his head and shoved open the door to the parking lot. His imminent departure raised not only the volume but even a hint of desperation in the scout's voice.

"So the only reason you came up to me tonight ... and the only reason you showed me a newspaper clipping from a game I played back as a kid ... was to try to convince me I should be interested in some fourth liner because he happens to come from a town with the same name as mine?"

"You should be interested because he's a hell of a young man," Willie snapped back, just as a bitter blast of cold air hit Stephen full in the face. "Stephen, if it helps, I can clothe the words in something more familiar for you. I can say he's a good kid with a big heart who works his butt off."

"He's an undersized centre with no shot. And if you really are the scout you claim to be, you'd know that hockey at this level demands a certain amount of skill before any of those tired old clichés about heart and desire can kick in to mean a damn thing."

"Ah, you're wrong Stephen," the original smile was back on Willie's face. "You're completely and utterly wrong. Casey is special."

"He's a goddamn fourth line centre!" Stephen now had the old man all but pinned up against the door jamb. "How the hell does that make him special?"

The answer was almost lost in the gusting wind and faded almost as soon as it left the old man's lips.

"Because he's the Messiah," Willie replied and disappeared into the frozen night.

~

The officer found what he was looking for, not more than two miles down the road, at the end of a set of erratic tire marks halted by the thick drifts of a filled-in lumber road. There, partially shielded from the highway by a dense thicket of evergreens was a beat-up rusted out Impala with a blown tire and a caved-in front left fender. The driver's door was open and a heavy footfall zigzagged down the snow-filled road and into the deep bush.

Left behind in the back seat was a baby wrapped up in the tatters of an old Hudson's Bay blanket … crying.

Part Two

Chapter One

Stephen stood frozen behind the microphone, dwarfed by the crowd of fifteen thousand on hand, shrinking further with the passing of each fraction of a second. Players, with families and friends, had all crammed into the bleachers of the Metropolitan Arena in St. Louis for this, the most important day in their lives. The smooth cement of the arena floor itself was scarcely visible beneath the mass of tables and chairs, each filled with half a dozen or more animated figures, many with heads buried deep in tables and charts; some talking on cell phones, arguing wildly with unseen adversaries.

At 11:15 the night before Stephen had made up his mind. But as he now stood there waiting for the commissioner's signal to proceed – seconds greeting him like hours – he knew his best recourse would be to block out the inevitable reaction; the shrugging gasps, the stares of disbelief, the ensuing laughter, in fact all the extraneous sounds the arena could throw at him … like he had as a kid.

He stepped up to the microphone.

"With their first pick of this year's amateur draft, the Toronto Centennials are pleased to select Casey Bruford, centre, from Prince George of the Western Junior League."

~

The PR secretary called the hastily arranged press conference to order and began with a written statement from general manager Bruce Hellyer, reiterating the strange set of circumstances of the previous three months that had seen the team's associate scout for Western Canada promoted to the role of Interim Director of Player Personnel, and therefore, in charge of the entry draft. (A story the attending press had already committed to memory and feasted on in far greater detail back when the appointment was first announced.)

"As you may recall, our previous Director of Personnel, Ted Markowitz, resigned his position this past April over a difference in philosophy with management." (Hellyer was a hands-off country club manager, lacking any innate sense of decisiveness; Markowitz was a detail-oriented workaholic constantly screaming for more direction and continuity in the organisation's hockey operations.) "Following the frustration of a disappointing conclusion to last season …" (the Centennials ended the season with eight straight losses and missed the playoffs for the third straight year) "… where expectations never came to fruition …" (Hellyer had traded away their best prospect in the minors for an aging winger who had gone pointless throughout said losing streak) "… those philosophical differences came to the fore." (Following the last game of the season – a dismal 5–0 loss to Ottawa – and after chain-smoking three packs of cigarettes and clearing out his desk in advance, Markowitz marched into Hellyer's office and gave a full analysis of the depth of his boss's incompetence.)

The eager young reporter in the front row could sit still no longer.

"Mr. Hellyer, were you aware this …" he consulted his note pad "… this Casey Bruford would be your first selection?"

"Mr. Loggins," the press secretary spoke up in a somewhat scolding tone, "Mr. Hellyer will take questions after his statement. Mr. Hellyer …"

"Yes … thank you," the GM grumbled, pausing to clear his throat and dab at the sweat beading up on his forehead. "Differences came to the fore at season's end and I took the opportunity to shuffle and revamp personnel." (Several of the other scouts marched into Hellyer's office the day after

Markowitz was let go and also voiced their displeasure. They too were shown the door.) "It was management's thinking that the sphere of player develop-ment would be in capable hands – on an interim basis – with our young and upcoming scout from Western Canada." (Stephen had been on the road when the mutiny had taken place.) "That it might gain him some valuable man-agement experience with an eye towards the future ..." (He was already on salary.)

"Questions ..."

~

The knock on the hotel room door had come around 9:30 the night before and Stephen, knee-deep in spreadsheets, rose wearily to answer it. Not a day had passed that he had not stopped to relive the details of his encounter with Willie. But while the scout's interest had remained keenly piqued, acting upon the old man's bizarre request to pick Casey had been nothing more than a hypothetical consideration – a moot point given the reality of Stephen's powers within the Centennials' chain of command. That is, until the curious circumstance of Markowitz's firing and his sub-sequent promotion to temporary director fortuitously intervened. He had been scouting a playoff game in Moose Jaw when he received word of his reassignment and while the promotion would have been received by any other professional scout as an honour deserving of immediate celebra-tion, Stephen's very first thought was of the old man's eerie wish.

He had decided he would use his tenth-round pick – the last pick of the day – to select the young centreman and no one would even bat an eye. Everyone in the business understands that severe speculation starts creep-ing into the drafting process as early as the third or fourth round with the odd selection of a hotshot scorer from Junior B, or a slough of little-known junior nationals from breakaway republics in eastern Europe. By the final round there would be very few left in the arena to hear Casey's name and those that were would be too weary and sleep-deprived to care. In the meantime, he would attend to the team's sorry need for help along the blue line. Parkinson's wrist had healed nicely over the spring, his office conditioning looked impressive and his worth was once again sky-high. Stephen was ready with the Centennials' first pick.

The knock repeated, more loudly, even before Stephen had a chance to reach the door.

"Hang on!" he snapped as he grabbed and yanked on the knob, thinking it likely Mitch Prudhomme or Les Morris, the two other scouts Hellyer had assigned to assist his interim director. As usual, the General Manager would not be attending himself – July being his month in the Muskokas.

"I'm looking for a hockey scout named Stephen Gillis?"

The face in the doorway wore no discernible expression, but was framed strikingly by straight long black hair, greying slightly at the temples and pulled back into a long ponytail which dangled off-centre over one shoulder. The man wore a grey tweed blazer over a plaid shirt. His jeans were faded and matched the denim knapsack slung over his arm. Stephen did not recognise the man and would have been more immediate in addressing that fact had he not been so drawn to the stranger's impeccable posture. Though he was of a height equal to Stephen's own, the scout perceived him to be taller … straighter.

"Do I know you?"

"Mr. Gillis, a man named Willie Skilliter sent me. He assured me you would know who he was."

Stephen's chin dropped at the sound of the old man's name coming from a voice other than that inside his head. Without so much as a "come in" the scout began scrambling about the room, gathering up stacks of papers that had been scattered across the carpet and draped over the suite's easy chair. "I've … I've met the man," he stuttered as he quickly stuffed his shirt-tail back inside his pants. "In fact, I've been trying to find him. Do you know where he is?"

The stranger paused, a troubled look introducing itself onto his handsome features.

"To be truthful … we've never met."

The response brought the manic tidying effort to a sudden standstill.

"Mr. Gillis, my name is David Thompson and I am from the *Mowachaht* band of the *Nuu chah nulth* tribe. We come from the outer coasts of Vancouver Island. We, among many other groups from that region, are commonly, though erroneously, referred to as Nootka. I am also a professor of anthropology at the University of British Columbia. I specialise in West Coast excavations of ancient native village sites."

"So how do you know about Willie?"

"That, I'm afraid, will take some time to explain. And while I can appreciate that you are a very busy man at the moment, I have come here to request an hour of your time."

Stephen nodded slowly and gestured for the man to take one of the chairs just cleared. With eyes glued to the stranger, he took up a spot opposite him, sitting stiffly on the edge of the bed.

"I must begin by saying one overwhelming thing," the stranger stated, removing his wire-rimmed glasses and rubbing at his eyes, "… and I am in no way comfortable doing this. You see, although much of my research is of my own ancestry and although many of my findings often support the anecdotal beliefs that say a grandmother or an uncle used to tell me, my approach and my methodology is that of an academic. I choose and I strive to maintain a detached focus in my work and to do so it is imperative that I be removed from being part of that which I am trying to study. It is an approach that has served me perfectly, Mr. Gillis … or at least had served me perfectly up until two weeks ago … when the dreams with Willie began."

He paused a moment, his eyes darting up and down as if some wall were in the way of safe passage.

"You met Willie in a dream?" Stephen's eyes popped up as the last of his gathered spreadsheets slid from his hands to the floor.

"Trust me, Mr. Gillis, the reasons for my sitting here, talking to you, hit my ears far more strangely than they could yours. As I said, I am an anthropologist, and while that field lies at the crossroads between physical and social science for many, I have remained a staunch empiricist who demands to examine, weigh and measure things before I enter them into my considerations. Why is a difficult question. Self-adjudicating one's own methods always is. Perhaps it's because I choose to elucidate rather than glorify, perhaps because so much of what I study is wrapped in legend and mythology, I feel I must be as tangible as possible. A good deal of folklore from west coast natives after all involves strong belief in the spirit world, which is fine as a social paradigm within which my research must be understood. However, when something as weightless as a dream attempts to capture my own attention in the here and now, I must confess my first instinct is to reach for Jung or Freud on my office shelf."

He shook his head and again sighed deeply. "He has appeared in a nightmare that has been repeated continually over the past few weeks. In the latest occurrence, the night before last, he was insistent that I would find a hockey scout named Stephen Gillis here in St. Louis and I should talk with him before his player draft took place."

"Why? What did he say?" Stephen said and leaned forward eagerly.

"He said I was to make sure you used your first selection to pick a player named Casey Bruford."

It was Stephen's turn to shake his head. "You don't follow hockey, do you?"

"I know the game Mr. Gillis, but no, I don't spend my time following it. I did, however, devote the majority of the flight here to the sports pages of yesterday's *Vancouver Sun* which ran a lengthy pre-draft report for each professional team. Yours centred around a player named Bill Parkinson as the obvious choice for your first selection. The Bruford boy's name was nowhere to be found."

"He's not widely considered a prospect," Stephen soft-pedalled. "That's why I can safely wait and use a late-round pick –"

"No! Willie was clear about this. He said it was imperative you commit to Casey as your first choice."

Stephen stared at the floor for a considerable time. "I'm sorry, it's just not possible," he said finally, staring blankly at the mounds of data circled at his feet. His guest, seemingly prepared for the scout's hesitation, leaned closer, elbows to knees.

"Mr. Gillis …" he barely spoke above a whisper. "I am not one to act rashly on whims. Furthermore, I'm not a man given to sharing his life with total strangers. But … he knew *everything* about me. Not just details of my past and of the people I grew up with. My own subconscious could easily supply those. But things that had yet to occur. Things I had no means of knowing yet. Mr. Gillis, if you have indeed met this man as you say you have, then you too will understand … it's as if he knows more about me than I do. So believe me when I say to you, I have not made this journey lightly."

"Neither have I," Stephen heard himself say and his eyes lifted to meet his guest. "What happens in the dream?"

"It always begins identically. I'm standing at the front of a fairly vanilla-looking community hall. There are fluorescent lights in rows down a white ceiling. Cement block walls painted beige. The hall is located outside of Gold River, towards the north end of Vancouver Island, however I didn't discover that fact until a week later when I was up there scouting potential dig sites and I happened to stop there and ask directions for a certain logging road. That was the first instance I realised I was dreaming reality. Discovering there actually was a player named Casey Bruford was the next. Then finding you here –"

"So is Willie in the hall?"

The professor nodded. "He's there to hear me lead a discussion with a number of band chiefs regarding the repatriation of native artifacts. That much of the dream is plausible enough. There has been a recurring call among the coastal peoples to reclaim items from the lakes adjacent to the village of Yuquot on the outer coast. They were sold to the American Museum of Anthropology back in 1904. Many pieces pertain to the Spirit Quests and the purification ceremonies of the whale hunt. Wooden carvings, rough-hewn rattles, human skulls and bones, *soul catchers* they were sometimes called, all taken right out of the whaler's watch houses themselves, as were many implements of the hunt itself. Harpoons with mussel shell tips and sealskin floats. Rope woven from strips of cedar. My ancestors were proud whalers, Mr. Gillis. The only coastal people to brave the hunt. So … in the dream I begin with a rally cry, speaking on how such artifacts have no meaning locked up in darkened vaults deep in the bowels of a Manhattan institution, so far from the culture from which they derived their existence and their purpose. I preach how they have been buried and forgotten beneath the eroding force of indoctrination. No longer talismans and icons, but now mere property, held from us by the greatest of levellers – white man's law. Willie sits right there in the front row, alongside all the chiefs wearing an old grey parka and a blue knitted hat, and no sooner have I finished my speech when he stands up, introduces himself and proceeds to inform me he is there on behalf of a future chief, a man named Casey Bruford. But the expression on his face isn't a happy one. He points this accusing finger at me and tells me to save all my haughty jargon for the university where it belongs, with *Mamat'n'i* learning; white man's learning … paper learning. He demands to know what my intentions are – if my goal is merely to recapture these items as artifacts to be institutionalised in a museum closer to home, or worse yet, he says … to be prodded and poked and measured in some laboratory. Or do I truly aim to return these sacred pieces to the woods and the shores from whence they came … to the secret shrines meant only for the select few to lay their eyes on. Do you see what he's asking, Mr. Gillis? He's asking me whether I am there first and foremost as an anthropologist or as a *Mowachaht*. He's making me choose."

"So what do you say?"

"I never get the chance. I open my mouth to respond but every time I'm interrupted by a loud bang at the back of the hall and two policemen barging in the doorway at the back of the room. For the first few nights, that's when I would awaken."

Though the man spoke confidently Stephen thought he detected a slight quiver in his breath, a faint stress to his voice … creeping up and trying to betray his steady calm, trying to press down his formidable posture and sink his shoulders into the folds of the upholstery.

"Mr. Thompson is it?"

"Doctor … Doctor Thompson, yes."

"Doctor ... maybe we need a drink."

~

"Mr. Hellyer, were you aware that Stephen Gillis was planning to use the first selection of the draft on a player who wasn't even rated in the top two hundred and fifty by Central Scouting?"

"It was decided that during Mr. Gillis's interim posting, all player development and drafting issues would be left in his hands."

"Mr. Hellyer ... Mark Loggins, Frontier Sports Radio."

"I know who you are! What's your question?"

"Well, like everyone else in the room sir, I was just wondering whether this is orthodox procedure for a professional sports franchise. As a rule, shouldn't the ship be steered from higher up the chain of command –"

"The ship, young man," Hellyer pointed a bony finger towards the reporter's tape recorder, *"as you so put it, is busy running the day-to-day business operations of this organisation! We simply left player selection in the hands of our scouting and development team!"*

"So you fully endorse Mr. Gillis's selection of this Casey Bruford?"

Hellyer paused to further dab the gathering perspiration that threatened to roll from his forehead down the bridge of his nose. "This organisation upholds the process of drafting young men and granting them the opportunity to compete and develop, with the hope they will mature and make valuable contributions to the Toronto Centennials hockey franchise."

"So there was no discussion?"

"No damn it! There was no discussion."

"And what is Mr. Gillis's status in light of yesterday's performance?"

Hellyer paused again to wipe his entire face, this time drawing a very deep breath. "Mr. Gillis has been reassigned back to the position of associate scout," he sighed.

~

Dr. Thompson sank back into the thick padding of the easy chair, the ice in his half-emptied drink jiggling around the plastic cup that he rolled between the palms of his hands.

"Sure you're OK with just the water?"

Thompson nodded. "The thing is, I would never chair a meeting like that. Especially using rhetoric like that … 'the eroding force of indoctrination'? Please. For those very reasons of scholarship that I mentioned earlier, I have never aspired to be what you would call a fiery activist. Nor have I cared to be terribly politicised in my work. And even if I were …"

His voice trailed off into silence as he thought for a moment. His head fell back against the recliner. His eyes closed. "And yet I must ask myself, if I had been older, if I had grown up back when the residential schools still plucked us from our families and herded us away for eleven months of the year, might I not be more willing to cry out against cultural genocide, make speeches regarding the calculated dismantling of our native heritage?"

"That makes a difference?"

The professor nodded. "Native residential schools – that educational system – left behind a legacy of shortcomings even the most die-hard of apologists for Indian Affairs cannot deny. We probably would have been sent off to Gold River. Myself and James Richard … James was the only other my age left in our village. And we would have been gone by the age of seven, to be taught by instructors and clergy with very few expectations for our potential. We would have chopped wood, painted sheds; we would have had a litany of regular chores. And of course we would have been apart from our parents – parents who had gone through their own childhood being similarly stripped of their culture. Then, at eighteen, with the pagan within thoroughly tamed, we would have left school to fend for ourselves in the supposedly civilised society for which we had allegedly been groomed. Perhaps we would make it. Perhaps not. Perhaps we would trickle back to our original homes – as our mothers or fathers did – knowing nothing about our heritage and even less of the world at large. Needless to say, since I've been having these dreams, I've been left to wonder – academic exploits notwithstanding – if I am not yet a product of this legacy too. I … and James Richard both."

He closed his eyes once more, this time tighter as if wincing at a sharp pain.

"James was raised by his grandmother. I'm not sure what became of his mom. Nobody is really – apart from the fact she was gone shortly after she gave birth. His father on the other hand … well, if you believe all the fables told around the outer coast, his father would have been someone in whom you would have taken great professional interest."

"Good hockey player?"

"The best on the Island as a kid, or so they say. However he died young, just before James was born in fact. It was a stand-off with police if memory serves. He was trying to flee from some run-in with the law. In any event, James grew up fatherless, which wasn't exactly a rarity I guess. But he also grew up angry. As a kid he was the school's resident bad-ass – whenever he got around to showing up, that is. As an adult, well, I believe he preferred booze to shift work at the cannery or out on the fishing boats. Unfortunately through it all, from kid right through to adult, I was his unwitting rival."

"Second string bad-ass?"

"Me? Anything but. I wanted nothing to do with him. Even when we were quite young James was three inches taller and thirty pounds heavier than I was. He had unusually broad shoulders, a huge set of hands, and he seemed perpetually ready to challenge me for what I guess he perceived as a particularly unsatisfactory snobbishness. Believe me, a good deal of my childhood was spent plotting out routes to and from school that would detour any potential confrontation. But those times I simply couldn't avoid him – more than likely in front of the general store or near the docks – I'd walk by and I'd hear the snide comments; the *apple* references whispered amongst him and some of his older drop-out friends."

"Apple?"

"Red on the outside. White through and through. It was always just loud enough to ensure I would hear. And always with the hope that with a reaction out of me some form of entertainment might ensue. Some sign that his words could sting a snotty little brown nose whom he believed kissed the ass of everybody who had kicked his. Fortunately that rarely happened, for while my fear of James was very real, it contained no measure of respect. I didn't plead for him to stop stealing my cap or my textbooks during yet another game of 'apple in the middle'. I certainly didn't plead with him to be my friend. I simply wished he didn't exist. At some level, I guess deep down he knew that."

"Dr. Thompson?"

"David."

"Sure, David ... look I don't want to sound rude here, but most everybody got beat up on the schoolyard at one time or another. And I'm not sure what any of this has to do with Willie ... or with me for that matter."

He nodded understandingly and reached for a couple of quick sips of water. "After about three or four nights of dreaming, I stopped waking up at the point when the police arrive at the hall. Instead they address me by name and take me aside to report a man – a native answering the description of one James Richard – had been seen in the Port Alberni area lurking near the home where a red Dodge Satellite had been reported stolen. It is expected, the constables inform me in no uncertain terms, that I should be forthcoming with any information that might be relevant to the case."

"So what do you tell them?"

Another sip, then a guzzle. "I tell them what I just told you. About growing up. I tell them that these childhood anecdotes are the only association I have ever had with the man. That we grew up to live in completely separate worlds. The officers seem to take me at my word but as they turn to leave, I see Willie in behind them. He's staring daggers right through me, shaking his head in disgust."

"Why?"

"Because ... he knows that I'm lying."

"About what?"

"About what …" the professor repeated with a sigh, shifting himself restlessly about the chair, uncomfortable with the slippery slope of detail that his tale was necessitating. "Mr. Gillis, for as long as I can remember I have excelled in school. Maths, literature, science, it all came quite naturally. Through day school, then secondary school in Port Alberni where I boarded with an uncle who worked the lumber docks. Then came university and the scholarship from UBC. Needless to say, Vancouver was a foreign world. The size of the city. The crowds … twenty-some thousand students on campus alone. My first lecture had 300 students … more than my entire high school. I began gobbling up survey courses with plenty of appetite but very little strain or satisfaction, and of course precious little interaction with others. History, sociology, philosophy … and naturally Native Studies, which I can admit now I took strictly as a need for a bit of rooting; to keep my 'apple' status, as declared by the James Richards of the world, nothing but a spiteful myth. I would be *Mowachaht*. I would be a scholar. I would make one the other."

"Make which one the other?" Stephen asked hesitantly.

"Ah, our friend Willie's question," he replied weakly, then tilted his head back and continued in a louder, almost mocking tone.

"Our very first lecture began with a short lesson in *Nuu chah nulth* vocabulary. *Haw'iih* meant chief. *Quu'as* referred to people, or perhaps to a specific pride of a people. *'Or a people's pride for a people,'* I heard a student to my left whisper. *'Or a people's pride for a great cup of coffee,'* another joined in until soon the whole row was snickering and shaking out silent convulsions of laughter. Unaware, the lecturer continued on. 'Inherent in a term like *quu'as,*' he explained, 'is the understanding of respect. Such respect was sometimes called *Iisaak* … the respect for the spirit present within all things.'

"'*Or the respect for being able to mix their spirits,*' the first student whispered again, setting off a lengthier round of tittering, until one student noticed my silence, then the colour of my hair and skin, and began a domino effect of nudging down the row of desks. It felt like a spotlight had been fixed directly upon my seat. There amongst the supposedly brightest young minds of the province … and I distinctly remember the campus recruiter enticing me with that very phrase when she came court-ing me back in my high school … there amongst those whom I naively believed had to have endured their own bouts of stolen caps and sabo-taged school books just to make it to this supposed refuge of higher learn-ing … there I sat, completely alone."

The professor's voice trailed off again, his eyes lost in a trance of rec-ollection for what seemed to Stephen a great length of time.

"Dr. Thompson, uh … David," he began carefully, "I certainly don't mean to make light of anything you had to go through. I mean, in my line of work, I've heard more than enough racist stuff. Hell I had a minor hockey coach that wouldn't even let any native kid try out. Not to men-tion more than a few old-school scouts in the trade with their theories on Indian players not being coachable … how they'll probably only drink away their salary. It's all a load of shit, especially given the fact most of those fossils spend much of the day stuck to a bar stool in some hotel lounge themselves. But you were talking about your dream before and I'm sorry but I'm still not getting what this has to do with Willie calling you a liar."

"We're getting there," he replied and rose to pace slowly about the room to collect his thoughts, seemingly of a need to choose his next tack very carefully. "You know, I might have packed up and left school right then – hopped the first ferry back to the Island, and a bus for the outer coast, just like all my neighbours and relatives had before me – if I hadn't happened upon anthropology. I declared it my major after one week of lectures. Later that year when the faculty received government monies to begin field work into the study of pre-European coastal village life, my professor picked me to work alongside him on the summer digs. Over the next few years, anyone who cared to listen … and as it turned out, those who didn't … were treated to a steady monologue on my part outlining term papers, thesis chapters, proposals for future excavations. Outside of a handful of grad students and professors, that audience was limited to my mother and …"

"And?"

"– and my younger sister Jocelyn. We kept in touch by mail, seeing as school consumed far too much of my time for visits home. Always some pressing deadline, some class to tutor. Even during the summers, when I was on the Island, only an hour away, I was always too busy at dig sites. Soon enough it would be fall and I'd be back at school studying all week and cataloguing artifacts all weekend."

The tempo of his pacing increased as he spoke and with it came an urgency apparent to Stephen just as the professor's footfall gained a set rhythm … five steps out toward the kitchenette, five back toward his chair.

"I guess I always just assumed she would be interested in my work," his voice softened. "But as time passed, especially after she got to high school, her letters became shorter and increasingly impassive. During the fall of her senior year, at my mother's request, I agreed to look into enrolling her at UBC and getting her away from the go-nowhere influences we knew could hold her down. I arranged to get copies of her transcripts, sent her the syllabus with suggested classes for her to try. I even looked into leasing a two-bedroom apartment near campus so we could stay together."

He was down to four strides … then three, turning faster, eyes planted on the floor ahead of him.

"I was a fool," he spat out condemningly. "I learned for certain later, but I guess at some level I had always known that my sister was not like I was. She didn't apply herself. She would never just pick up some book and leaf through just to see what it was about – I guess her level of general curiosity wasn't predominant. And yet, there I was, imagining her immersed in university life, her world opening up for her far beyond her sights on a job at the local tavern or the weekend drinking binges down at the shore."

He was almost down to a pivot. His drink sloshed from the rim of the glass down his arm.

"As her graduation drew closer, her letters waned even more. Nothing more than quick notes really. Just short, meaningless superficial things. By April, even those had stopped. She had not bothered to send her marks on for admission. Her application was still incomplete. She had no interest in visiting the campus. It was a few weeks after that when my mother walked up to a neighbour's home to borrow his phone. She told me how Jocelyn had dropped out of school, how she had been extremely agitated and unhappy for quite some time; something my mother had at first attributed to apprehension over moving to the mainland and attending school with the white kids."

He broke the rhythm of his footsteps and planted his feet in front of the hotel room's generous bay window, rubbing his forehead vigorously.

"Mr. Gillis, I must commend you on your patience with me tonight. I realise I am rambling on at great length."

"Don't worry about it," Stephen replied quickly, more at odds at that point, in fact, with the professor's break from his narrative. "Are you OK to go on?" he added. "You need more water?"

"No ... no," the professor waved him back into his chair without taking his eyes off the dim outline of the horizon that rolled beyond the brightly lit skyline. He was struggling now. The words tried to choke him and he needed a series of quick hard swallows in order to gain the fortitude to continue.

"She had always been subject to his ... swagger. From the time she first started developing curves. The muscular arms. The big shoulders. There was something about him that was irresistible ... intoxicating."

"Who?"

He turned back toward Stephen with tear-filled need for enlightenment to greet the scout silently, lest he have to say the name.

"You mean James?"

The professor shrugged helplessly, his shoulders slumping forward, his hands falling to slap against his sides. "He had a defiant charisma I guess. Invisible to everyone but those whom it charmed. Like Jocelyn. I was told she used to put herself in advantageous locations, make herself available to meet him. Even when she was a kid, just twelve or thirteen, and he was this brute of a man-child, she would hover nearby the bonfire beach parties, biding her time. Maybe he would show her a bit of attention, maybe he wouldn't. Inevitably he'd end up drunk with some of the older girls from town, falling all over each other. They'd end up down on the beach and disappear down the shoreline for the night. The year Josh turned seventeen ... that April ... it was finally her turn. Two months later, a trip to the doctor in Gold River confirmed that all the agitation hadn't just been nervousness over college. The following October – around six months pregnant I guess – she sneaked out of our mother's house and left the Island for good. Since no one could find James either, it was assumed they had gone together ..."

His voice broke and for several minutes all he could do was ward off the laboured contractions of uncontrollable sobs.

"Authorities in Edmonton," he could barely force the words out, "they found her that winter. She was huddled in an unheated basement apartment ... sprawled across the floor and drenched in blood from her own wrists. They told my mother the room was empty except for an old mouldy mattress ... and an empty bassinet."

He bolted for the washroom and doused glass after glass of water over the back of his neck and all down his face, rubbing it in feverishly with several of the hotel towels, scouring his features until his nose and cheeks and eyelids looked red and burned. Then he flung himself back into the room, landing back in the easy chair, his eyes squeezed tightly shut.

"Each night I dream that I'm running after those policemen," he whispered. "Screaming for them to tell me what they know about my sister. But as soon as I run outside that community hall, I'm suddenly no longer on Vancouver Island. Instead, I'm standing on a deserted highway in the middle of a blizzard ... with Willie right beside me. 'Where are we?' I ask him and he tells me we're in northwestern Ontario and he says it like it should be obvious. Then he tells me about you; about your job as a hockey scout. He informs me exactly when and where I can find you and insists I must go there and convince you to make a player named Casey Bruford your foremost priority. And true to form, I'm full of questions. Why would I do any of this? Who is Casey Bruford? Why would I care about him or some hockey scout? Willie turns to me and with this self-satisfied smile he says,

Because it's your Spirit Quest. And with that, the old man simply vanishes, leaving me there in the middle of the road alone with the faint sound of a car engine cutting through the wind. Soon I can make out a dim glow through the storm; a set of headlights that seem to be coming at me far too quickly given the weather, and yet still picking up speed. When I finally see the outline of the car, it's swerving all over the road … coming right at me. I go to jump out of the way but my feet are stuck in the snow and when I look down to see what's catching them, I find them frozen up to my ankles in a pool of blood. Each night I awaken just as the car is about to strike."

He was shifting around painfully in the chair and Stephen rushed to the washroom to fetch more water and a dampened towel. "A 'Spirit Quest', what is that exactly?" he called back into the room, anxious to maintain all the details of the story in his head.

"In ancestral times, a chosen boy would retreat to the woods all alone for a rite of purification and passage into manhood. He would pray and fast and seek the favour of the spirit world in the hope of being allowed to join the Whale Hunt. But like I said, while I have made a career of studying my ancestor's ways I have never been an active participant in my people's traditional beliefs, so I don't see –"

"He told me Casey was the Messiah," Stephen blurted out suddenly before the crutch of caution could grab back the words.

"What?"

"Willie said Casey was the Messiah … and I'm not what you'd call religious either."

There was a silence as the two men stared at one another, during which the professor seemed to regain a measure of calm. "I think he's in the car," he said slowly.

"Casey? Why would Casey be driving through northern –"

"I didn't say he was driving, just in the car. I think the dream is old. Twenty years old to be exact."

"But he'd only be –"

"– a couple of weeks old."

Stephen remained motionless, working through the waves of consequences rolling through his mind, until his eyes shot open. "You think Casey's your sister's child?"

His guest nodded. "I believe this is what the dream is trying to tell me."

"So who is driving? James?"

He rose and the pacing resumed again, only this time it was a purposeful active stride at double the speed, one Stephen could imagine him shifting into during an impassioned lecture on some aspect of his chosen field. "I've done a fair bit of sleuthing since the dreaming started. Harassing detachments of the Ontario Provincial Police mostly. I called Thunder Bay a number of times, first asking if they had any records or reports from twenty winters ago about reckless driving charges, or maybe a car accident involving a vehicle from out west – either an Alberta or BC licence plate. I asked them about missing children's cases. I even asked if they had anything involving a man named James Richard from Vancouver Island. They said no to all counts but also told me that some of their files would have been purged since then. And they did suggest I try around to some of the other detachments. So I tried Fort Frances, Dryden, Sioux Narrows and then finally Kenora."

"Kenora?"

"That's right," the professor continued, too focused to notice his host suddenly turning very pale. "They didn't have anything on file there either but I talked to a Constable Ross up there who remembered his partner finding a baby in an abandoned car in the middle of a blizzard. He even remembered the date. January 17 – the same day as The Crash, as he called it. One week on the job and still the most gruesome highway fatality he's ever seen."

The professor's account was interrupted by the sound of a glass of Scotch shattering on the floor.

"What is it? Mr. Gillis? Stephen … what's wrong?"

Chapter Two

"You're listening to 'THE LATE SHIFT' on The Frontier Sports Radio Network. I'm Mark Loggins, along for the ride until 2 a.m., taking your calls on this balmy summer night, giving you the listener a chance to have a say. Let's go to Jimmy on a car phone out in the west end … Jimmy!"

– Hey Mark, just wanted to say first off how much I love the show. Listen every night.

"Good to hear. What's on your mind, Jimmy?"

– Well I know it's the off-season and all, but I want to talk about the Centennials.

"You sure you want to get me started, Jim-Man?"

– So what the hell were they thinking?

"Jimmy … if you could tell me, we'd both know, you know what I'm sayin' buddy? I mean I've covered the Cents for five years now, on the beat during the season, at training camp, at the amateur draft. And I thought I had seen everything, with respect to this organisation's level of incompetence, and I mean from the top with Hellyer, right on down."

– Well this is why I listen to your show, man. I mean don't get me wrong, I bleed blue and white, but I still want somebody like you to tell it like it is. I mean, I'm sitting at home last month, keeping an ear to the radio to see who

we get in the draft. You guys kept talking about that big defenceman from out west ...

"*Parkinson.*"

– Yeah, that guy.

"*Oh could we have used him Jimbo?*"

– Tell me about it. They were sayin' how the Centennials had been watching him all year and how he was, like, this sure-fire pick.

"*And I'll tell you somethin' else Jim ... something else that just burns me up. Just off the top of my head, I can think of a dozen highly regarded players – hell a hundred, just here in the Ontario league alone, not to mention Quebec, American college ranks. Europe. Geez there were a couple of Swedes turning the scouts' heads back at the world junior tourney last Christmas. But when it finally came time to step up and select one of these quality prospects ...*"

– Yeah ... who the hell was that guy?

"*Casey Bruford – played fourth line in Prince George.*"

– No, I mean the guy who made the pick.

~

The vast gulf between the world that discussed Messiahs and Spirit Quests, and that which concerned itself with wins, losses, profit margins and salary arbitrations weighed heavily on Stephen Gillis throughout the summer. That which had spoken so strongly to him in the quiet light of a St. Louis hotel room, those words that had proved irresistible in their reinforcement of the scout's own encounter with Willie, were now being tested severely by the strain and scrutiny of fluorescent office lights, contract offers, training camp pre-reports and a host of other practical concerns that made professional hockey the bureaucracy it was.

He and Dr. Thompson had left things open. The professor, weary from both the personal and geographical journey he had undertaken, had requested Stephen not contact him unless the scout managed to locate Willie's whereabouts. Stephen agreed on the basis that the professor do likewise, and on the further condition that he be contacted if anything more became known about Casey's birth, his abandonment or his subsequent adoption. He mentioned nothing, however, of his motives; nothing of his father's death; nothing of a car crash on the Trans-Canada that also occurred two months before a certain Charles and Liisa Bruford adopted a twelve-week-old native boy allegedly found abandoned in a car outside of Kenora, Ontario.

But as the dog days of summer dragged on, Stephen grew to regret much of the arrangement, for in the continued absence of Willie himself, the professor was his only ally; his sole confidant. Without him, the upcoming season offered no sustenance beyond the flat world of conventional hockey thinking as served up by team management and by press row – those warm bodies who lined the arena rafters each and every game night – not to mention the luxury boxes and lounges leased by grand corporations and jammed with wide-eyed impressionable clients, visiting-from-out-of-town investors or company subcontractors, each rewarded with a one-night pass to the game. They come replete with padded chairs; broadloom; a sofa for some of the larger units; a TV monitor for replays, but also with a remote control in case the attending party grows bored and needs to turn the channel to catch a bit of something else; a bar with an extensive beer and wine list and a patient wait staff to read off and serve the appropriate vintage or to tempt any children with chocolate ice cream – Dutch, Belgian, Swiss. There they talk of year-end statements and bottom lines; of politics, broached from the angle of their particular businesses. They discuss the folly of social nets and high taxes. They lament the slothful who manipulate welfare and maintain a carefree existence, financed, they decry, by the hard work of tax-paying men like themselves. They make allusions to greater ills befalling the land. They speak of the increasing number of people begging for change outside their hotel ("They won't leave you alone"), of Quebecois sovereignty claims ("Damn whiners"), perhaps of Native land claims ("If they want more money for booze, they can build another casino, like up there in Orillia"). And, of course, each and every one knows precisely and in great detail, what ails their beloved Toronto Centennials. They point at Hellyer and to problems of mismanagement; they all agree the Cup will only grace Toronto ice when revenues are spent correctly to acquire players with the necessary attributes to succeed. The cost will be high, perhaps even reflected in a price hike for luxury perches such as theirs, but they all accept this as a necessity because there in the plush world of private boxes Hockey is Business. And success in Business comes with a price. And even if the game before them turns into the plodding neutral-ice drudgery of a score-less tie, these tenets will not be questioned. No one will discuss the merits of having attended. They will talk instead of the team earning a point; of getting the job done. They will talk of toil, but not of thrill; of the end, but not the means. They will stare into the ice with stone-faced seriousness. They will follow the game steadfastly … because that is what they do.

These were the people who scared Stephen the most. Those whose voices he heard on those occasions when the glare of fluorescent doubt tried to blind him from the power of Willie's words or the strength of the professor's vision. These were the voices of sleepless nights, offering con-stant cost-benefit analyses for his decision to draft a 150-pound centre-man whose best efforts had produced but a 20-point season.

~

"We've got Rocco on the line from Scarborough. Rocco, talk to me man …"
– Yeah, hey Mark, I just wanted to know when the Centennials' training camp starts.
"Ooh Rocco, you been out of town, guy? Rookies reported five days ago. The full squad starts two-a-day skates a week from Friday."
– Oh OK. 'Cause I was sittin' here listening to the show and I was just wondering if you think any new guys will make the team this year.
"Well … I'd like to say so, Rocco. Especially after finishing out of the play-offs last year, but the truth is, there's not much out there, buddy. A couple of defencemen might challenge for the seventh spot on the blue line … Pickerell from St. John's, Isherwood over from Vancouver's farm system. Maybe, Mario

Pelletier in net ... maybe. Apart from that, I can't see anyone making any sig-nificant impact."

   – *What about that guy the Cents took in the draft?*

"*You mean Bruford?*"

   – *Yeah.*

"*Whoa Rocco, you really have been out of the loop.*"

   – *So he's got no chance, right?*

"*Seeing as he was reassigned to St. John's after only two days of practice, I'd say, no ... he's got no chance. In fact, if you ask me, from what I saw at the rookie scrimmages, this guy'll be hard pressed to make the farm team.*"

~

It was early November when Stephen finally boarded a flight for Newfoundland to go and see his chosen one play professionally for the first time. And there was grave cause for concern. Casey had been held without a point through his first dozen games and had, in fact, seen very little ice time for the past six. It took until the 8:37 mark of the second period – Stephen remembered checking the clock – before the kid finally received the tap on the shoulder and jumped over the boards to take his first shift, the draw coming just outside the visiting Albany team's blue line. He appeared slightly bulkier to the scout's hopeful eye – possibly 165 pounds. Possibly. However, on any given night, he was still probably the smallest on the ice. Given Stephen's firsthand experience of life in the minor leagues, he could not but wince at the thought of any number of 220-pound defencemen only too eager to baptise the young draft pick with elbows and face washes, the likes of which he had never encountered back in junior.

   And yet, despite the scout's worst fears, Casey's initial shift went well. Extremely well. From the faceoff, he managed to bat the puck out of mid-air and through the legs of the opposing centreman, slipping deftly around his opponent to chase the disk up the right wing. An Albany defenceman quickly moved to the outside to cut off the rookie's progress by shouldering him into the glass. But with unsuspected agility, Casey ducked to the ice and slid on his stomach along the boards. Struggling to regain his feet, but now free of the attempted takeout, he swatted a backhand pass up ahead of him in the direction of a yelp from his hard-charging linemate. The desperate swipe travelled tape to tape, and the Albany defenceman pivoted quickly from the boards to race back into the play. Casey's winger, realising he would be cut off, sent a bullet pass right back onto the rookie's stick, completely wrong-footing the rearguard. Now in the clear, Casey swooped in on net from right to left, pulling the goaltender into a sprawl across the face of the goal – stick paddle down, pads stacked – to defend against the anticipated deke. But with a quick cry of his own, Casey alerted his winger and dropped the puck back in the direction from which he had come. His team-mate (an eight-year man named McKeough, whose game included lots of goal-mouth savvy but precious little else) had followed behind at the ready and he fired a bullet to the top right corner for the game's first goal and Casey's first point as a professional.

Before the young centreman had finished skating back along the players' bench to run the gauntlet of congratulatory gloved high-fives, Stephen's mind was already hard at work editing the goal. True, Casey had shown quickness on the draw, but if he had lined up against a Messier or an Yzerman, his stick would have surely been pinned for the count. And while the give-and-go was good, if the defenceman in question had been a Blake or a Pronger (or even Parkinson, the voice in Stephen's head teased) instead of a first-year free agent out of Michigan Tech, Casey would not have squirted free. Furthermore, the scout in Stephen now in full-swing mitigation, a front-line top-league goaltender would have stayed at home on the near post and guarded against the drop-pass, maybe even poke-checked Casey before he had time to make the play.

It wasn't the way Willie would have reacted. Stephen knew this. And he could all but imagine the old man's voice in his ear, urging him to just let loose and belly-yell along with the locals now roaring triumphantly and punching the air directly in front of their perch along the rails. But he was still a scout, damn it. And having done the vocation of conventional scouting the unspeakable horror of drafting the little-known forward in the first place, it was surely time to return to the here and now. It was still his job to evaluate and monitor the kid's skills, to gauge his progress with complete and objective criticism. Surely, that was the only way anything would come of him. For Casey to have any chance at all of success in St. John's and beyond … for there to be any hope of proving Willie right, the boy would need his play critiqued solely with the context of the top league's swifter level of play in mind. He would need to be coached continually, developed constantly. He would need … *need to be fathered* Stephen thought he heard the old man whisper from right behind him – right at the very instant the crowd erupted again and the blare of the arena's celebratory horn was unleashed a second time.

Stephen looked up from his notebook to find himself on the receiving end of a hearty back-slap from an engaging old fan in a sou'wester who was only too eager to describe in ecstatic detail how "the scrawny kid" had just pulled off the very same move right off the centre-ice draw. Batted the puck through the other centre's wickets and dumped it hard into the right-hand corner. The goalie had gone behind the net to play it, but the puck took a crazy bounce and came off the corner dasher on the very same angle it had gone in … right back to a streaking Casey Bruford who deposited the ricochet into the open net.

"And the kicker!" the old-timer continued, "The kid pulls off another belly-flop on the way in … got behind that big Number 3 Albany's got out there on the blue line. Number 3. Shit, we had this Jesus team in here for the semis last year and I'm here to tells ya, nobody could get around that big bastard … nobody!" He paused to catch his breath. "Mind you … nobody's ever thought of droppin' on his gut!"

This was fair enough, Stephen allowed. Every kid who ever laced up his skates for a rep team spent ten minutes out of every hockey practice executing the arduous belly-flop drill – usually, it was believed, as filler right after stops-and-starts and right before wind sprints – but very few ever found a practical application for them.

"Hey!" the fan stopped short his commentary and shook a rather bony hand in front of Stephen's face. "You're that feller … that scout from Tronna! The one gettin' all kinds of grief for pickin' this lad so high in the draft."

Stephen nodded to all counts, but offered nothing more.

"Paper made it sound like you went crazy … but I dunno … looks ta me like yer either some kinda genius or I'd say this kid's tryin' his damnedest ta save yer butt!"

～

Casey set up one more goal before the second period ended, then went on to add a goal and two assists in the third for a six-point night which brought reporters from the *Telegram* and two local radio stations hustling to his dressing room stall. Stephen also made the trip to the locker room, squeezing in behind the door against the wall, spectator to the jubilance of the 6–1 victory. It was a scene he had watched countless times as a player. Everyone from the players right down to the equipment manager and the stick boy laughing, joking, singing along poorly to three or four competing stereos that filled the dressing room with an indecipherable din. Everyone, that is, except the coach.

Ron Schott had slipped into the locker room, swearing slightly under his breath when the door found resistance in the form of Stephen's shoulder. He was a short and terse man who had been around the game far too long to let one lopsided win get the better of him. Coaching stints in junior, then the university ranks, then the minor pro leagues had long since weaned the cheerleader out of him. He had been an assistant in Moncton until that franchise folded, followed by stays in Binghamton, Hershey and Maine, before he finally landed a head job on the Rock.

"Guess we all finally got a taste o' what you saw in the kid," he mumbled to Stephen around a tired wad of gum. "Kid's been knocked around pretty heavy, but this'll go a long way to settle him in."

"Helps when you teach him the sweet spots on the boards," Stephen returned in kind but the coach just shrugged him off.

"To tell ya the truth, I didn't know our corners had a bounce like that in 'em, but the kid's been out there after practice the last two days, firin' pucks by the bucketful at the boards … usually from way outside the blue line. Told me some old-timer in the stands stopped him after his last game and suggested that given the lad's size, dumping and chasing might be the best route to go. Said the old guy told him how Lindsay and Howe used to play the carom in the old Olympia to perfection. The kid did the rest himself."

Casey caught sight of his scout during the middle of his second radio interview, just as he was explaining to a reporter how he hadn't felt this good about his play since he notched four points in one period against Kamloops the year before in junior. Seeing the rookie's enthusiastic smile, Stephen called across the noisy room to offer congratulations on the scoring outburst, plus a slew of other soft-ball comments that most assume scouts are paid to say. How the organisation would be keeping a keen eye on his play, how continued hard work would bring nothing but good things. Used-car stuff, uttered at arm's length.

Part of him would have preferred another conversation, had the rest of him not frozen his feet to the floor and his shoulder to the wall. A more private conversation to help satisfy the thousands of questions spinning round the man's head. Questions about a car crash and a baby adopted into a northern Ontario home. About the lad's knowledge or opinions – if he indeed had any – regarding Spirit Quests, or Messiahs or whale hunts. Questions about the mysterious old man who had suggested the dump-and-chase; whether he had offered his name; if he had worn a toque and an old coat; if he had been carrying a tattered old scrapbook around in a shopping bag. Whether, by chance, he might have mentioned Stephen's name.

~

– *Is this the radio show?*

"*Well this is a radio show. You're on 'THE LATE SHIFT'. What's on your mind tonight?*"

– *I want to talk about Stephen Gillis.*

"*Ah yes, our beloved scout turned director of player personnel turned scout again. Still my favourite example when it comes to what's wrong with the entire Centennials organisation.*"

– *Which is why you shouldn't use your program to single out Mr. Gillis alone.*

"*Hey, on this program we call 'em like we see 'em, and when it comes to this team, there's more than enough blame to go around. Now I don't fault Gillis for getting hired; that's Hellyer's mess. He could have found a qualified, experienced hockey man months before the draft. But instead he waits till the last minute, and for the sake of saving a salary, he moves over a junior scout with less than four years experience. Where I do blame Gillis, is his cranial cramp on draft day. Casey Bruford? What's up with that? There were at least a hundred players available ... hell, two hundred with a better shot at making the Centennials. It's obvious the guy panicked. Couldn't handle the job.*"

– *Have you ever been a scout, Mr. Loggins?*

"*I don't think I have to be a scout to have an informed opinion, if that's what you're asking me. I spend a lot of time covering this organisation and I think I know when –*"

– *So tell me then, when you watch a game, do you see the ice as a mirror?*

"*Meaning what?*"

– *A mirror whereby each rush up the ice exists only within the context of the defensive strategy that awaits it?*

"*Well, as profound as that sounds, I'm not sure what it has to do with anything. But I will say this. If this is an example of how your man Gillis spends his time assessing talent, I say it's no wonder he drafted the way he did. We have to go ... we have a lot of people on the lines.*"

– *But wait ... there's so much more involved here.*

"*Next caller ... Mike in Etobicoke ... you're on 'THE LATE SHIFT'.*"

~

Walking to and from arenas had always been Stephen's preference, though as a professional hockey player it had branded him as something of an oddity. So too had his penchant for arriving at games or practices at the last possible moment; and for being the first to shower, dress and leave the rink once that game or practice had been completed. Yet these were but the tip of the iceberg when it came to Stephen Gillis and his list of idiosyncrasies – constraints by outward appearance but survival instincts as far as he was concerned. He had spent four years in Peoria and during that entire time had rarely strayed from his two-room rental just three blocks down the road from the coliseum. Its convenience and simplicity offered too much in the way of inertia for him to live otherwise. He was close to a shopping mall should he ever dare to make a significant purchase. Several fast-food outlets could be found in a line around the corner to keep him sustained with a modicum of variety. There was a bank where his directly-deposited paycheques were made accessible. And of course there was his best friend, the sign for the ramp to the Interstate out of town perched on the light standard not more than a hundred yards to the north. On painfully slow days off Stephen found himself staring at that blue-and-red badge just outside his living room window, tempting him with the freeway's proximity. The daily view of a means out of town ... an out. As the years went by, those stares grew longer and longer. While the minor leagues could seem like a promising training ground for bright-eyed rookies, for a road-weary veteran two or three seasons of bus travel could soon suck all hope of promotion. In Stephen's case, that hopeless-ness translated into a deep irresistible desire never to put down roots. For him, a sense of the temporary was completely necessary to make his remaining playing days palatable; like a kid away from home for the first time, he shrank his world into a simple, clearly-defined radius so that nothing of his surroundings could be construed as permanent. He avoided memorising Peoria's street or traffic patterns. He kept his car in the drive-way unless absolutely necessary. He passed on deals for townhouses and condos in more upscale suburbs, meeting new neighbours, socialising ... dating. His last two seasons he rented month-to-month when even the idea of a lease felt like too much a commitment. He likely would have continued to do so had the Centennials not put an end to the ordeal that was his career by answering his whim of an offer to join their scouting staff.

Stephen's room-mate on road trips had always been Eddie Burtnyk, a short squat thirty-something winger from Winkler, Manitoba, who could stickhandle in a space the size of a broom closet, but sadly hadn't the foot speed to skate out of one with any significant pace. At five foot eight, 170 pounds, Eddie was plodding along in his tenth season of minor pro by the time Stephen came along, allowed to roam up and down the same wing year after year largely because management knew he was still good for thirty-five goals and because Eddie himself still loved the job. The travel, the road trips, the taverns and the arenas, all of it ... and in that order. His first few years rooming with the man, Stephen had just assumed a career in Peoria was simply far more than Eddie could have expected out of life back in Manitoba. It wasn't until their fourth season together – during one of their highly infrequent meaningful conversations – that the veteran confessed to possession of a CPA certificate which he had started by correspondence his last year in junior, and had completed during the off-season. Apparently he had even attempted some accountancy work back home in Winkler after two years of minor pro but nine-to-five employment just couldn't compete with his passion for the game. Without as much as a single momentary delusion about a possible life in the bright lights of the big leagues, Eddie returned – happy as a shit-laden pig – to carve out a career in the bus leagues, starting out in the lowly old Southern League, with a weekly paycheque of $300 and stops in such exotic locales as Albuquerque, El Paso, Lubbock and Shreveport. Artificial oases of ice separated by vast expanses of bayou and sage brush and cacti. Where the sport made a few local businessmen a few dollars, but where the game itself made very little sense.

Eddie's "wild man" reputation was a wide one. There was the legendary tale of a state trooper pulling over the team bus outside of

Louisville after Eddie had been busy throwing half-filled cans of beer out the window. The officer, not anticipating such a forthcoming reply, had boarded the vehicle stone-faced and militant, asking the players if they had happened to notice the $500 fine for littering posted on a sign not half a mile back down the road. "Sir, yes Sir!" Eddie jumped to attention and barked out with suspect deference. "But we just drove through Missouri and Ohio Sir! And their signs are at eight-fifty, so we thought we better take advantage of the prices – Sir!"

He boasted a bottle-blonde in every port of call. From Salt Lake City, ("name's Larlene … tits to die for, but Mormon so I had to tread careful") to Muskegon ("those twin sisters that are always sitting behind our bench? Met me at their door wearing nothing but a replica of my jersey."), Eddie boasted them all. And Stephen, feigning sleep, was always the first recipient of the slurred post-coital scouting report, usually around daybreak when Eddie managed to stumble back to their motel room. The only saving grace was that the veteran never brought his dates back with him. On Stephen's very first road trip – an overnight to Milwaukee – the ground rules had been set in stone after Eddie, with more than a few backslapping promises, eagerly offered to share the wealth of a couple of "hot possibilities" whom he insisted would put out the moment you showed them your jockstrap. The look on Stephen's face must have been enough to tell Eddie that his roomie may as well have been gay or a priest or both, for it communicated in no uncertain terms that when it came to post-game exploits Stephen would be permanently on the disabled list. The two kept the understanding and such an offer was never broached again, the only repercussion being the birth of Stephen's nickname for the rest of his playing days, delivered with a grin on Eddie's face the next morning at practice. "Say hello to *Newt*," he announced with a grin before proceeding to explain – for the sake of some of the team's slower forwards – how it was short for "neutered." Stephen didn't mind. Somehow it served as a secure buffer instead of a tenuous bridge between himself and his team-mates. And that, too – like the sign for the Interstate right outside his apartment – helped to keep him in the game.

He had been anti-social. He knew that. A loner, his team-mates said, though in his heart, the term seemed overly lofty, implying some sort of stoic independence that, despite outward appearances, he had actually never come close to locating. Not as a child, not as a player, not now. And despite all the grand mystique of hockey; all the talk and romance, the tradition and the mythology that writers, commentators and pundits used to express their passion for the game, none of it could stand up to his strain. He had no fables to lean on. No memories of rustic childhood scenes, no frozen rivers hosting carefree games of shinny; no gathering of village sons and daughters on snowy banks to watch and play. For some these may have been more than myth, but not for Stephen Gillis. All he had known were arenas. Cold January morning arenas with grey steel girders and empty cavernous echoes. So many times he had tried, but failed to recall the day he learned to skate. That moment when after hours – maybe even days – of trying to negotiate some semblance of balance, a magical equilibrium suddenly presented itself with the promise of a lifelong friend. Balance had always just been a given. A birthright beyond the horizon of his memory. A means ... not an end. And as such, he could not reach the next question that asked why. Why had he wanted to learn in the first place? He learned because his father had learned. He played – and now scouted – because that is what he does.

～

Stephen strode quickly down the empty street, looking for the sign of the variety store he was certain he had passed on the walk from the hotel to the arena earlier that evening. A growing heartburn had begun to climb up into his throat, which experience had diagnosed instantly as the result of too much arena coffee far too late in the day; it was a condition which would soon require some over-the-counter relief if he were to get any sleep that night. Adding to his discomfort was the fast-turning weather which had scattered a typical St. John's fog in favour of a surging wind that sent a wall of rain right through the inner lining of the scout's trench coat.

As the storm intensified, and with his hotel still six blocks away, Stephen soon turned his search toward the more immediate desire for shelter and sloshed his way across the road and down a side street toward a couple of dimly lit storefronts. The first turned out to be a closed breakfast counter without an awning or eave from which to wait out the downpour. The second, although darker, had more promise, thanks to a small overhang atop a windowless front entrance. Stephen ran beneath it and pinned his back up against the door which, to his surprise, gave way, lurching him backwards into the crowded, cluttered inventory of a tiny sundries shop.

"At the game were ya?" an elderly lady called out without bothering to look up from her newspaper, chewing away on what appeared to be her own false teeth.

Stephen peered about the confines and felt lost in time. The store was completely wooden … from the walls, to the floor, to the shelves and counters. Illuminated by nothing more than two 100-watt bulbs strung without fixtures over a couple of support beams in the ceiling, it consisted of two short aisles stuffed to the rafters with what appeared to be a little bit of everything and yet, nothing in particular. Cluttered plastic toys were strewn beside dozens of pairs of rubber boots. Model airplanes sat next to jars of jams. Laundry detergent with pickles; chutneys with assorted woollens. And all along the front, next to the door, stood a combination magazine/candy rack that creaked quite loudly when Stephen stepped on any of the floorboards nearby.

Immediately his eye fell to the headline spread across the top of *The Hockey Forecaster* magazine (displayed right beside a fine array of lozenges that promised certain relief for a litany of ailments). "GET THE INSIDE SCOOP FOR ALL YOUR OFFICE POOL PICKS!" it promised boldly. Stephen lifted out the top copy and leafed through the front pages, past a wasteland of advertisements for sports memorabilia and wagering, until he located the chapter that mattered. "MARK LOGGINS RATES THE AMATEUR DRAFT! ALL THE PROSPECTS … ALL THE TEAMS!" The caption lured him, and against all good judgement the scout flipped page after page until he came to the painful but expected assessment of his own work:

> When it comes to prospects in the Toronto chain, the cupboard is pretty bare. Certainly the recent instability within the organisation's management and player personnel department hasn't helped the situation. But when temporary director of player personnel Steve Gillis – and we stress the term temporary here – used the team's first pick in this year's entry draft to select a player that no other team is known to have rated at all (a player they could have waited and signed as a free agent) … well the move speaks volumes for the levels of incompetence that are entrenched in this once proud franchise.

Stephen fired the magazine back onto the rack with such a force that he sent what had been a carefully fanned-out display of body-building publications flying across the floor, an act for which he apologised quickly. He dropped to his knees to right the casualties of his tantrum. This included fishing for the issue that had deflected off the scout's shin and onto a lower rack displaying a number of locally published paperbacks. The first, a tall flimsy book whose title boasted *The 400 Best Newfie Jokes of All Time,* had been knocked over in the process and its momentum had, in turn, struck a farmer's almanac next to it, and then a couple of self-help books, all of which created something of a domino effect right down to the end of the shelf. Stephen scrambled across the length of the row, propping back up the entire line while the clerk looked on impassively, offering nothing further than a cursory "you got 'er" when he reached for the final book.

It was a dusty little paperback and it caught the scout's eye instantly. The Old Straight Track Revisited: Understanding the Theory of Ley Lines. Stephen let out a gasp and tossed the book back at the shelf like it was a burning ember. He stumbled to his feet and began pacing up and down in front of the rack nervously, his clipped footfalls filling the shop with a chorus of heel clomps and floor squeaks. Ever since that night in Prince George, a very small part of him had greeted each morning with the distant hope that this would be the day Willie showed his face again, if for no other reason than to tip the balance of resolve back in the young scout's favour, to offer up a subsequent breath of affirmation by divulging the purpose and meaning behind this entire strange journey. Stephen had taken up the search for the old man with renewed vigour following his meeting with David Thompson, but it had been to no avail. And the task was made all the more difficult – in public libraries and record halls at least – by the fact that the sports media had turned his curious draft selection into their *cause célèbre,* and in so doing had made Stephen's face something of a poster child for the folly that was the Toronto Centennials. And yet, now coming face to face with a little book about ley lines … in an out-of-the-way variety store in St. John's of all places … felt anything but coincidental. Perhaps Casey's six-point performance had something to do with it. Perhaps the curious story of the stranger offering the boy advice after practice also played a role. Perhaps given the events of the past eight months as a whole, Stephen Gillis simply could no longer believe in something as implausible as coincidence. Regardless, he was struck with a sudden sensation in his spine that convinced him in no uncertain terms that this tired-looking dusty paperback had been sitting there on that bottom shelf waiting specifically for him. He strode up one aisle and down the other in a slightly agitated state, feeling the damp of cold sweat soak through the back of his shirt collar as he worked through the wonder of his realisation.

"If yer lookin' for the Girlies, the boss says I gotta keep 'em back behind the counter," the saleswoman called after him, interpreting the scout's nervous excitement in a completely different direction. "An' if it were up to me, you fellahs wouldn't be able ta gawk at dem naked young t'ings at all …I'm close enough ta hell havin' to sell 'em as it is –"

But Stephen didn't hear her. Grabbing the book and without even the slightest thought for his change, he threw down a twenty, bundled his purchase tight to his ribs inside his coat and sprinted from the shop, back into the drenched night.

~

The introduction began straightforwardly enough. One summer day in 1920, a journeyman miller named Alfred Watkins – a man well schooled in antiquities – was hiking high up in the hills of Herefordshire, England, when he scanned the countryside and for the first time noticed something quite startling. In a region where ancient burial mounds, mottes, ancient hill forts, well sites and the like still managed to peek out from beneath the onslaught of modern times, he observed that many of these places seemed to align; that when connected with the eye, or with a straight edge along a map, they suggested the very routes and paths by which prehistoric peoples must have travelled. For the next few years, Mr. Watkins devoted his life and energy to searching out and studying these alignments. He scoured over survey maps by the hundreds, plotting as many of these ancient pathways as he could find and naming them *ley lines* or *leys* whenever no less than five significant landmarks formed a straight line. (A valid landmark being any one of seventeen physical remnants of ancient civilisations which Mr. Watkins himself had laboured to compile in his first publication on the matter, *The Old Straight Track*.)

"But as important as Mr. Watkins's efforts were," the text proceeded, "they were yet a foggy first glimpse through a frosted window. It would be the next generation of ley hunters, following along and building upon the pioneering of this man, who would uncover the key components missing from the groundwork of their founder."

Stephen Gillis might well have gleaned the nature of these key components that very night, had his eyes not grown so heavy ... had he forced them to remain open beyond the foreign jargon that greeted him over the page in the next chapter's first paragraph. *Geographical eschatology ... spatial millenarianism ...* terminology splattered down without so much as a hint of a definition; as if the author – one Agnes Albright – either foolishly assumed the reader would know these phrases implicitly, or was realistic enough to believe the only person likely to pick up the book in the first place would be one as zealously schooled on the topic as herself. Regardless, the result was text insufficient to overcome the wave of sleep fast overtaking the weary scout. Within minutes, he had drifted off, spread-eagled on the hotel bed, still wearing his trench coat … with the book lying open across his chest.

~

"It's 1:15 in the morning and this is 'THE LATE SHIFT' coming to you across the country on Frontier Sports Radio."

– Hello?

"Yes, you're on the air. Go ahead caller."

– Mr. Loggins, we spoke earlier tonight.

"Uh oh, sounds like the president of the Steve Gillis fan club is back again."

– I was trying to speak to you about the necessity for chemistry when it comes to the art of scouting. Now the example of the '3D' line of the Montreal Junior Canadiens back in the 70's comes to mind –

"I'm sure it does, caller, but I think we all got your point the last time. You think I've been too hard on Gillis for wasting their highest draft pick on a scrawny kid from out west. I don't happen to agree, but your point is taken, alright? Now, we have a lot of other callers trying to get through so unless you have something further to say –"

– I am trying to tell you that there are elements to the game of hockey that you, as a radio announcer, could not know anything about.

"Really! And what exactly am I missing?"

– Now there's no reason to get defensive.

"Hey pal, if you're going to come on the air to insult my intelligence, I think I am perfectly within my rights to ask you what makes you an authority to make that call!"

– Well as a matter of fact, you could say I used to dabble a bit in the recruiting business –

"Oh yeah? For who?"

– That doesn't matter.

"No, you brought it up. Who did you scout for?"

– Look I didn't call to pick a fight. I merely wanted to discuss the element of chemistry.

"So what? Stephen Gillis went out on a limb because he felt some chemistry for Bruford?"

– It's possible.

"Well caller, all I can say is he must have one wicked crystal ball if he thinks this guy will ever make it to the top."

– Maybe he will, maybe he won't. It all depends on the strength of the chemistry. Maybe he never makes it out of the minors, or maybe he's a future all-star … the next Great One … maybe the Second Coming himself –

"Yeah, and maybe you should get some rest."

– St. John's was playing tonight, were they not?

"We have to go!"

– How did they do?

"Let's go to our next caller."

– Perhaps you should check your sports' wire –

(Click.)

~

He's back in Saskatchewan. He's watching a group of children playing shinny on a frozen river. Willie sits in the snow bank reading from Ms. Albright's paperback, his eyes dancing excitedly across its pages. His mouth moves along with the text but if he is indeed reading aloud, Stephen cannot make it out. Nor can he hear any shouting or laughter coming from any of the youthful rose-coloured faces scrambling about the ice. The only audible voice is the chillingly familiar, disembodied drone of angry instruction … *"GET YOUR HEAD IN THE GODDAMN GAME! YOU'RE KILLING ME HERE!"*

"But I'm not even playing!" he tries to shout back but chokes on the words. He throws his arms skyward in frustration, but on their way back down they land upon a lectern that has suddenly appeared in front of him, stuck deep into the snow bank. He looks down and sees he is wearing the powder blue leisure suit his mother bought for his year-end bantam hockey banquet – the year before Kenora. His forearms stick out well past his shirt sleeves and the striped tops of his white tube socks show well below his cuffs. He grips the sides of the lectern tightly and begins …

"With their first pick of this year's entry draft …"

"*NO!!*" The cry comes from his mother, sitting on a community-hall stacking chair in the middle of the river where the game had been only moments before. The shinny, the children are all gone and she is alone, dressed in a long black dress, with her head in her hands, rocking back and forth violently. Behind her, at a distance, stands his father, the prairie wind whistling through the shreds of skin hanging from his torn and mangled body. He is blood from head to toe.

"With their first selection," he continues, "the Toronto Centennials are pleased to select Casey Bruford, centre, from Prince George of the Western Junior League!"

"*NO! NOOOO!!!*" his mother cries out again and collapses to the ice. "*YOU'RE KILLING ME HERE!*"

~

He awoke with a start, huddled on the bed in a kneeling position, fighting for his breath. The fingernails of his left hand were dug into the plaster just above the headboard. The white knuckles of his right gripped the spine of the paperback. Immediately he fired the book into an open suitcase.

It would be quite some time before he picked it up again.

Part Three

Chapter One

To: sgillis@centennials.scout/west.ca

Dear Mr. Gillis,

Greetings from the Hendrickson home and on behalf of the Alliance of Christian Athletes.

Congratulations are in order for the success that your faith in young Casey Bruford has garnered for the Toronto Centennials franchise. My wife and I lead the Toronto chapter of the Alliance in a prayer meeting every Wednesday evening and we always make a point of inviting any new players to join us in worship. However, in addition to sending an invitation to Casey, I thought I would extend this opportunity of praise to yourself. It strikes me that our group would be truly inspired to hear how the Lord blessed you and put you in the path of this talented young man. Furthermore, I have always liked the idea of using a time of prosperity as a springboard to dedication and/or renewal to God's Word.

We would be thrilled if you could join us for a time of worship and fellowship. We meet at 7 p.m. at the Faith Tabernacle Hall on Airport Road. If your scouting scheduling permits, we'd love to see you there.

Yours in Christ.
Peter Hendrickson
Hisglory@hotmail.com

~

The stretched white chassis of the limousine edged to the curb. The driver, equally long and stately in his dark and neatly pressed tailcoat, emerged from behind the wheel with his cap carefully placed bill-forward beneath his left arm. He stepped smartly to the rear of the vehicle and, bowing from the waist at a carefully measured right angle, reached to unlatch the back-seat door handle, its polished chrome glistening impressively in the early morning sun.

Stephen Gillis's eyes shot up out of the doorway, first to the patiently dispassionate expression of his driver, and then further, to the towering office buildings that shaded the downtown core. As usual, his latent prairie sensibilities required a moment of orientation; an adjustment to the shadows and the skyline's absence of horizon, where at first glance every direction appeared to be identical – canyons formed by glass fronts and concrete, crevices of business far below the light of day.

A striking young businesswoman approached immediately, introducing herself simply as Sharon. She thanked the driver with a simple yet rather cryptic nod, then instructed Stephen to follow her inside, requesting that he ignore the congestion surrounding the double wall of elevators in the centre of the lobby and proceed instead to the single oak door on the far left back wall marked *Restricted Access*.

~

To: sgillis@centennials.scout/west.ca

Dear Mr. Gillis,

I would be interested in getting together for some background on your association with Casey Bruford. Especially after the start the kid has had. I've pitched to my editor for a full back-page piece in the Sunday edition so some depth from you would come in handy. I can meet you down there at your office, or over lunch if that's easiest. Let me know by Tuesday, if you can.

Doug Lefebvre
Sports writer
Toronto Sentinel

~

It was three weeks after his breakout performance when Casey received the call. In those intervening twenty-one days he had played six more games for St. John's, scored an incredible ten goals, and helped set up another thirteen. When two Centennial forwards serendipitously went down to injury at the end of a long road trip in which Toronto went winless in five contests, these numbers proved more than enough to warrant the promotion. Casey was summoned for a November 25 match, a Saturday night encounter against Colorado.

He was expected to be used in spot duty only – an extra forward for the coaching staff to substitute in, should anyone in the regular four-line rotation need a bit of a breather. Three or four shifts at the very most. Absolutely no one anticipated the performance they were about to be treated to – not the coaches, not the players, not the television commentators or sports writers, not even in the wildest dreams of the harried young associate scout who watched the game nervously from the far corner of the team's private box. Nevertheless, against all odds, against all expectation, Casey, on his very first shift, pulled the same faceoff move he had perfected in St. John's with the same success, tucking the puck between the opposing centre's legs, banking it off the boards behind a defenceman, then sliding between the rearguard and the side wall so he could hop to his feet and swerve in on net to pot his first career big-league marker – after only six seconds of playing time. By game's end, the young centreman had set new franchise records for most assists (4) and points (5) by a rookie player in his first game. The next night in Philadelphia, he would follow up his debut by scoring twice and setting up another. Three days later in Washington, now playing up on the second line and the first penalty killing unit, he would help hold the other team's attack at bay while scoring an empty-net goal himself – converting his own rather odd-looking cross-ice carom off the end boards – to seal a 2–0 win.

∼

To: sgillis@centennials.scout/west.ca

Dear Mr. Gillis,

I would welcome the chance to interview you for a story we're considering for our next edition. If you are willing we would like to follow you for a day or two as you go about your business of scouting hockey talent. (We would not ask you to alter any of your scheduling; we have sufficient budget to travel wherever your job takes you.) Given the meteoric start of Casey Bruford last week, our sports editor has convinced me that we would do well to run a piece on how the complexities of player evaluation have grown in our national sport. We would appreciate your help and input. Regards.

Jeremy Lyons – Managing Editor
Canada at Large

∼

They rode the elevator in silence, an express lift with one-way glass that shot them up past the dwarfed rooftops of the surrounding skyscape in a matter of seconds; past the sixty-four floors of offices between them and the ground, directly to the penthouse suite. They strode through two oversized doors of solid mahogany, then down a long dimly lit hallway that seemed to turn left at gradually increasing intervals, slowly leading towards what seemed to promise some hidden centre core. In the intermittent mirrored panels that trimmed the rich dark cherry-wood walls, Stephen could faintly make out his own slightly hunched form wading somewhat laboriously through the deep pile of the broadloom, and could see how its slumping shape was at striking odds with the quick efficient gait of the expressionless woman leading him. Brief though the images were, they were sufficient to leave him doubting his decision to come; sufficient also to send the scout scrambling to revisit the motivations that lured him to respond to such a peculiar request in the first place. Certainly there had been the allure of meeting the man himself. He was, after all, a self-made multi-billionaire mogul whom everyone in the country had heard of, the vast majority willingly perpetuating his business empire merely by tuning into at least one station of his spectrum of cable channels each and every day. And yet he was a man whom precious few people anywhere could recognise. He was an enigmatically steadfast recluse; a hermit who advertised no part of his personal life and who, for all his success in the world of telecommunications, seemingly took painstaking care to keep his face as far as possible from the light of the very cameras through which he had forged his kingdom.

Risking another glance toward the reflection of his rather awkward frame, Stephen suddenly realised that beyond these curiosities lay perhaps nothing more than his own imagination's doing. Nothing more than the strange, now suddenly vague and untenable extrapolations of the man's character based on the supposition that because his business acumen commanded immeasurable respect, he would somehow be forthcoming in his reasons for seeking a private meeting with a mere associate hockey scout. The now-questionable belief that whereas a Willie Skilliter chose to depart every bit the stranger he was when he introduced himself, and whereas a David Thompson had to slug through the lofty if not cloudy jargon of academia, this man would surely leave no doubt. He would be straightforward in his approach. Businesslike. Questions answered directly. Knowledge shared freely, with open lines of communication. A real player's coach.

~

Stephen Gillis
c/o The Toronto Centennials Hockey Club
Suite 500
1st Ambassador's Place
6 Front Street, Toronto

Dear Mr. Gillis,

An unusual series of circumstances has given me great interest in you. This Bruford player, who until very recently had been dismissed by every other scout, coach, and alleged hockey pundit, must have struck you in a very curious way. I would be interested in hearing about your decision to draft this young man.

I will be sending a driver to your office on my behalf tomorrow morning at ten-thirty. I will instruct him to wait outside the main exit with his cap held under his left arm. I will instruct him to wait there fifteen minutes, after which time I will assume you have no interest in discussing the matter.

Should your absence, however, be simply a matter of a scheduling conflict, please mention this to the driver and I will endeavour to set up an alternative time in the very near future.

Sincerely,
Robin Touchwater
President
Frontier Communications Inc.

~

He slid out from under the solitary beam of his desk lamp in the otherwise unlit room. His gingerly appearance – so far from the physical image Stephen had honed of a ruggedly featured self-made man, fit and trim beyond his years – caught the scout completely off guard and thereby impregnated the next few moments with a considerable degree of awkwardness. He was, to say the least, dramatically stooped – with his torso bent low beneath a pronounced set of bony shoulder blades that appeared to be the only internal support for his otherwise limp-hanging suit jacket. His knees did not seem either to straighten or lock as he shuffled across the floor. When Stephen took the shaky palm outstretched in greeting, he could feel considerable sway in the man's balance.

"Thank you for agreeing to see me," he wheezed. With painfully small steps he ushered Stephen to an overstuffed sofa, then edged back behind his desk where, with a carefully aimed lean, he managed to unfold with a thud back into the heavy upholstery of his own plush armchair. He peered at length from behind a huge pair of thick-rimmed glasses which seemed exaggerated against his thin wrinkled forehead and hollowed-out cheeks. His shaky hands hovered over what appeared to be a copy of Stephen's faxed reply to his invitation. Further silence ensued, to Stephen's mind pervasively so, setting the scout's nerves in motion to search for some compelling words to instigate any semblance of conversation that might help curb the discomfort of the moment.

"Do you watch my network, Mr. Gillis?" he asked suddenly, his halting raspy words serving to startle and further tongue-tie the poor scout. "Yes? ... No?"

"Not much I guess."

"And why would that be?"

Stephen shrugged. "I don't watch much TV in general. Maybe when I'm out on the road and I want to catch up on things ... I did try your news channel a few times, but I guess I found it a bit too ... brief, I guess you could say."

"Too brief," the elderly man repeated with a puzzled look. "Can you explain what you mean by that?"

Catching himself just as the nervous rubbing of his palm into the arm of the leather sofa began to have a less-than-desirable effect, Stephen straightened out his posture, cleared his throat and swallowed hard before beginning again.

"Well don't get me wrong, if you want a quick hockey score or the temperature outside, yours is fine ... great even ... uh, I guess. It's just when you want to know about something in a bit more detail ..."

Aware that his host was now leaning out over his desk with a rather curious grin on his face, Stephen paused to see if disdain might be anywhere to be found in the man's keenly attentive stare.

"Go on, Mr. Gillis," he urged. "You can't offend me with an opinion."

"Well … take this morning for example. I turned on your morning show. I don't know why … because I knew I was coming down here, I guess. Anyway your news woman read off three or four headlines, but before I heard anything about them, the camera whirled around to some weatherman, who told me he was just about ready to give me the forecast, but first he had to send it over to the traffic desk where some other guy told me about a few problems in the east end. But before saying where they were, he introduces me to some other person standing outside on the street, who proceeded to tell me who the very first newscaster was going to interview later on in the show."

"Think of it as good puck movement," his host offered, his smile having shifted slightly left of centre in his amusement.

"Felt more like a big game of keep-away, from where I sat."

"But therein lies the allure of television, Mr. Gillis. It's not what is on your screen at the moment that matters, but the anticipation of what comes next. My industry is about nothing more than keeping viewers curious. And that, as the axiom goes, is all about form rather than content. Quick camera cuts, flashy graphics and music. Sexy, controversial sound bites. In short, candy for the eye and the ear. And brazen though it sounds, this axiom pertains to news gathering just as much as it does to music videos or Hollywood gossip shows."

"So you're saying it doesn't matter what somebody's watching, so long as they're watching it on your network?"

"Come now. You too deal in a competitive field Mr. Gillis. I am merely telling you the specifics of mine. But just because I adhere to their existence, I would ask you not to make the mistake of believing I – or anyone else in a position similar to my own, for that matter – is responsible for concocting them. No one snowflake takes the blame for an avalanche, Mr. Gillis, so the saying goes. Trust me, the further one rises in a position of power, the more they realise the truth of such a proverb. We are all, in the end, just pawns. Myself included."

He paused a moment to collect his thoughts, removing the glasses from the end of his nose and rolling them slowly between his trembling palms.

"I have a staff of two dozen senior producers to whom I grant carte blanche. Simply let their own thirst to dominate the airwaves be their fuel. That morning news show you mentioned is one of our most successful flagships. A production staff of over forty eager beavers each ignoring their homes, their spouses, their children, the outside world around them; each expending at least twelve hours of energy every day, working out the best camera angle or the most effective lighting ... making sure the shots of each anchor also show the bustle of TV news-gathering over their shoulders, writers and editors typing madly, working the phone lines ... that sort of thing's so in vogue these days."

"Geez."

"Geez what, Mr. Gillis? What are you thinking?"

"I'm thinking it all sounds so ... mindless."

"Mindless?" His voice cracked suddenly with hoarse, high-pitched excitement and he struggled forward to lean out over his desk on his elbows. "Do you really think so Mr. Gillis? Because if you do, this would be a smashing place to begin."

The man's sudden outburst did more to startle than engage the scout, and feeling vulnerably overcommitted to his opinion, he instinctively wavered, trying to mitigate his way back to a safer footing.

"Well maybe not mindless. I mean I'm sure a lot of hard work goes into that show –"

"Consuming then?" his host shot back with eager impatience. "Thought-numbing? As if a critical mass were close at hand and the entire world of telecommunications was about to meet its end in the colossal heave of one great, collective cosmic sigh of self-imploding boredom?!"

He looked up just in time to note the considerable confusion washing across his guest's face. "Please do not be alarmed, Mr. Gillis. This is all just by way of introduction," he said with rather a disarming smile.

"But I don't think I understand – because if what you're saying ever came true –"

"Oh believe me, it will indeed become true Mr. Gillis. And on an inevitably grander scale than even my enthusiasm can express."

"But wait a minute … if you're talking about the death of TV –"

"TV, radio, Web sites, podcasts, the information highway."

"But that would take in your own TV networks as well, right?"

His host nodded emphatically. "Presumably, right at the top of the list, yes."

"And after all you've worked for … you'd be alright with that?"

The elderly man once again let his body weight fall back into the button tufts of his office chair with an unavoidably undignified thump and resulting coughing spell. At length, after several whoops of breath to clear his throat, he let out a long and – to Stephen's ear, possibly put-on – sigh, and continued.

"Mr. Gillis, I invite you to look around this office," he said, pausing a moment to allow the scout to do just that. Stephen's eyes were only then adjusting to the dim windowless surroundings where blackened undefined corners merged with the murky greyish walls. Gradually, as his host waited and afforded him the opportunity to peer from side to side and over each shoulder, Stephen became aware that in every direction grew the vague outlines of vast bookshelves, stretching the length of the office from floor to ceiling, completely filled with dark heavy covers of thousands of well-aged editions.

"I've read them all at least once, you know. Many of them on several occasions. Theses, tomes, texts … each one hypothesising about the mysteries of the universe. Philosophers, theologians, psychoanalysts, astrologers, speculative physicists, dreamers, shamans. Some offering mere droplets of insight. Others taking on vast oceans of ideas. But each and every one nevertheless hoping to persuade the others to come and swim in its waters. Now

… I have here in front of me your rather lengthy reply to my invitation, in which you were bold and forthcoming enough to mention some very curious ideas regarding hockey *chemistry*. And while I am not certain that I have fully gleaned your meaning or intention, suffice it to say you endeavoured to relate the experience of scouting to reading a road map. Well for what's it's worth, Mr. Gillis, all these works you see surrounding us are also road maps. Road maps of reality journeying from the infinitely microscopic to the eternal. The tragic reality, however, is that the journeys these maps promise will never truly be attempted, let alone followed, until modern civilisation is ready to revisit and appreciate their ambition and their detail. That is to say, their *content*, Mr. Gillis. And for that to happen, our fascination with form and our thirst for impassive, instantaneous stimulation – for glossy graphics and jingles, for home video accounts of car crashes or tornados, for stunt plane disasters – the whole lot of it must first be ushered to a well-deserved funeral. And as a self-appointed pallbearer, I have no problem trying to use my position to force the process. You said at the outset that you don't watch much TV. Believe me Mr. Gillis when I tell you I find this extremely encouraging."

"But this is crazy. I mean anything I ever saw written about you went on about how television is your whole life –"

"And hockey is yours. Tell me Mr. Gillis, how do you feel about the state of your industry?"

For a brief moment his grin and eagerness were gone, replaced by a sharp stare seemingly aimed to wedge apart Stephen's lips and force out some sort of reply. After several seconds of silence, when it grew evident that none was forthcoming, the elderly man let out another of his sighs.

"This is what I want," he said matter-of-factly, returning his eyes to his guest's letter. "Over the course of our next few visits, I wish to hear of the events that led to your selection of the Bruford player. Further, I would request you resist any urge to cater your account to what you perceive to be my sensibilities. Forgive my bluntness in this matter, but it may very well come to pass that we'll have a great deal to discuss and I am not a young man, so age necessitates a certain degree of directness."

As if on cue, his instruction came to an abrupt halt, displaced by a string of coughs and then an extended choking sound as he endeavoured to clear the stubborn cling of phlegm from his throat. The attempt proved contrary to its intention and instead instigated a second round of hacking, which took several minutes to subside before the man could safely swallow and fully gather his breath.

"Very well then, to your letter," he proceeded finally and worked himself back up over the pages spread across his desk. "You mentioned here that you were first made aware of Casey's talents by a chance meeting with a rather unusual character –"

"Willie."

"Right … Willie. You also point out that this person went on at length with respect to a notion that professional sport has assumed the mantle of religion in modern times. However, you never connected this, nor the bits about the road maps for that matter, with whatever insight you garnered from them that granted you the foresight to pick an unknown like Casey Bruford."

He pushed the letter away from the conical beam of his desk light and with a grin once again peered up into the scout's face over the flimsy wire glasses, which he had returned to perch crookedly on the hollowed cartilage of his nose. With that look Stephen suddenly drew up breathless as a flash of a possibility entertained his imagination and sent an anticipatory chill cascading from his forehead through his arms and back. The lightning quick thought struck him head on. Perhaps the mighty Robin Touchwater, wealthy recluse and self-made billionaire, had also crossed paths with and been likewise tempted by a man in a frumpy old parka with a bag full of newspaper clippings in hand? It suddenly made so much sense. Just as Willie had successfully challenged the conventions of his scouting practices, and just as he had persuaded an ultra-rational anthropologist to follow the suggestions of his dream life, so too must he have encountered and tempted this telecommunications mogul with the pitfalls of his own empire. Perhaps he even knew of Willie's current whereabouts. Perhaps he would direct the scout to him so he could finally ask all the still unasked questions … illuminate the still shadowy mystery of Casey's rise to glory.

"Nevertheless, I find all of this extremely noteworthy, Mr. Gillis, because I, in association with a group of speculators and futurists, have devoted much of my private life to the pursuit of a certain possibility; a possibility that what we are witnessing around us today in so-called modern society is, in fact, civilisation fast filling up. That Mother Earth as a whole sits heaving under irrevocable strain. And very recently a sport-as-religion insight very similar to your own has been revealed to us as a significant symptom of such strain.

"You see, Mr. Gillis, sport is a mirror by which civilisation reflects itself. More than the arts, more than painting, sculpture or music; certainly more than theatre or cinema. For although all of these passions are derived from the world which they observe, at the end of the day all but sport are, inescapably, nothing more than constructs. Fabrications woven by a scriptwriter or playwright, designed to take an audience on a journey that he or she, as creator, has already pre-ordained. Sport, however, carries no specific predetermination. The outcome of the drama is as unknown to the participants as the crowd who gather to watch. It is self-woven as it goes, and for that reason over and above any other pastime, we willingly hitch ourselves along for the irresistible ride. Now on a different but still related plane, I believe sport gains its power when it successfully ritualises the very tenets from which a society derives its meaning. The purest of these to my mind, and indeed the most enduring, is athletics. The track and field events symbolise basic practices and imperatives that have endured from our distant and primitive origins. The sprints symbolise the speed required for survival. Field events like javelin and the hammer bring in the exercises of the hunter, as do their more modern relatives of archery and target shooting. Pole vaulting, long- and high-jumping are reflections of the obstacles thrown in man's path. Distances to be forged and heights to be scaled if food, shelter or safety is to be ensured. Likewise are the disciplines of wrestling and boxing although, in a sense, they reflect obstacles of a different order … man's struggle against his own. The fight for dominance over common territory, from cave to grassland to a circle of mats or a roped-in ring.

"In our western culture however, team sports seem to have effectively usurped individual competitions for our mass attention. Games in which victories are determined with far more complex goals and sets of rules. Football is forever the convenient example here, with its blatant approximations of militaristic conquest. It is a warrior's dance of a dozen separate but simultaneous skirmishes, all undertaken as means towards the shared goal of securing control of a field of battle and maintaining possession of the agreed-upon grail – in this case, an oblong piece of inflated pig leather. Baseball's context, by contrast, is far more subtle yet nevertheless completely tied to the burgeoning mechanistic age of industrialism in which it was born. Think about it. A pitcher throws a ball. A batter swings and hits that ball, thereby initiating a series of pre-programmed production-line manoeuvres. A shortstop pedals to his left, scoops up the ball and tosses it over to second base where his fellow infielder has run to receive it just ahead of a charging baserunner. He, in turn, fires the ball on to the first baseman, who upon the batter's contact has trotted back to his station and stretched out as far as possible to receive the throw. In behind him, the catcher has jogged down behind first to back up the play, lest the production line break down somewhere along the way. And what about basketball? Well it's a different manifestation yet. Much less static. Much more concerned with flow and momentum. It remains, at its purest playground form, a dance of individual expression and skill, the cutting edge of which is born of the cramped quarters of inner-city America. Athleticism and beauty peaking up to blossom through the cracks in the crumbling underbelly of the industrial dream. Far to the opposite end of the spectrum are the playgrounds of the advantaged … the vast greenery that's home to the world of golf and cricket and tennis with the gentility of conquered uniform grasses and the high maintenance of its landscapes, where only the most complex of games with the most intricate codes of etiquette are allowed to flourish with the luxury of time and space."

"And so what about hockey?" Stephen interrupted.

"What indeed," the old man replied with a shrug. "Certainly there are elements of much of the aforementioned. The earliest professional leagues were play-toy possessions of the advantaged. Timber barons mostly. And the game certainly can be warrior-like, though it is also full of grace and creativity. In fact, it seems to be a game uniquely capable of being simultaneously artistic and angry; beautiful and yet cold. Like winter herself perhaps."

Stephen leaned forward in his chair nervously, his anticipation unable to sit through any further discourse.

"This group of people you said you worked out these theories with …" his voice quivered, "Is Willie Skilliter one of them?"

The man removed his glasses again, tossed them down on the desktop and rubbed at his eyes.

"Oh I was fearful of this. Especially after reading your reply. Mr. Gillis, would I be correct in assuming your motivations for meeting with me today revolve around the hope that I might have information on where you could find this man?"

In his discomfort and uncertainty, the scout managed to nod and shrug at the same time.

"Then I am sorry Mr. Gillis, but I confess I have never met anyone by that name. However, lest you despair, may I say that I believe this is actually a point in our favour."

"How is that?"

"It may well be that your friend Willie has independently tapped into the same energies and currents that lie within a number of significant revelations recently bestowed upon myself and my associates. If this indeed were to be the case, then certainly it would lend legitimacy to both our experiences. Yours and mine. Can you understand this?"

But Stephen's head had drooped towards the floor, still limp in the folly of his recent hope.

"I don't know," he mumbled. "I'm afraid I'm a bit out of my league. I'm just a hockey scout."

"That is an absolutely correct statement my good man. However whereas you take pains to self-impose limitation with such a phrase, '*just a hockey scout*', I would counter, from all that I have learned, that you are in fact, '*wholly* a hockey scout'. I hope you will forgive the intrusion, but I took the liberty of having Sharon run something of a background check on you and her findings were most interesting to say the least. You were born in Saskatchewan, raised as an only child, by your mother alone after your father was killed in a car accident. You have never married and have no children. You have never been employed in any capacity outside of the game of hockey."

"And this is supposed to help me how?"

"Quite simply Mr. Gillis, regardless if by design or by default, this sport is obviously your life. Now, it is true that given what you put in your letter, the boundaries of that life have recently been stretched and challenged. But while you might tend to believe this has occurred despite your limited breadth of vocation and experience, I would argue quite the opposite. I believe you have been afforded a glimpse of revelation specifically *because* you are so immersed in the game. That you, as only a very select few are ever privileged, have transcended your experiences and glanced at a deeper and fuller reality. But as I tried to make clear earlier, to explore this possibility fully, I will need to hear your story, told soulfully in the everyday jargon of the hockey world that begot it. I believe it was the philosopher Kierkegaard who argued that for a man to fully explore his divinity, he must first be completely at ease in his everyday surroundings. So it must be for you Mr. Gillis. I have no need for contrived, woven tales for I seek nothing but the natural weaves and braids that make up our deepest relationship with our Mother Earth, and indeed our cosmos. And if what I sense of your experiences is correct, I believe the aims of our separate paths have synchronously aligned. Perhaps we can help each other. I with your search for this Willie person ... you with a missing piece to our most important puzzle."

"What? What puzzle?" Stephen sputtered finally. "Look, this all sounds fascinating but it's a little much to take in. And to tell you the truth, I still don't really know what you want from me."

"For now, nothing more than the truth," he replied, his grin returning and broadening mischievously at the corners of his mouth. "So ... to work."

And with a quick nod he was off, allowing his guest no further opportunity to digest or rebut all he had just heard.

"Now I should tell you that just like every other sports fan in this city, I was extremely impressed with the immediate impact young Mr. Bruford had on your team. However, my interest wasn't truly piqued until someone on my staff informed me that for the two weeks prior to Casey's meteoric debut, someone had been calling the phone-in shows on our Sports Radio station on a regular basis offering eloquent speculation about how young Casey was destined to suit up for the Blue and White because of a symbiotic connection he had with the man who had first scouted him. How that connection was – and I'm quoting from one of the transcripts here – 'manifest in terms of a chemistry that transcends hockey and has its underpinnings in the very energies of the Earth herself'."

"Wait. That sounds like something Willie might have said."

"Perhaps yes ... perhaps no," the old man replied slowly while, with all the careful deliberation of a small child stamping her very first envelope, his shaky hands endeavoured to re-attach the little yellow post-it note from which he had read the quote, back on the top sheet of Stephen's letter. "Nevertheless ... it was this person's insight that compelled me to contact you."

The piece of paper securely back in place, the old man proceeded to shuffle through the top few pages of the scout's lengthy response, as if seeking out a specific line or passage. Stephen knew well which one. It was the one he had stewed and fretted over, adding and deleting on several drafts before finally summoning enough reckless courage to include it. It was the one now plainly visible beneath the beacon of the man's lamp, highlighted and circled in bright red ink.

"You wrote here that Willie referred to the boy as the Messiah," he noted impassively, his voice offering the scout a hint of neither scepticism nor affirmation, as if either option were equally plausible and worthy of consideration.

"I know it sounds crazy. I mean why the hell would some Messiah waste his time playing hockey?"

"As opposed to what?"

"I don't know. Feeding the poor. Healing the sick. Overthrowing some dictator –"

"Mr. Gillis ... Stephen ... while I'm sure you must thirst for an answer to that question, I'm afraid it is not my place to impose upon you with my ideas of what constitutes being a Messiah. For now let us simply treat your friend Willie's statement as a starting point and explore from there. Now, you are a dedicated hockey scout, so if one is to believe you were indeed chosen to bring Casey Bruford into prominence, then one must also believe that your sport is integral to the process in some deep and essential way."

"I guess ... maybe," the scout conceded thoughtfully. "Except I don't think Willie was after anything good."

"What do you mean?"

"Well, whenever Willie started comparing something about hockey – or any sport for that matter – to something about religion, it was always negative. Like it was some sort of sign of doom."

"Whose doom? Sport or religion?"

"I don't know. Both maybe? All I know is ... he had this scrapbook full of newspaper clippings. Stories about the down side of pro sports. Riots, brawls, player walkouts. But he was also down on a lot of religious issues. The way preachers talked. Told other people what to believe. That sort of thing."

Touchwater nodded knowingly.

"Perhaps he has reason. Both roads are well fraught with danger. A charismatic's preaching can, after all, ring in the ears of his followers so sweetly, they soon begin adoring the sound of his voice more than the meaning of his words. Similarly, a sports fan can live and die by his favourite athlete's exploits, deifying him because of nothing more than an ability to skate or run or throw a ball, forgiving him any indiscretion – drug trafficking, assault, rape – with instant absolution … saved by the sheer sweetness of his athletic skill. This is why I prefer shadow over lime-light Mr. Gillis. A man in my position can all too easily stop seeking the energies that fuel him; spend his life instead emulating the persona that inevitably builds up around his success. From there it's but a dangerously short skip to the role of converter really. Through the years, I have come to learn much about the man whom I greet in the mirror every morning. Chief amongst these lessons is the understanding that he has no place in the persuasion business. Of course many of my more strident critics would dismiss this point as complete nonsense, citing my involvement in radio and telecommunications as persuasion of the first order. And while it's true they do not know me even as clearly as you do already, Mr. Gillis, I am always willing to admit my reclusiveness may yet prove to be noth-ing more than a self-serving contradiction. It's difficult to judge really. One's humanity is, after all, a continual debate … a constant conversa-tion."

He checked his watch and appeared startled slightly by the time. "Goodness, it's getting on, and I have meditations to attend to," he stated and began to rise gingerly to his feet, faster than he ought to have, as the motion caused yet another bout of coughing from deep in his chest.

"I would like to leave you with one more thought," he sputtered through the congestion. "A reiteration of sorts, I suppose, but neverthe-less. Please do not assume you have been burdened here with something beyond your scope. Instead, I urge you to follow the journey in the ways that you know, so that the secrets of its meaning and direction will unlock in the natural measure of their time. Oh and one more thing … quite important really. As I'm sure you can appreciate, the matters I attend to here in my private office are not quite ready for public broadcast, to put it mildly. So for now I would expect you to keep our association in the strictest confidence. Now … please wait here and in a moment Sharon will be around to show you out. I will be in touch when I need to speak to you again."

And with that, he pressed a switch on the base of his desk lamp causing one of the bookcase sections to unfold and reveal a doorway bathed in greyish blue light, scarcely brighter than the room the two were in. Without a further word, the old man waddled through it and disappeared, leaving the entrance to close again and Stephen Gillis to sit alone … in the dark.

Chapter Two

To: sgillis@centennials.scout/west.ca

Dear Mr. Gillis,

I am writing to thank you for the example you've shown in scouting and drafting a player like Casey Bruford. My son is an eleven-year-old centreman on the Nepean AAA peewee hockey club and it's refreshing to see a professional recognising that heart and desire are still more important attributes than a player's height and weight.

My son and I have drawn a lot of inspiration from the example you have set. Clint is pretty small himself, so despite his natural ability, it took a fair bit of convincing before his coach agreed to card him for the rep team. But when I see the effort the young Bruford kid puts forth, I realise all the persuading and all the sacrifice is worth it. Because I'm sure you'll agree a boy just can't get the development and coaching he needs at a house-league level. Thanks again.

Sincerely,
Clint Young Sr.

⁓

To: sgillis@centennials.scout/west.ca

To Stephen Gillis:
Scout for the Toronto Centennials

    I'm a college basketball player going to school down here in Pennsylvania and I have to do this communication studies project to help my tutor keep my grade point average over 2.5 so I'm eligible to play. She said I have to write a paper that compares my goals in life to somebody else's, but she said I can't use anybody who plays basketball. She says it has to be somebody different. So I got thinking I could write you. See I grew up in Regent Park in Toronto. Not what people down here consider to be basketball country. All my team-mates think cause I'm on scholarship from Canada I must have lived in some igloo or something. Anyway I'm still a big Centennials fan, even though it's hard to get you guys on TV down here. But when I saw that article in *Sports Unlimited* about how nobody but you paid any attention to Bruford I thought I could write about you. You know, get the scout's perspective. See my goal is to get drafted and play pro basketball even though our conference gets about as much TV coverage down here as the Centennials. But I got the highest scoring average on the team in our first three games, and my plan is to stay positive throughout the year, cause all that counts is our conference tourney. If we could win that, then it would be a trip to the nationals in March where my game could get some major exposure. I guess you could say I'm looking for a ticket like Casey got from you. Some of the guys say I'm dreaming, but I look at it as my master plan.
    The way I figure, Casey must have had a plan too. And you must have seen it, cause you're the only one who thought he was any good. Was it all his attitude? Or just hustle? I need to know cause I want to sort of incorporate him into my plan. And I can also use it for my paper, cause like I said, I gotta keep up my grade point average and my tutor says I can't write about basketball.
Thanks a lot.

Cedric Manville
Lehigh University

～

To: sgillis@centennials.scout/west.ca

Greetings …

from a fellow seeker whose path is as the wind and whose visions are not his own. I have felt your pain. I have dreamed your mother's tears cutting through the howling winter wind. Your feet frozen in blood-stained ice. But take heart. For I will buoy your resolve, even when the hour grows darkest, for it is surely set to blacken. We dwell in critical times, my brother, but by nothing other than sheer grace, ours has been ordained the task of the usher. To bid revelation near. Listen to Brother Touchwater and do not be afraid, but know that he is as we both are – sojourners aloft on the wings of destiny.

I have dreamed the day and hour. I have seen the multitudes gathering by the thousands on either side of the battle plain. Those who come only to watch, will be unable to flee. Those who keep The Watch will be spared. Keep this in faith.

Brother Amos

～

"Any questions from our first meeting?"

"No, I don't think so," Stephen quickly replied as he eased back onto the sticky leather of the same sofa he had occupied on his first visit ten days before, where the same spell of accommodating obedience still resided. In fact, hundreds of questions raced through the scout's consciousness, as they had done ever since the two first met, bombarding him in the middle of the night as he sprang from the sweat-soaked sheets, shaking with the images of a blood-frozen river and a widow slumped and wailing before a mangled corpse, its venomous screams the only remaining signs of its life. The urge in those dark hours – as it was now again in the uncertain shadows of Mr. Touchwater's private suite – was to race back for some manageable daylight. It was not to sit and linger in the cacophony of vulnerability that seemed intent on surrounding him. He felt no innate ability to conquer the onslaught, to amalgamate the buzz in his head into one overall question that when answered might quell his building confusion. So instead he sat stiffly silent, his shoulders slumping in somewhat of a cringe, like a half-pint centreman deciding to turtle in the face of the 230-pound enforcer he had just unintentionally provoked.

Winter had come with a vengeance that afternoon, turning the streets of downtown Toronto into snow-blown wind tunnels – conduits clogged with slushy dark brown sludge, impassable clusters of skidding or stalled vehicles and cumbersome streetcars creeping along at micro-distances per hour. Touchwater's office, however, remained unaffected. The room temperature seemed staggeringly warm – warmer than Stephen had remembered it being previously – to combat the old man's throat and chest ailments, he assumed. And of course the windowless room had no vantage point for the storm. It was instead still lit by the single beam of the desk lamp shining down on the ink blotter beneath the old man's wrinkled hands, where Stephen's letter still sat, though now greatly adorned with what appeared to be scores of hastily jotted margin notes.

"Casey is still doing well I see."

"Four more games. Ten more points," Stephen supplied.

"Splendid. So then … to continue our task. Today I would like to turn our attention to this whole idea of these ley lines. It's been rather refreshing these past few days, I must say … brushing up on my Alfred Watkins. Quite the antiquarian, he was. All about uncovering the pathways that ancient cultures used in getting about. Formulating criteria as to what constituted the points whose alignments might prove these paths. However, I'm afraid as founder of ley ideology he was far more stringent than your friend Willie. Watkins insisted on the alignment of at least four or five sites – be they a ruin or a hill fort or what have you – before he would grant status for a true ley line. According to your letter Willie offered you but two. Your hometown and an alleged birthplace for Mr. Bruford, which, by the way, I wish to ask you about presently. Now as I'm sure you realise, any two points on a map can be joined by a straight line and therefore cannot claim to be proof of a ley. You did, however, go on to describe how Willie tried to make a connection between these two locations on the basis of their mutual proximity to 49 degrees north latitude – your town at 49 degrees 10 minutes; the BC locale at 49 degrees 22 minutes. And I suppose there may be something to this, especially when this is considered alongside what I believe is the far clearer portal of inquiry. That is to say, the matter of the shared place name. Estevan and Estevan Point. I find something deliciously synchronistic in this. Much like the old St. Michael's line that ley proponents love to hang their hat on. Seven independent points all in a line in southern England and all named after the same saint. I had Sharon do a little research yesterday and with respect to the origin of your hometown's name there seems to be a difference of opinion. One side holds that the community was named in honour of two men who served as president for the CP Railroad, one George Stephen and a W.C. Van Horne. The other maintains it was created solely for Stephen, who apparently used 'Estevan' as his telegraph name. Now as for the boy, I confess I'm still somewhat confused."

Touchwater fumbled to the second, then the third page of Stephen's file. "Yes, here it is. You say here that Willie claimed he was from Estevan Point on Vancouver Island. This despite the fact Casey himself calls Thunder Bay his home. Now I know since his rise to stardom the media have been making a meal about his story; how he was abandoned soon after birth, found on the open road and then raised by a single parent. So are you telling me you believe this young man was actually born on the west coast and transported halfway across the country before any of this occurred?"

Stephen squirmed loudly against the leather beneath him. "Well yes," he sighed nervously, "shortly before the player draft I learned there was a possibility Casey may have been taken from a home on Vancouver Island."

"The boy admitted this to you?"

Stephen shook his head slightly. "That's the thing. I'm not sure he even knows."

"Well then how do you?"

The scout opened his mouth, much of him of a will to tell all; about Thompson and his dreams about Willie, about the frozen highway and James Richard. But blocking the way of his resolve was an impossible image in the scout's mind. It was of the professor, sitting beside him in the shadowy office listening to this billionaire's vague notions. Perhaps it was the memory of the anthropologist's persistent need to temper the accounts of his dream-life with testimonies to his career as a rationalist, or perhaps it was the recollection of how ill at ease he was as a scientist bowing to the urge to come find Stephen in the first place. For the expression Stephen envisioned on Thompson's face was surely not one of acceptance, and as quickly as the wishful wave to communicate candidly had splashed upon him, it receded, leaving the scout no choice but to leave the professor's name out of the story altogether.

"A man I met from out there," he shrugged, his eyes focused squarely on his shoelaces. "He teaches at UBC. He's native too, just like Casey."

"Really?" the old man replied, his eyebrows dancing upward suddenly. "This is very interesting. Very interesting indeed … and I should like to hear more about this man. Once you feel sufficiently comfortable to share such information, that is."

Stephen looked up sheepishly just in time to see the corners of his host's mouth break into the mischievous grin that he remembered so clearly from their first encounter.

"I also put Sharon to work on the origins for the name of Estevan Point."

"Well if my town was named after railroad builders, wouldn't that place be the same?" Stephen spoke up with considerably more comfort, having been let off the hook in such an agreeable manner.

Touchwater shook his head with what seemed unwarranted excitement. "Except the CPR wasn't built past Port Moody on the mainland. Furthermore, Estevan Point isn't an incorporated town, but merely a landmark along the outer coastline. No, it turns out the name has no historical connection to your town whatsoever. It is in fact far older; named for Esteban José Martínez, a lieutenant on the first Spanish exploration to the area back in 1774."

Stephen slunk back in his seat, the constant ebb and flow of confusion pushing forth again.

"No cause to be glum, Mr. Gillis. This is exactly the type of association we're looking for."

"But you just said there's no connection –"

"No historical connection Stephen. No deliberate connection. The association therefore, if it does indeed exist, lies between you and the boy, perhaps evolving even as we speak. Perhaps seeking to mesh with the connections and associations of many other seekers. This is what *we* are about my friend! The points of experience where cause and effect are torn away, and the weave of a stronger fabric is found anew. Or, as a ley hunter might say, where the invisible line has been made visible –"

"I have a question now," the scout blurted out, shooting up his hand, just as another image of David Thompson's disapproving face flashed across his mind.

"Yes Stephen."

"Who do you mean *we*?"

"I beg your pardon?"

"In the first meeting you mentioned there are people you associate with about this … stuff. And just now you said this is what we are all about, but apart from telling me in no uncertain terms that Willie wasn't one of you, you haven't mentioned anything about this group of yours. So, I was just … kind of … curious …"

The smile gone, Touchwater stared blankly at his guest for a considerable length of time, leaving Stephen unable to decide if he was asking for information that the man considered obvious or simply irrelevant.

"Very well," he replied finally and with his patented heavy sigh checked the watch slung loosely around his shrivelled wrist, then reached down into a side drawer. Slowly and laboriously he lifted out a considerable stack of file folders, wincing as he negotiated an elbow back out of the drawer and up onto the desktop. Just when Stephen began to wonder if he should rise and be of assistance, Touchwater let out a mighty grunt and jerked the entire pile up over the edge of the desk, letting the files fall from his hands in a rather unceremonious heap. He then opened the top cover and began leafing through several loose pages, most of which seemed to be copies of letters carrying the same Frontier Communications letter-head that Stephen remembered from his own original invitation.

"Let me see here … this is Cameron Dawkin's work. He's something of a Templar Knight fanatic … studies that whole realm from an estate somewhere along the coast of Dorset in England. And somewhere in here I have Marjorie Doyle's. She's a freelance journalist out of San Francisco who specialises in lost wisdoms. I guess our most noted associate would be none other than Harland Mortimer, author of *The Seven-fold Path,* and all the subsequent self-help companions that followed. Certainly you've seen them. They're in every magazine rack of every grocery store from here to New Zealand, which is where Harland resides, by the way. In fact it was Harland who first steered me from the path of business tycoon and aspiring communications despot to the role of Watchkeeper, although I will amend that by stating it was in no way through the sentiments found in any of his mass-market self-awareness paperbacks. No, our association dates well back beyond the so-called success of those publications. Back to a letter he sent to me – as he did to men of influence throughout the world, I later learned – convincing me of the existence of cosmic forces at work in the universe that are far greater than any of those we dare to manipulate and conquer. I should also note that Harland is the man who has recently steered me towards this interest in the interconnected ener-gies between popular sport and religious fervour. He sees both as prime societal manifestations of the vast cosmic energies that currently sit under severe – if not irrevocable – stress. A pressure point in the seam of history, poised to split open the very fabric of civilisation … or so he puts it. Since this revelation he and I have been working constantly with others in The Watch. Bartholomew Wolfe, the former Jesuit who founded his own spir-itual movement with a number of renowned Buddhist monks, he's one. And though you have chosen not to bring it up, I have no doubt Brother

Amos will have sent you his own poetic take on things by now. He calls the mountains of Peru his home. However, with all this said, I would caution you strongly to resist the urge to define this so-called association too rigidly, for the only true common component of The Watch – indeed its sole *raison d'être* – is nothing more than the shared need to explore those elusive energies which underlie the drone of modern existence; those which shape and fuel people's most essential connections between one another, and indeed between themselves and the cosmos."

"And you think I fit into all this somehow."

"Recent events have suggested this, yes."

"What events?"

Again Touchwater reached into the drawer, this time pulling out a wafer-thin remote control, and with one press of its keypad, set a series of operations in motion. The entire library shelf to Stephen's left suddenly retreated backwards, then slid sideways into the inner wall, revealing a wide-screen television monitor which had spun around to face the two men. Then, using a second remote, the old man launched a programmed series of news clips all spliced in quick succession – sporting events with eager cheering crowds, news footage filled with images of mobs and riots, confronting police and military forces. It all strobed past the scout's eyes far too quickly for him to recognise much in the way of specifics until the sequence came to an abrupt halt, stalled frozen on a still-shot. The frame depicted a small rural high school on a hill overlooking a sweeping vista of farmland in the background. Stephen remembered the scene.

"Hey, that's that school in North Dakota. The one that was in the news. Didn't some kid go crazy inside and try to shoot the place up?"

"Well not exactly …" Touchwater replied, the image of the picture reflecting back against his glasses and forehead, actually warming the dark room behind him in a bath of bluish light. "His name was Simon Plagenet. He was a fifteen-year-old *Chippewa* and a student at the school. Simon's father John had been incarcerated for most of the boy's life, serving time for his involvement in an armed stand-off with FBI over land rights a dozen years ago. Apparently the boy blamed much of the considerable sorrow in his own life on what he saw as a wrongful separation from his father … he grew up impoverished, with an alcoholic and rather violent mother. And on the morning of Wednesday, November 22, two days after his father had been denied parole for the third time, young Simon, who had somehow managed to procure an entire arsenal of rifles, went down to his school and for three days held an entire classroom hostage while he demanded his dad's immediate release."

"But the news said nobody was killed, right?"

"Initially no," Touchwater sighed. "But three days later, on the following Saturday night, and after he had let the last of his captives go free, the boy pressed the barrel of his rifle up under the roof of his own mouth. Now, that same day I received a rather excited phone call from Harland down in Christchurch. Rugby being his sport of choice, he had planned to take in the match that day as his beloved All Blacks were scheduled to host the Scottish national squad in an exhibition match. But things turned tragic almost from the outset, and in the aftermath, my friend confessed to an overwhelming compulsion to contact me about what he witnessed that afternoon. The match had begun in traditional Kiwi style, with the home side performing their ritual *haka*. It's a pre-game warrior dance based on ancient Maori tradition."

"Yeah I think I've seen that on TV."

"Then you'll know it includes a number of gut-wrenching screams combined with slow exaggerated leg movements and squats, not to mention some rather hideous facial contortions. All very aggressive, all very choreographed, and all designed to intimidate an opponent and whirl their own spirits into a frenzy. On this day however, just as the squad launched into their routine, a most disturbing incident occurred. The All Blacks' captain, a Maori himself and, according to Harland, quite an outspoken advocate for aboriginal rights, suddenly came to a complete standstill, threw back his head and with arms stretched out skyward, screamed at the top of his lungs. He then fell limp to the pitch where he was pronounced dead immediately."

"What? A heart attack?"

The old man shrugged. "If Harland knew, he never said. You see, my friend was far more preoccupied by what the captain had shouted before he died."

"What?"

"Well, first he cried out a word that Harland thought sounded like *OMMEAMEE*. Next he yelled out the word *RUGBY.*" The old man paused for no other reason that Stephen could see than to milk the moment for all its dramatic worth.

"There was something else?"

"Yes. Simon Plagenet's name."

Touchwater adjusted his glasses to focus on his guest and better gauge the impact of the story. His squint found Stephen chewing hard on his fingers, putting in the work necessary to believe it all.

"So the rugby player must have heard about the kid on the news."

Touchwater grinned and shook his head slowly. "Harland didn't even know anything about the hostage story or who the boy was until I told him. In fact I had Sharon check the news logs of all the Kiwi broadcast stations and newspaper reports. No one down there had picked up anything about the Plagenet boy from the news wires. No, the reason Harland called was strictly to see if I could shed some light on the first term the Maori player screamed. *Ommeamee.*"

"Probably something in his native language."

"One would assume, yet after hours of sleuthing, my friend had been unable to locate the term in any Maori dictionary or text or resource book whatsoever. I, on a completely different tack, set out to explore the North Dakota angle, delving much further into the backgrounds of both Simon and his father. As I said, the Plagenets were *Chippewa,* or *Ojibwa,* if you prefer the other anglicisation. I also became quite intrigued when I learned that the town where Simon's father grew up, and indeed the town where the boy was born, happens to sit no more than a few miles from the geographical centre of the entire North American continent. Even more curious, is that the town's name is *Rugby.*"

"So you think this rugby player and the kid had some kind of connection?"

The old man pressed the palms of his hands out toward Stephen as much to quell his own over-excitement as to hold back the scout's questions. He gulped for a few short but necessary breaths and continued eagerly. "Well I still wanted to be cautious so I had Sharon explore the matter of placing this word *ommeamee*." He drew another breath, long enough this time to pull out a handkerchief and dab at the moisture now beading on his brow. "Incredibly ... the only match she uncovered was *Ojibwa!* A word meaning 'people of the peninsula'. This word has also been anglicised popularly. You would know it as 'Miami'."

"As in the city?"

"Well this bit of news just set us in full motion, Stephen. Immediately Harland and I and several others of our Watch began a world-wide search for any other noteworthy events occurring that day which involved *Ojibwa* people, or natives in general ... especially if that event had anything whatsoever to do with some aspect of sport."

"And?" Stephen urged impatiently, now as far to the edge of the sofa as he could safely manage.

Touchwater smiled warmly, opened yet another file and began leafing through sheets of notes. "One ... a group of archaeologists were to meet with the mayor of Miami, Florida that day regarding a proposed act to protect what is believed to be a massive artifact find sitting directly under the city. Experts believe the site pre-dates all European contact by many centuries. There is some speculation it might even be Mayan which is of great interest because ... Two, a faction of native Chiapas nationalists in southern Mexico also chose that Saturday to reclaim and occupy a Mayan ruin just north of the Guatemalan border. Meanwhile, Three ... in Salt Lake City, a large group of Latter-Day Saint adherents made up almost exclusively of native Utes voted to break away from the Mormon Church. An original tenet of the church's founder, Joseph Smith, holds that the American Indians were actually the manifestation of the lost tribes of Israel and it was the newly splintereds' belief that this tenet had become lost in the complacency and comfort of middle-class religion. Interesting though – and let's call this Three A – included in the congregation was a running back for the Brigham Young football team who showed his support by going out and rushing for an unexpected 245 yards against the University of Wyoming that day before he handed in his pads and burned his jersey immediately afterwards. Oh yes … and Four …"

The old man stopped to gather in all the loose files, pushing them one by one to the far side of the desk until only one remained. He tapped his forefinger repeatedly across its top page, but kept his beaming gaze fixed straight ahead lest he miss the precise moment when the scout's eyes shot up wide. "That's right, Mr. Gillis … on that very same Saturday … Four … an upstart rookie hockey player abandoned at birth … a young native overlooked by every professional hockey scout save one … is summoned from the minors for his very first big-league game. He scores on his very first shift. Collects five points by game's end."

Touchwater fell back into the plush folds of his chair.

"This is why you're here. I need to learn what you saw in the boy. And furthermore I need you to keep watch over him. To listen and note the ways in which he explains his successes. If he speaks mostly of luck and good fortune. If he views his meteoric rise as some sort of gift or birthright. I need to know what fuels him to excel. Approval? Anger? A sense of mission or destiny, perhaps? Why the look Mr Gillis … is this a problem?"

But the scout had failed to hear the question, the old man's request having suddenly melted into a distant drone. Dulled too seemed the bluish light still emanating from the TV screen but no longer washing the room in the warm bath of possibility, where for a brief moment, a mere hockey scout might entertain the notion of being elevated from unwitting pawn to chosen shepherd for a future Messiah. Dulled because the mere consideration of taking such a notion back to the cold shrill halogen and unimaginative fluorescence that lit the world of professional hockey was an impossibility. Stephen had never been comfortable talking to Casey. He had always kept contact and conversations both infrequent and brief – no longer than the congratulatory phone call he offered on the day after the draft or the momentary exchange back in the St. John's dressing room after Casey's first breakout game. Anything more would surely put the scout in the path of the undeniable question. The one that up until Casey's promotion and success, reporters had had a field day with … the one that Stephen's own superiors never felt he had fully explained. But whereas the scout had managed to steer through the professional minefields of his peers and critics, he could never imagine surviving what Casey himself, beyond all others, would surely demand to know. He was, after all, the player in question; the fourth-line centre plucked from one of the worst junior teams in the country. Surely he more than anyone else must have known how ridiculously slim his chances were of being drafted at all. How preposterous a scenario it was to have learned his name was the first one called from that podium in St. Louis. What could Stephen possibly say when the young man demanded to know why? Tell him he believed the lad to be the Messiah? Tell him about Willie and his scrapbook? About Thompson and his dream? Tell him all these shady tales right out in the open? Right there beneath the shadowless light of an arena locker room?

"Mr. Gillis … Mr. Gillis, are you alright?" Touchwater repeated, peering out into the vacant trance that had now engulfed his guest's face; a face that for the second time that afternoon, with the forced haste of dishonesty, answered far too quickly.

"No … no … everything's fine," he replied, all but lunging for the exit. "But if we're about done here for today …?"

"Done? Why I've only nicely begun to –"

"Don't bother Sharon. I remember the way out."

"But Mr. Gillis … Stephen …"

Chapter Three

Stephen Gillis
c/o The Toronto Centennials Hockey Club
Suite 500
Ist Ambassador's Place
6 Front Street
Toronto ON
M7D 2E4

Dear Mr. Gillis,

For quite some time I have felt a deep need to correspond with you. Throughout my career I have lived and taught with the belief that there is a deeper calling to the realm of Sport. From your comments made in recent articles regarding the element of chemistry in the pursuit of talent, I could not help feeling you are of a similar belief.

The chase of the meaning of "team" is a philosophical challenge that has guided my career. It is also a challenge I give all my recruits upon their arrival at this small college where I teach football. (I prefer the term "teach" to the far more manipulative connotations associated with the word "coach.") The young men whom I select are chosen essentially by their eagerness to explore and to find this meaning; to be as one in our creativity on the field; and to celebrate that *whole* as win or lose, it miraculously outshines the sum of the attributes each individual brings to my football field every autumn Saturday afternoon.

I would welcome any input from your experiences that might assist me in enabling and empowering my student-athletes in their creative journey here. I look forward to hearing from you.

With many thanks,

Dr. Charlie Frost
Prof. of Sports Psychology
Dornhoeffer College

~

MEMO: from Adam Benning (ABENNIN)
Director of Player Personnel

to scout staff
.cc Stephen Gillis (SGILLIS)

Please note the general meeting of all minor pro and junior scout staff will be held January 3 through January 5. To best utilise our time and resources, it is necessary that all outstanding interim scouting reports be filed to my office for review no later than December 15 as I will require those two weeks to familiarise myself with all prospect assessments. I would therefore encourage you to make these reports your top priority so that we may best address the needs of our overall player development and proceed into the upcoming year with clear vision and goals.

~

Stephen Gillis
c/o The Toronto Centennials Hockey Club
Suite 500
Ist Ambassador's Place
6 Front Street
Toronto ON
M7D 2E4

Dear Mr. Gillis,

I received your letter in the mail last week. I must admit I find it a rather curious request, you wanting me to tell you about Casey when he was a boy. I would have thought you could just ask him yourself, but then again I guess you're probably too busy, off scouting more boys all over the country.

I will be frank, Mr. Gillis. I haven't had much contact with Casey these past few years. We had a parting of the ways back when he was fifteen. It was a difference in opinion over how much hockey he should be playing. The result was him running off to board with my sister's kids in Winnipeg, where he caught on with a junior team there. Tier two I believe you call it. From there he was spotted by the Prince George people.

But I have to say, even if we were still close, I wouldn't know what to make of all your questions about his birth parents. Or where you would get the idea he was from BC He was found abandoned up here in a snowstorm on the Trans Canada highway. Surely you knew that, what with all the newspapers going on about it. Casey came to us two months later as a ward of the state. My husband and I had taken on four foster children over the years and child services knew us and trusted us. With Casey, there was just something about the timing that seemed right and we decided to adopt him as our own. Unfortunately Charles took sick and passed away when Casey was only three years old.

I did the best I could, Mr. Gillis. Raising him, taking in more foster kids from time to time, and holding down a job with the post office. Sometimes I had to drop him off at the arena when I had a late shift. I know that may not sound like the best, but he loved it there and I knew he was out of trouble. He was a good kid, Mr. Gillis. When I took on the other children, he would help me with dinners and lunches for school.

Did his paper route on time every day. And the more I think about it, the more I realise that's all you or anybody else needs to know. So I'm sorry but I just don't think you need to get all concerned about who my boy's birth parents were because the truth is, I never stopped Casey from searching for his real mother and father, or learning more about his native roots. He'd always smile and say it was good enough to have me for a mom. Me! An old Finnish woman who married an Englishman. Like I said, Mr. Gillis. He's a good kid. Plain and simple.

Sincerely
Mrs. Liisa Bruford
Thunder Bay ON

~

To: sgillis@centennials.scout/west.ca

Dear Mr. Gillis,

    I am ten years old and next spring I'm going to try out for a baseball team where I live in Victoria, BC Did you ever play baseball? I hope so, because I don't think I would ever try if it wasn't for you because you let Casey play hockey on your team and he's native just like me. I'm the only one in my school though, because my mom had to move us down here to live with my aunt. She's a cleaning lady on the Vancouver ferry. She said I should write Casey and ask for his picture and autograph. But I wanted to write you too.

Sincerely,
Allen Williams

P.S. – I'm going to try out for shortstop and pitcher.

~

"Mr. Gillis … good. Please step in."

It was December 19, over a week since Stephen's last visit and through the wrinkles and the tired lines sunken into deeply hollowed eye sockets – a condition that the scout thought must be exacerbated by countless days spent scouring over books in the dim environs of his office tower – the old man's face actually appeared brighter. His step out from behind the desk, while still laboriously slow, was somehow more balanced and steady.

"We have made a monumental breakthrough," he blurted between rather giddy gulps of air, like a child priming to describe the favourite bit of his very first matinee. "And I dare say should it continue to unravel so exponentially, very soon the time will be upon myself and my associates to speak of our findings openly. History is stretching, Stephen. Stretching in preparation of shedding her tired skin … you look awful by the way."

Stephen shrugged weakly. "I haven't been sleeping."

"Well perhaps our meeting will take some of that pressure away," Touchwater replied quickly with what the scout considered a rather dismissive tone. "I must say, I was quite uncertain whether we'd ever be talking again after your hasty retreat last week. But the fact you have agreed to one more meeting tells me you have discovered some interesting details in the interim. So tell me … what's this Casey Bruford like?"

Stephen rubbed his temples, pressing hard on the circles ground around his eyes; the same spots that had housed his migraine of the last five days, imbedded and impenetrable to all over-the-counter medication.

"Well … he's gone without a point his last four games. So I'm starting to hear the critics griping again. Saying he was a ten-game wonder. I get the sense that's the opinion around the office too. Especially with Benning, the new director of player personnel. It's to be expected really. The checking's got closer and some of the teams have seen him a second time, so they're giving him more attention. Casey's not that big a player either, so I imagine he's feeling the wear and tear."

Stephen took a moment and sighed wearily. "What else can I say … he's a good kid. Pitched right in with some charity events. Seems to make time for the fans. Gives reporters all the time they want, win, lose or –"

"Stephen please!" Touchwater's palms fell with their full weight against his desk. "I did not call you back here so you could regurgitate a string of tired sports clichés. Did you even take time to talk with the boy? I mean really talk –"

"And say what?" The scout shot back defensively. "Tell him he's scheduled to save the world?"

"You could be circumspect."

Touchwater's stare was once again bearing down, paralysing Stephen with uncertainty as it pushed away whatever hint of clarity still remained. He fidgeted with the upholstery, turning his head this way and that, looking for any object to emerge from the darkened room that might serve as a counter focal point to the old man's gaze. Only after centring on the edge of a wastebasket peeking out from behind the corner of the desk could he gather himself with sufficient leverage to offer any sort of reply. And even then it was in his smallest of voices. One from distant corridors in his memory, predating by far Stephen Gillis the scout, or the minor pro journeyman forward or even Stephen Gillis the collegiate first-line centre. It was a voice that had, in fact, rarely been heard, having never risen even as high as the lettering on the Estevan Home Hardware dressing room door back in his hometown before it was inevitably shaken down by deep blue streaks of fatherly concern.

"This isn't easy for me," he whispered finally and allowed himself enough latitude to slump back against the sofa. "On top of everything else, I've been getting a lot of letters lately. And, well they're kind of … confusing."

"What sort of letters?"

"Well … fan letters, I guess you could say. Like that one from Brother Amos, right out of the blue. Only it's not just him. It's a lot of people … from all over the place."

"That's good. People are connecting with you."

"No, people are freaking me out. I mean it's Casey they want. I'm just a scout –" Stephen caught himself just as Touchwater brought a finger to his lips. "What I mean is, Casey's the one who has them all intrigued. Why don't they just write him?"

"Because they're all obsessed with how you knew. Trust me Stephen. People in the messiah-hunting business, people like myself who try to map out the steps of the cosmic dance, even your run-of-the-mill sports fans ... we're really all quite alike. When someone like Casey comes along we worry that we may have missed out on something grand because our own sensibilities were too dull to give him a try. Believe me, it's a dullness we usually are more than willing to dress up in some seemingly very healthy guise, cloaking it in terms like practicality or rationality. But we do so at our own peril. For when someone truly and unexpectedly exceptional finally does come our way, we can't fully bring ourselves to believe it on our own. So instead we head for the bloke who looks just like one of us yet who was nevertheless able to take that leap of faith. People can't quite believe such a hockey talent could have been hidden so long. They want to understand how you knew. They think you have a secret Stephen and they want to be a part of it because, as I'm sure you know, once someone becomes intrigued by a secret, they will go to great lengths to discover more."

Touchwater chuckled gleefully, pausing to gaze over to the confused expression that Stephen worried was now etched permanently on his face.

"Very well then," he announced presently, "let us quickly get to business – for, as I said, our time may indeed be quite short. Now ... since we spoke last, our association has learned of a great many more events, all having occurred on the weekend of November 25, and all having something to do with native culture and/or sport. For example, it seems that at approximately 7:30 on that Saturday evening in November – the same time Simon Plagenet took his life – a rally was under way in Washington, D.C., in which representatives from a number of native groups had gathered to protest the continued use of a term perceived to be derogatory to natives as a professional football team's moniker. In leading the demonstration, the primary speaker was apparently quite eloquent in punctuating the ignorance involved in maintaining such a stereotypical blanket description for the North American Indian, especially for a team whose largest racial component was African American, and who ran around playing a game that shared its deepest roots in the very Euro-centric sport of rugby. All very interesting, given the incident Sharon dug up from the same day out in Brandon, Manitoba. Evidently a recreation league hockey game got out of hand and deteriorated into an ugly brawl between one of the town clubs and one from the nearby reserve. Six players and three spectators were sent to hospital. The story making the rounds alleges that the entire debacle started when the town's coach referred to the opposition repeatedly as 'them fuckin' redskins' in rather boisterous and inebriated tones. Meanwhile down in South America there was unrest in La Paz, Bolivia. Youth gangs made up primarily of indigenous peoples chose a city soccer derby to launch a series of home-made smoke bombs. And in New Mexico, there were a number of native groups organising highway blockades, two of which apparently denied many travellers passage to the stadium hosting a nearby college football game. In fact, from tracking news wires and Internet dispatches all over the world, we have uncovered more than two dozen additional incidents from that day. All involve aboriginal unrest. Many also deal with a sporting event. Taking the same cue as your friend Willie did to explain your connection with the Bruford boy, Harland and I immediately began investigating the possibility of a geographical pattern for all these simultaneous happenings and we started by looking to see if any or all of them formed some sort of ley line. The results, however, were weak. In almost every case, the locations of three or four occurrences aligned, but that was all. Furthermore, there was no logical pattern to all these disparate scattered lines. At least nothing powerful enough to dismiss the possibility of geographical happenstance. So next, we began exhausting every possible non-linear pattern we could think of. From pentagrams to circles; constellular depictions of shapes and images common to the folklore of a whole host of native peoples, we tried playing connect-the-dots with all of them, but with no real success. A spoke-wheel pattern turned out to be the only configuration to offer anything in the way of hope and we gave it quite a workout, starting with the town of

Rugby, North Dakota as the hub, given its association with the Plagenet boy and its distinct proximity to the geographical centre of the entire continent. But even then, very few of the other locations lined up to form any satisfying semblance of an outward radial pattern."

"Well then why do you sound so damn optimistic?" Stephen asked quickly, fighting to get the query in during one of his host's hyper-gasps for air.

Touchwater responded by squeezing further together the muscles in his face and squinting a smile that surely borrowed from his youth.

"I am optimistic, aren't I?" he chimed with a giggle and then instantly dropped his voice to a whisper, slinging his head low as if further discretion, beyond even the sealed-off environs of his office tower, were yet required, as if what he had to say next was so earth-shattering that the walls, the light fixture, the very books upon the shelves of his sequestered refuge could not be implicitly trusted. The effect was dramatic and an unexpected shiver shot up the scout's spine; a strangely familiar blast that doubled him over with elbows on knees and left him just as he had ended up with Willie in Prince George; just as he had been upon learning of Thompson's dream-life in a St. Louis hotel suite.

"Everyone in our association received correspondence from Brother Amos two days ago," the old man hissed. "Correspondence concerning imminent cosmic intervention. His message was at once both a blessing of The Watch's collective efforts and a call to further step up our pace. You see, Brother Amos is both mystic and visionary. He's a former Oblate monk who now pursues speculative histories and eschatologies, but with the understanding that these pursuits can be accessed only through mystical union with Mother Earth and the energies she channels. The result is a powerful and beautiful gift of prophecy, one which we have all come to trust and rely upon. So when the good brother contacted us the day before last, speaking of the imminence of cosmic intervention ... perhaps only weeks away, perhaps days ... well Harland took the call completely to heart. Immediately we deputised the services of an equally enthusiastic friend, a cartographer currently residing in Wales. Together he and

Harland renewed their convictions and began working on a possible modification to the spoke-wheel configuration, and may I add … with unbelievable results."

"Wait … hold it … modifications to what? I'm not following."

"It was the Welshman's idea, Stephen, and it was brilliant. You see, he had always had a feeling that the spoke-wheel pattern was on the right track – if you'll pardon the pun. He found it in keeping with the direction of our search, which is after all, a will to reduce a number of common events to a central core. He did, however, feel that our premise of the town of Rugby, North Dakota being part of that central core was something of a red herring. So instead he went right back to the original ley lines we had plotted – those tracks with three or more points on them – and then approached the matter with the supposition that perhaps all these separate lines, when extrapolated out beyond their current end points might possibly share a common point of confluence. Where the sum of all their energies would be destined to combine."

Stephen threw up his hands and pleaded once more. "No … please. For once I want to make sure I've got this. Are you telling me all these places form a whole bunch of lines and that all those lines actually intersect in the same place?"

Touchwater slapped his palms down against the top of the desk, rocking forward in his chair. He opened his mouth to reply and Stephen heard the eagerness to his breath, the last remaining seam holding back the waves of overwhelming emotion welling up within.

"Stephen …" he whispered, hoarse with excitement, *"It worked!"*

And with that he broke into a moment of uncontrollable laughter that seemed destined to turn into tears had a coughing spell not brought the pre-emptive need for calm. Stephen waited as patiently as he could while the man whooped loose a few good grunts of stuff from deep down in his lungs, then pulled out a handkerchief to wipe and probe his nasal passages for any residual debris. Finally the suspense could leave him silent no more.

"So where is this place?"

Touchwater still didn't respond immediately, but with one mighty heave, managed to swivel around in his chair and wrestle from the side table behind him a monstrous atlas laid open to the first template, a map of the world as a whole. Stephen jumped from his chair and bolted over to inspect the map from closer range, noting immediately that a vast network of straight lines had been drawn over the topography, each meticulously traced in fine red ink; each with a number of points marked in bright green felt and highlighted further in fluorescent blue. Brandon was connected by one of the straight red lines with Salt Lake City and the eastern islands of Fiji. A second line dissected Christchurch – the city where the All Black team's captain had died, as a margin note explained carefully off to the side – angling away to the northwest past southern Burundi and Liberia in Africa. A third close by joined a point in Congo to Miami, Florida and Las Cruces, New Mexico. There were many others too. Many others. Easily over a dozen by the scout's quick count. Each made up of clearly highlighted points and captioned with a brief but thorough account of what specific event occurred there on the day of November 25; a riot in Indonesia, matched with both a confrontation in the Faeroe Islands between Greenpeace activists and local whalers, and an independence rally in Hawaii; a march in the national sports stadium of Malta, in line with ethnic skirmishes in northern Syria and the Afghan mountains. Every episode helped form the points that made up the series of straight lines … Baja, the Galapagos Islands and the mountains to the north of Santiago, Chile; Washington, the Ukraine and northern Kazakhstan; the coast of Brazil, Medellin and the Guatemala-Mexico border … and amazingly, each one of those lines – just as Robin had promised – had been extrapolated outwards to reveal one common point of intersection for them all. Stephen's eyes darted to the broad block letters emblazoned in gold ink, obliterating the details of over half the state of California.

"Pasadena," the old man whispered proudly, with a quiver of excitement in his voice. "And if all this were not a sufficiently dynamic synchronism … it turns out the city's name … Pasadena? It's *Ojibwa*. I swear Stephen, it's true. Founded and so named by a group of settlers from

Indiana. Imagine ... a group of white Euro-centric farmers from the 1800's complete with that century's sensibilities no doubt, come west with the mysterious will to choose the *Chippewa* term for 'valley' in naming their new home ... *Pasadena* ..."

He cooed the word over three or four more times, letting the sound of it meander off his lips and hang in the space between them – like a small child blowing bubbles – swallowing hard in between as he tried to keep his enthusiasm from running any wilder, lest it trigger yet another coughing spell.

"Wait a minute ... Pasadena?"

"Yes Stephen. Go on ... what just struck you?"

"The last letter I had from the monk. It ended with something about huge crowds gathered to surround a battle on both sides. Pasadena's where they play the Bowl game. Do you think –"

Touchwater leaned back into his chair, the grin on his face now rivalling the Cheshire cat.

"College football's New Year's fixture. And this year it will decide the overall National Championship. Do you follow the college game at all Stephen?"

"A little bit. Isn't Arizona up against that little school who surprised everybody all year?"

"Central Michigan University. Team nickname? You won't believe it. *The Chippewas.* And I dare say they sound like an entire herd of Casey Brufords the way they have come out of nowhere. Being ranked as one of the weaker programs over the years, they managed to find their way onto the early schedules of a great number of traditional powerhouses this past season; considered easy prey for schools trying to pad their records I would think. However, to bend a tired old cliché a little further, a funny thing happened on the way to the end zone."

"Yeah they turned the tables on everyone didn't they?"

"Notre Dame, Ohio State, Wisconsin ... 47–9 over the University of Michigan on national television. They finished the year undefeated."

Touchwater stopped short the summary to note his guest's face buried back in the atlas, his concerned eyes dancing desperately over all the lines traced there. "I gather from your expression you're now wondering where Casey fits in to all of this?"

"I don't see anything about him on the map," the scout replied leadingly; however the reassurance he sought was not forthcoming. The manner in which his host spent the next few seconds clearing his throat, Stephen found most foreboding.

"I am afraid … at least as of yet … Casey is not part of the pattern."

"What the hell do you mean, he's not –"

"Now Stephen. I am saying 'as of yet' … please be clear of that before frustration gets the better of you."

"The hell with that. What about all these undercover trips up here at your beck and call. Christ, you came looking for me. Not the other way around!"

"Because your experiences with Casey were worthy of extended scrutiny. But the fact remains that despite their undeniable intrigue, they have failed to connect with the corpus of our revelations."

"Because they don't fit some goddamn pattern?"

"Stephen please. I called you in today to see if perhaps you had discovered something more about Mr. Bruford's mentality, something that might have proved illuminating with regard to our work. Furthermore, I have divulged to you the direction and the scope of my endeavours with the same confidence and candour as I would one of my own associates in The Watch, and I have done so strictly because I believe your co-operation during our times here together deserves no less."

"But what about Willie? I mean I thought the whole point of me being here was because you also believed Casey was going to become this … this … Messiah. I mean that was the one thing Willie was completely clear on. It was the last thing that he said to me and I had the distinct feeling it was on purpose."

Touchwater sighed as he grabbed his spectacles from their perch on his nose and tossed them down beside the atlas.

"Forgive me for what I'm about to tell you because, even as I consider it, I realise it carries the danger of sounding like nothing more than trite fodder. But as I sit here and listen to you responding to what must seem a rather ungracious slap in the face, I can think of no other way to explain my position. Stephen, are you familiar with the parable about the five blind brothers and their pet elephant? Where each brother only has access to feel one portion of the beast's anatomy? It's Eastern in origin I believe, and goes something like this. It seems an argument began amongst these brothers over what constituted the correct description of an elephant. The brother who had hold of the trunk was convinced an elephant was a long and slender animal. The one grasping an ear insisted it was wide, flat and floppy. Meanwhile the brother with his arms around a leg argued tooth and nail that the animal was a thick, muscular column shape. And so it went, with each brother convinced of his own description based on his individual experience, and yet with each also greatly limited by the scope of his faculties. My feeling is that at the end of the day, the same should be said of your friend Willie. For while it cannot be denied he tapped into the irrepressible currents of Mother Earth's energies, I believe he succumbed to the very human fallibility of assuming his experience was the ultimate expression of those currents when in fact it was but a brief shadowy glimpse. Of course he would describe Casey in the grandest terms possible. A *Messiah* no less."

"And what about you! You have no problem throwing around your own big cosmic terms –"

"Please hear me my friend. I'm not saying he's wrong. It is true, part of an elephant is indeed wide, flat and floppy. But unfortunately most of it isn't. And as for my use of grand terminology, please understand I do so only after careful and soulful exploration. All of which means that as fond as I was in having you visit and discuss your experiences about a curious old visionary who believes he knows the Messiah, I simply cannot ignore The Watch's revelations in order to cater to these experiences when revelation is leading me elsewhere. The result would be nothing more than self-serving fiction and as I said at the outset, I have no interest in weaving tales. Believe me, Stephen, we tried to place Casey into the pattern in every way possible. Using the alleged birthplace on Vancouver Island, Thunder Bay, Prince George, Toronto, even St. John's. Nothing aligned with any of the other points."

"So that's it then? I'm just through here?"

"I want to thank you deeply and sincerely for these meetings. And I would still ask you to leave the names and phone numbers of any locations you're likely to be in the next few days."

"Why?"

"Because as I have tried to make clear throughout our visits, nothing should ever be ruled out completely when one deals in the world of revelation and possibility. As Harland pointed out just last night when I discussed the matter with him, it's not as if Casey's performance was one of a whole list of intriguing events from the night of November 25 that turned out not to match up with our hub-spoke pattern. It was in fact one of only two – the other being an account from Easter Island. It seems people on two separate ships alleged to have seen the ancient statues there lit in a fiery glow. But please understand, while this, in and of itself, may give my colleague some warrant for caution, the undeniable imminence of our pattern's fulfilment makes the scheduling of any more meetings an impossibility –"

"Why?" Stephen interrupted. "You haven't ever said anything specific."

"Stephen you're upset and defensive."

"No. I'm tired and I'm pissed off. So tell me. Other than some long shot college playing in the Bowl game, just what the hell is supposed to happen?"

"What indeed. There is still much to that question, I'm afraid. And I must now attend to its answer. Keep good watch my friend. Perhaps one day soon the answers we crave and the mysteries that give us thirst will all be made known. Now if you'll forgive me. I have much yet to consider."

And with that, the aged Robin Touchwater fell silent and shrank down behind his reading glasses, dropping his head down between his sagging shoulders, the irrepressible grin having returned to his face again as he sat re-examining the red-lined pattern that graced his map of the world.

Stephen rose slowly for the door, carrying with him an empty but burdened weight of someone jettisoned. Someone left behind. Perhaps it was this feeling which sponsored the scout's final words – unexpected even to him until he spoke them … so quietly … gazing back one last time from the shadows of the room, his hand already clenched on the shiny brass knob of the office door … the last words Stephen would say to the man in person.

"He's a good kid."

"I beg your pardon?"

"Casey Bruford … he's a good kid."

"Oh yes … yes, of course. Now if you'll pardon me …"

Chapter Four

MEMO: from Adam Benning (ABENNIN)
Director of Player Personnel

to Stephen Gillis (SGILLIS)

A reminder that all player evaluations were to have been submitted by last Friday. To date, I have received all European, minor pro, collegiate and eastern junior reports. Please forward what files you have completed and make the balance of these evaluations your top priority.

∼

Stephen Gillis
c/o The Toronto Centennials Hockey Club
Suite 500
Ist Ambassador's Place
6 Front Street
Toronto ON
M7D 2E4

Dear Mr. Gillis,

I guess my first letter was not direct enough so I'll say it plainer. I'm not interested in discussing my son's life with you or with any acquaintance you feel obligated to send by. Who is this Willie Skilliter person anyway and why did you send him to my door? He claimed to be a scouting associate but judging by his appearance, I'd say he looked more like a homeless drifter. Why you thought he would have any more success than you in prying into Casey's affairs, I'll never know and nor do I care to. I'm just writing you once more so you can tell him to stay away from my house. (I'd call him and tell him myself except I can't find a listing for him anywhere in the phone book.)

The same goes for you.

Liisa Bruford

~

To: sgillis@centennials.scout/west.ca

Dear Stephen,

Just a quick note to let you know we're all still thinking of you and to remind you that our invitation still stands. Wednesdays at 7 p.m. out at the Faith Tabernacle on Airport Road. God Bless.

P. Hendrickson
Hisglory@hotmail.com

⁓

Back in his car is where they started in earnest, seeping up from beneath the pretences of his professional duties. Blood-red images set against a frozen white backdrop creeping insidiously from their previous dream life confines, spilling onto the wide screen of his windshield; interrupting the steadfast simplicity of the open road to play out his fears like some never-ending movie. His only refuge was the roadside truck stops for marathon sits with watered-down coffee refills – his usual preference for hot turkey or an all-day breakfast omelette having proven impossible to keep down ever since Nipigon. That was the day, while en route to his daily perusal of the sports pages, he just happened to glance at the article splashed across the first page of the *Toronto Sentinel's* religion section. "CULT GLUTS NEWS WIRES WORLD WIDE WITH PRESS RELEASE PROCLAMATION".

And below it, the press release in question.

THE WATCH HOUSE – AN OPEN PROCLAMATION

We cast our eyes upon the horizons that burn just beyond our touch. We have seen portents of coming revolution; not by the hands of mankind, but indeed by the very channels of energy of Mother Earth herself, upon which we unwittingly surge and ebb, adrift on a sea of dreary sleep. We have become lost in the minutiae of the everyday; drowned by powerlessness and neutered from hope. But a surfacing is near. The small and the meek will lead the way. They will crumble our violent ways and open our hardened hearts. Let the crowds and their cheers give way to silence as we wait.

We remember you, Simon Plagenet. We welcome The Utah Circle and their journey of faith. So too, the indigenous of the Yucatan, those who fight on in Washington, and in Miami … and all around the World. Soon will be reborn the lost wisdoms that the very soul of Mother Earth craves to reclaim. And we hold reverent still the dance of young Casey to the north and thank Brother Gillis for offering it to us.

To those who hear, we invite you to awaken now, for time is short. Once we too were asleep, but now the Earth calls us to seek out the pathways of her power.

BROTHER AMOS
THE WATCH

With the newspaper clutched under his arm Stephen had sprinted from the diner immediately, jumped into his car and steered down the nearest gravel road to work on the business of regulating his heart rate in private. A public statement from The Watch was unexpected enough. But that his and Casey's names were included made no sense at all; not given the tone of his final meeting in Touchwater's office.

It was but a stroke of good fortune that he was out on the road and away from the Toronto media spotlight when the article came out. Benning's memo had helped, despite its needlessly terse and condescending tone. After all, Stephen had never before been late in submitting interim reports, whereas the same could not be said of several of his senior colleagues. They were notoriously tardy year in and out, without anything in the way of a tangible reprimand, although (as the voice in the scout's head now pointed out relentlessly) none of those old-schoolers had ever been implicated as a member of some sort of religious cult. Nevertheless, Stephen Gillis had grabbed at opportunity when he saw it, for he immediately began the task of fudging work schedules and travel itineraries, cooking his day planner with a busy play-by-play for one more whirlwind swing through the west before the new year – a goalie in Brandon, a winger in Prince Albert, The Viking Junior Tournament in Camrose, the under-17 tourney hosted in Nanaimo … all so that under the guise of his profession he could once again climb back into his car, disappear into the highway's hypnotising ribbon of familiarity and thereby shrink his confused world to a more manageable size …

That, and the matter of the urgent e-mail the scout had received only an hour after his return from the farewell meeting in Touchwater's office.

~

To: sgillis@centennials.scout/west.ca
From: Dr. David Thompson, Dept. of Anthropology, UBC

Have located James Richard – or at least evidence of him – out at Estevan Point on Vancouver Island. Contact me as soon as possible. We need to meet.

~

The charter's pilot gripped the wheel casually, seemingly unfazed by the fact his boat was using as much energy to jack-knife over the building wave crests as it needed for forward motion. It wasn't until well over halfway into the outward journey that he chose to comment on the darkening skies closing in from the north and west, and by then Stephen's innate land-locked sensibilities were hard at work. He fought to squint through the burn of the sea mist and focus on the outlines of the trees and mountains that loomed in the shadowy grey of the sound. But rather than steadying his already churning stomach, the massive silhouettes only seemed to augment the lurch of the boat. He tried breathing deeply but struggled to find adequately dry air; a condition that he had encountered on the drive out through the claustrophobic rainforest the previous day. The discomfort served only to amplify the ever-circling doubts in his head, making him take sceptical stock of how, in the span of a week, his implausible journey had led him from the posh penthouse of one of the nation's wealthiest, most powerful barons, to the open deck of a small tug that hugged the shoreline of the Muchalat Inlet searching as long as possible for modest protection until she turned to chug her way into the open mouth of Nootka Sound. And if that were not disconcerting enough, there was the detached, off-putting silence of the man sitting across from him; the man who had invited him into these inhospitably foreign environs in the first place.

~

They had met early that morning in the far end of the empty parking lot at the community hall in Gold River. Stephen pulled in the drive at ten past seven. Thompson had been waiting for over an hour.

Their reintroduction had proved awkward. The scout had been first to extend a stiff and unsure hand which the professor responded to in kind, revealing beneath his arm the folded front page of the Vancouver sports section. *The Saviour and the Scout* read the banner across the top of the page, sending a chill up Stephen's spine that convinced him, with no more necessary proof than the damning shape of the copy blocks themselves, that it was yet another hatchet piece, as relentless an account as he had read in the Calgary papers the previous day ... Regina the day before that.

"So what's that one got to say?"

"That you suffer from delusions of grandeur. That you're a scout who played a hunch well, but that the magnitude of the favourable results has left you, quote *straining the bounds of your own sanity to account for your good fortune.* End quote."

"Great."

"And they interviewed some old room-mate of yours from a team you played on in Illinois. He seems to believe you turned out the way you are because of a prolonged absence of sexual relations in your life."

"Burtnyk said that?"

"In so many words, yes. He also kept referring to you as *Newt.*"

Stephen sighed and nodded. "My nickname. Stood for neutered."

"Yes, I gathered."

The walk to the pier had also been uncomfortable, filled with a silent tension that seemed magnified by the hollow clop of their lumbering strides resonating off the slippery wood of the dock; unbroken, even when the outfitter emerged from his small office at the end of the pier to greet the men and introduce them to Kenton – his assistant, who would pilot them for the day. Kenton too could not faze the silence, despite his valiant stream-of-consciousness attacks. He complimented the two men on their sensible attire of toques, gloves and rain slicks; segued to how so many of his clients – especially the Americans up from Texas and Florida – would either arrive in the dead of summer with a parka under their arm, or show up for some late November excursion in a T-shirt and Bermuda shorts; but that being said, he and his wife had surely enjoyed their last vacation down south ... a cruise out of Miami ... a discounted deal that she had received through work where they had the choice of the Caribbean or

Alaska; but when you grow up next to the inside passage, what the hell's the attraction in Alaska …

There were a few more sporadic attempts of weather talk mostly – thrown back over his shoulder in the general direction of the two men, each huddled alone – until he was left with no other option than to surrender to their lifelessness, sink back into his captain's chair, and with a deft light grip of the ship's wheel steer the little tug towards the darkening cloud line.

And so it was left to Stephen to change the moment; to swallow hard and summon the strength and determination he had tried to accumulate over the past six days of driving – during which he had finally resolved to share *everything* with Thompson. *Everything* he had gone through … completely and vulnerably … in the same leap-of-faith manner the professor had demonstrated back in that hotel room in St. Louis. His meetings with Touchwater. The details of his own recurring nightmares. His father's death. Willie's cryptic knowledge of the day it happened. *Everything*. Like a farm kid on his first second-beam dive into the straw mow, the task required a few necessary false starts to build up nerve, but after a half-dozen or so of the requisite flinches, he leapt from his perch on the port side, diving headlong into exposition, beginning with a full account of the night Willie first walked up and spoke to him about his theories of religion and chemistry and sport. About *ley lines* and how they seemed to apply to his and Casey's birthplaces. He barely paused for breath, shouting over the din of the engine, as he relived the events of draft day and the night in St. John's where Casey had first broken out as a prolific scoring sensation. He endeavoured to describe the secret life of Robin Touchwater, revealing to the professor that he was actually a leader and catalyst for *The Watch,* and that he firmly believed something huge was about to happen that would affect all of mankind, the signs of which they believed had been revealed in an incredible number of events involving aspects of religion, native issues and popular sport, all of which had occurred on the 25th of November. Gathering more speed, he began spewing out, to the best of what still seemed very limited ability, the modified hub-and-spoke model, explaining how the location of these events had formed a great number of ley lines that all shared one common intersection point in Pasadena, California. He included Brother Amos and his prophecies. How they too were the results of a vivid dream-life. How they too seemed to reinforce Pasadena as the location where something monumental was destined to occur … possibly as soon as New Year's Day. He concluded with an account of his last meeting with the TV mogul. How his and Casey's story had been all but dismissed because their geographical settings failed to fall onto any of the leys that made up the spokes of the aforementioned hub pattern. How the mood of that final meeting was at complete odds with Brother Amos's newspaper proclamation which mentioned them so prominently. He told everything. Everything, that is, except the matter which first piqued his interest to start his unlikely journey in the first place; the matter of his father's death and Willie's implied knowledge of that event.

"But there's one more thing that I didn't even consider until I was halfway out here," the scout stammered on at his hyper-pace, fighting off the salt spray that accompanied his gulps for air. "Remember all those things you told me about all those artifacts you wanted to get back from the New York museum. Touchwater never mentioned anything about them."

The professor rose, wrapped his rain slick tighter around his body and, still silent, moved away from Stephen's barrage.

"– and I got thinking maybe it's because *our* story has to do with those artifacts. Maybe you wrote me and invited me to come out here because we're all still a part of it … and it's our job to find out how Casey and his people fit into that story. Me because I drafted the guy. You because you've dedicated your life to studying your people –"

Thompson's sensibilities could sit idly no longer and he spun around to meet Stephen's gaze with something of a wince.

"We need to clarify a few things," he responded in a voice commanding enough to startle Kenton into biting down on the lower lip that had been cradling several well-chewed cuticles. "Firstly, may I reiterate that my dedication is to anthropology. I seek only to illuminate understanding of past cultures of the Pacific Northwest. Not to renew or even celebrate the belief paradigms of my ancestors, but simply to understand them. Secondly, I do not seek to participate in any pan-native movements that try to group together disparate peoples whose only commonality lay in similar skin tone and similar treatment by the opposing Imperial forces who usurped their ways of life ... ways that previous to European contact had little or no relevance to one another. Furthermore, even if by *my people*, as you quaintly put it, you only mean those natives residing along the shores of present-day Vancouver Island and Washington state, I still have an immense bone of contention. One, I might add, that anyone who has read even a portion of the available anthropological materials on West Coast indigenous peoples would already be well aware of. Simply put, it's yours and this Watch group's preposterous ignorance that allows you to equate the social paradigms of *my people's* traditions with some so-called *lost wisdom.* Do you even know anything about the different bands that make up my tribe? Do you know the difference and similarities between the *Mowachaht* and the *Muchalaht?* How about the *Hesquiaht?* Or how about the *Nuu-chah-Nulth* as a whole and how they differ from their neighbours the *Saalish* or the *Haida?* Do you know, for example, how heavily stratified some of these societies were? That they enslaved the lowest castes of their very own? Bartered, exchanged, even killed them? Tell me Stephen, does this sound like the *lost wisdoms that the very soul of Mother Earth craves to reclaim,* as this Brother Amos so put it? And tell me, what would he think of us returning to the practice of whaling, given how whale populations have been so decimated by the Europeans and the Japanese for so many years? How exactly would that enhance the soul of Mother Earth? And just how enlightened is the practice of leaving young boys out in the woods to fend for themselves for a week or more, expecting them to fast and to rub stone and splinters into their skin until it bleeds? And after you've finished considering these questions, please take some time to reflect on what any of this has to do with you ... or me ... or our friend Willie for that matter."

"Willie is the only reason I drafted Casey in the first place. He's the only reason we met. And sure, Casey's scoring spree made him a media sensation, but if it weren't for his native roots Touchwater would never have been interested in him. I think we're all a part of this."

"Part of what? This movement you're so excited about seems to lack any clear definition."

"Robin called it history shedding its old skin."

"Did he?"

"And that the specifics would be revealed through events that involve sports and native issues ... and that it's going to be incredibly big."

"And this incredibly big event is supposed to occur on New Year's Day according to your monk's supposed vision."

"His dream, David. He has dreams, just like you do."

"But I didn't go looking for mine," Thompson said coolly and walked back to reclaim his original perch by the rail of the starboard side, seemingly undaunted by the growing spray that caromed off the hull and up into his face.

"I have no interest in these pursuits," he stated flatly, slapping his hands down on his lap for emphasis. "And frankly, I don't think you do either. As for your news that Robin Touchwater is at the forefront of these finely tuned fantasies, I am at a complete loss, just as I am over the unquestioning shining you seem to have taken to him."

"I told you. He's not what you would expect. I mean part of me was expecting some hard-assed businessman too ... but he's really just this tiny shrivelled-up old guy who can barely walk around his own desk. He has an assistant to do all his leg work because I think he suffers from some kind of bronchial condition. His breathing is really –"

"I'm sorry. I was too vague. I am not so much at a loss to comment on the man as I am uninterested in him. I certainly don't care about his personal appearance ... nor do I give a damn about his choice to live his life as a recluse. But his actions and their effect have been plain for all to see. And those actions simply don't point to this sage-like character you claim he is. My guess is the only reason you have come to know this man is because you happened to get in his line of fire. By selecting Casey he thought you gained some knowledge that he had not yet possessed. And while the specifics of such knowledge might be clothed in eloquent words about history shedding her tired skin, as far as I can see he's still trying to buy you out like the modern business mogul he is. The medium, I believe, is still the message in this case."

"Well Christ, David. Suppose you tell me what the hell I'm doing here then?" Stephen flung down his arms with a hard slap against his rubber rain gear. "Shit, did I just drive six days for the privilege of listening to you shoot down everything I have to say? What, is it because I don't have some research paper to back me up? Look you called me out here, not the other way around. So I'm just telling you what I've been through OK? But since that doesn't seem good enough, why don't we save some time and you tell me exactly why I'm here –"

"You are here because –" Thompson cut in, but just as quickly stopped himself, shaking his head in the direction of the distant shore that loomed ahead of them. "No," he said after a few seconds further thought. "You should wait."

"Fuck that, I've waited long enough!" Stephen snapped, whirling the professor around by the arm. But whereas a Robin Touchwater or a Willie Skilliter might have disarmed him with some mysterious smirk, Thompson's face was as stone grey cold as mountain rock. And so the silence returned.

～

Once out in the open sound, Kenton's voice returned, this time a steady stream of trepidation that droned over the slap of water on hull as he scanned the gathering skies and began twisting the channels of his radio for further information about the oncoming weather. It was with considerable reluctance that he agreed to proceed with the journey and manoeuvre his craft close to the south shore, allowing his two clients to lower an oversized zodiac with an outboard engine to the frothing surf below and shuttle across to a lonely patch of flat beach fifty arduous yards away. Had the pilot's skills not allowed him to negotiate so near, he surely would not have permitted the pair over the side, for conditions were fast becoming a dangerous challenge. The fog from early morning was now a dark and swirling cloud cover. The driving wind pelted sea spray hard into the faces of the men as they squinted for land over the edge of their inflatable craft. And by the time Thompson managed to steer close enough to stick his hip-waders into the surf and wrestle the raft the last few metres to dry land, the pilot couldn't be certain if either had heard his shouts to be back and ready to go in one hour, no more.

The professor led the way to the faint markings of an overgrown footpath that took both men up a steep incline and into the dank depths of old-growth forest. Congested monolithic firs shot straight into impenetrable curtains of cloud, fallen trunks of similarly threatening size oozed mosses of insipid green. For a flash of a moment Stephen tried to recall how he had first imagined the landscape of Casey's alleged birthplace. Whether he had, in fact, ever taken the time to hypothesise about it at all. If so, it was clear to him now just standing in its midst, that he must have leaned heavily upon some false image of woodland gentility; one that did not include the suffocating tangle of tree, vine and foliage that now greeted him. Nor the unnerving slightly haunting moan of the cloud-cloaked limbs that creaked away somewhere above, just beyond sight.

"Up there," Thompson announced calmly, pointing further up the trail. As they proceeded Stephen soon made out a tiny parting in the forest's canopy where a slightly larger portion of the day's dull light was allowed to filter down to the forest floor. There in the break of the trees were the remains of a shelter, some kind of lean-to that had at some point been walled in to make a cabin, but now sat dormant as did a nearby fallen Douglas fir whose branches had smashed and caved in much of the roof.

"This would have been a summer house," the professor stated in a solemnly dispassionate voice. "From here a chief and his family would have planned and prepared for their whale hunts. In the winter he would have moved them all further inland. For the past few years fishing trawlers have reported seeing lights on shore right down off the point here. Many accounts made it sound like quite a ghostly tale … with sightings of mysterious bonfires lit on shore. Some versions included a naked man seen wading out into the ocean surf, then fleeing into the woods whenever he realised he was being watched. My mother cleans in the hotel down in Port Alberni. That's where she's lived ever since Jocelyn died. She told me she had heard these stories for years but never gave them any thought until two weeks ago when she overheard a strange old guy in the hotel bar. He said he was a fisherman but she didn't recognise him as anyone local. And of course she hasn't seen him since. But he was nevertheless memorable by both his loud voice and his attire. It seems he wore an old flimsy parka and a toque … and carried around what appeared to be his entire earthly possessions in an old paper shopping bag."

Stephen's head snapped to attention, the professor's news instantly and effectively muting the discomfort of the forest's relentless sounds.

"Willie?" he whispered.

Thompson shrugged. "The man didn't offer a name. But according to my mother, he claimed to have been close enough to see the figure on shore before he darted for cover. And that the figure must have possessed a certain degree of shame, for as he ran he cloaked himself in an old hockey jersey, the old man said – as well as what appeared to be a blue-and-yellow baseball cap."

Thompson stooped to snatch up a small rock and pitch it into the darkened doorway of the old cabin, then with his head cocked to the side he waited for any snorting of interrupted hibernation or scrambling of startled claws. Satisfied after a moment of silence he pulled a battery powered halogen lamp from his sizeable pack of supplies and motioned for Stephen to keep his head low and follow him inside. In the middle of the structure's only room, directly beneath the concave ceiling was a weathered half-rotted table. Beyond it, the remainder of a small bed frame, void of any semblance of springs or mattress let alone bedding. The rest of the cabin – the entire far side in fact – was filled quite obtrusively with the metallic shine and reflective glare of scientific equipment. Brushes, trowels, tweezers. Envelope sleeves with samples of stone and bone and indiscriminate rust slipped within, some no larger than a postage stamp or a sugar packet. Attached to every individual finding was a small tag with a catalogue number and a series of measurements, achieved no doubt with the aid of the fine collection of calibrators, tape measures and portable scales that were laid out atop a tightly pulled tarp and placed in careful parallel and perpendicular angles to one another.

"This is my third time back," Thompson stated by way of explanation, and reached below the tabletop to open a small centre drawer. "As you can see, I've started the process of cataloguing. However, the two most illuminating items I left in here, precisely where I found them."

He pulled out first a blue baseball cap holding the brim up into the light so Stephen could note the UBC insignia, embroidered in bright gold letters across the crown. Beneath it, in a similar font, the name *Jocelyn* had been stitched with a finer white thread.

"I had this monogrammed for her seventeenth birthday. Apparently it was the only thing about the school she wanted anything to do with. I remember my mother telling me how she wore it everywhere. How the night she disappeared, so did her hat."

He stared at the scout a moment with a distinctly irritated expression that Stephen simply could not make sense of. Then without a further word he turned back to the drawer, this time to wrestle out a large and cumbersome scrapbook overflowing with stuffed-in papers all yellowed and frayed around the edges. From the professor's efforts in extricating the book, it was clear to Stephen he required it to remain open to a specific page which contained but one leaf of newsprint barely hanging by a strip of tape in the top left corner. The reason why became clear when it was dropped unceremoniously to the table with an intentional thud.

Estevan captures championship at annual Kinsman Midget tourney ... led by captain Steve Gillis and his four-point explosion in the final period, the Estevan Home Hardware Midget squad overcame a three-goal deficit to defeat the hometown Kenora Optimists last Sunday at the Coliseum.

Thompson dropped his head and began to pace.

"Look at the date of that clipping. The last Sunday in question would have been January 17. The same day Casey Bruford was found in an abandoned vehicle in Northwestern Ontario. Now I suppose this could still be dismissed as coincidence, but the fact that an article about you has appeared in what most likely is a refuge for the man who is responsible for my sister's death, well it tips the scales quite differently, wouldn't you agree? This after I threw aside all rationality – me of all people – and flew halfway across the continent to hunt you down just so I could introduce myself and proceed to spill my life story. And all that time you just sat there, clearly knowing far more than you ever intended to let on. Certainly more than that well-rehearsed apology you felt compelled to spew at me back on the boat! Well, it all ends right now. You wanted to know why I brought you out here? So you can tell me why the hell James Richard would have an article about your childhood among his possessions!"

But Stephen was not with him. For while the effect of seeing the scrapbook again was exactly as shocking as the professor had expected, the motivation for his surprise could not have been known until that moment when the professor flung his accusing gaze upwards in time to see the scout's hands begin to shake uncontrollably. Stephen leafed through some of the other pages and articles, slowly at first and then with a building frantic rhythm until he dropped the book altogether and stumbled backward into the rickety bed frame, his fall landing him dangerously close to the professor's careful array of specimens. His voice was but a hoarse whisper, delivered from behind a quivering chin as he jabbed the air directly above the book with his index finger over and over again.

"It's *his*."

"Yes Stephen. This is – or at least was – James's lair. Try to keep up –"

"No. *His* … Willie's. He had it with him that night in Prince George. He pulled out these very same articles for me to read."

Once again, Stephen began putting a good portion of the professor's work in peril as he paced about the limited confines, rubbing his hands through his hair rather violently.

"January 17 was also the day my father died … a car accident just outside of Kenora."

The professor stared for a moment, quickly trying to take stock of the motivations of the figure pacing before him.

"So this whole search … this is why you turned ghost white back in St. Louis when I told you about Jocelyn and my dreams? This isn't about finding some old man who convinced you to pick an unknown for your hockey team. This is personal! You think James had something to do with your father's death, don't you?"

"No … well yes, in the beginning … but it's all bigger than that now. Look, you have to understand!" Stephen's steps grew longer, his knees drawn up high towards his chest, further than his balance could safely negotiate. He began to stumble, his head and arms flailing loosely like the treetops above them.

"The weather was crap … there was a bad storm that day and the highway was full of drifts. And he was so … angry."

"Angry about what?"

"No! You don't get it! He shouldn't have been there! He wouldn't have been there if I hadn't …" Stephen slammed his hand into the scrapbook, snatching loose the news clipping that bore his name, ripping and crumpling it into tiny bits. "It wasn't worth it … FUCK!"

"Stephen, calm down. What wasn't worth it?"

"For Christ sake, I was doing my fucking best!"

"You're saying your dad was upset with you?"

Stephen opened his mouth to respond but could form no sound. With a few rapid blinks his eyes glazed over and, like a drug's instant answer to inconsolable disease, the scout stopped short his torment and stood frozen at attention.

"I gotta talk to Robin again," he blurted out suddenly and with no further warning bolted for the door. Thompson chased after, shouting out warnings to be careful. The academic's muscle tone, however, was no match for the leg strength of a former hockey player. Within seconds, Stephen was swallowed from view by the omnipresent mix of tree trunk and ground foliage, a development which would have been cause for greater concern had the blood-curdling screams not begun shortly thereafter, echoing from the direction in which the scout had vanished. The professor slowed his gait to a calmer walk, satisfied that Stephen had indeed not fled deeper into the forest, fooled by the directionless sounds of wind and ocean swirling overhead. He proceeded to a spot fifty yards ahead, tucked and hidden behind a mossy outcropping of rock and nestled against a gently sloping section of the forest floor. There, as the shrieks had suggested, he discovered the scout, backed up against the trunk of a giant cedar staring petrified into the hollow sockets and taunting grin of an irregularly-shaped human skull. The skull was perched precisely at eye level upon a roughly-hewn platform of branches, thatched together with kelp and seaweed, and affixed to a series of upright poles, many of which had sagged to rather precarious angles in the soft give of the earth underfoot.

"*Jesus Christ!*" the scout sputtered over and over, his lips trembling uncontrollably.

"You're in a watch house Stephen; a shrine if you will," Thompson stated with intended clinical calm, as he tried to allay the scout's panic. "Burial was not a practical consideration on the outer coast of BC. The region's wildlife – specifically the sizeable wolf population – was only too willing to dig up and make meals of people's mortal remains. So the deceased were placed up on racks or in tree branches for safety."

"*It's huge … it's … Jesus Christ!*"

"Yes. It's the skull of a man who appears to have had a rather wide head, but that's all. Human bones were often moved to the whaling houses as a demonstration of reverence or respect. This man's remains must have found such a fate. He may have been a chief or a distinguished whaler. Possibly a shaman."

Stephen could not latch onto the professor's reassurance. Had he the luxury of learning of such a place in the safety of a university lecture hall or the pages of a textbook then no doubt the rationality Thompson sought to provide would not have proved so faint as it was out there, set against the taunting malevolent voice of the wild – a voice which to Stephen now seemed attached to the demonic toothless grin before him. He reacted instinctively, recklessly flinging his head this way and that in a desperate search for some sign of retreat. But every direction looked identical, and in the confusion of the undergrowth his mind began to wander aimlessly. Suddenly he found himself longing for those safe shadows back in Touchwater's lair, where the darkness seemed so much clearer. Clean and safe. Like a noiseless buffer that could encapsulate everything that possibly lay beyond and reduce it to a manageable size. He longed for that simplicity, that clear definition. The open road. The prairie sky. His friend, the ribbon of highway paint, streaming steadfast through the snowy plains by day, faithfully out past the beams of his headlights by night. And all the while his head spun faster, back and forth, peering for any hint of light out of his horizon-less hell. Away from the growing cacophony of the wind and waves, now combined with a sudden awareness of bird and animal calls, all of which seemed to meld together deafeningly for no other reason than to supply an eerie defiance of delineation.

"I ... I gotta get back ... I gotta phone Robin ... I need to talk to Robin!" he mumbled repeatedly, settling into the same urgent pacing that had overtaken him back in the cabin, as he began to work over a series of contingencies in his head. If he could return to the boat quickly he could get Kenton to radio Gold River and the outfitter could maybe patch through a call. At the very least, he could phone from the docks when he returned, which would be another two hours; and perhaps if Robin would agree to meet with him, there would still be two days before midnight ushered in the New Year ... assuming he could get an immediate flight back to Toronto.

"Stephen, calm down and think about this a moment," Thompson urged. "Even if Touchwater is the guru you would have him be, if your stake in all of this is, as I said, personal in nature, why should he care about anything I've shown you here today?"

"Because at least he's got the guts to put it all together into one big picture, alright?" The scout shot back with a reserve of anger whose depth caught both men off-guard. "Look! I've been fucked with for the better part of a year ... first Willie, then Casey. Then you ... oh yeah buddy, you too! All of you only too willing to bend over backwards to play goddamn head games with the hockey scout, but God fucking forbid somebody should actually let me in on what it's all about."

"All what? You're going to have to be more clear if you –"

"I TOLD YOU! THE BIG PICTURE! *EVERYTHING!* WHAT THE HELL ELSE?!"

He was beside himself now, screaming at the top of his lungs, watching himself do so from some vantage point beyond, that, while offering a clear view, was nevertheless unable to intervene against the fury. His hands grabbed Thompson by the collar of his rain slick. It was a desperate clutch that lurched the scientist to and fro before slamming his back up against the unforgiving bark of a giant fir. The slap of the professor's rain gear against the tree echoed through the forest much like a child's sweat-soaked shoulder pad striking a dressing room door. And in that moment, the professor learned firsthand the instincts of a hockey man's wrath; became keenly aware of his coat being pulled up around his neck, until it threatened to swallow his head whole. But the fist he expected never arrived, its place taken instead by a shivering wagging finger pointed in front of his face.

"If all of this ... if all of this ... my father's death ... Casey ... Willie ... you and your goddamn dream ... if it's all just one big shit pot of a coincidence ... if none of it amounts to sweet fuck all ... then you tell me, why the hell did I risk my career to take Casey Bruford in the first place? I mean if the whole fucking thing is really just the product of my own goddamn mother-fucking imagination, why the hell didn't I just pick a sure-fire prospect like Parkinson? Because I sure as hell would have if it hadn't been for you showing up at my hotel. So you tell me ... if all this is just a fucking crock of shit, why the hell haven't I paid for it? Why the hell is this kid turning into the best fucking thing since Gretzky? Ah Christ, forget it!"

He tossed Thompson free of his grasp and with a shove that knocked the professor's head back against the tree bark, bolted for what seemed to

be the only sign of a subtle slope in the forest floor, the only hint of a possible route back to the shore.

"Stephen wait," Thompson called out, gathering himself from the
force that had freed him. "Whatever there is to be discovered, we can still
do it. Right here. Or we can take the book and the cap back to the labs at
the university if need be."

"THERE'S NO TIME!"

"No time? No time? There seems to be all the time in the world for
Ouija boards and crystal balls, and whatever the hell else the mighty
Robin Touchwater and his friends pass off as methodology! Stephen, you
have to believe me, this man is nothing more than a deluded romantic.
He's trying to wedge history – and from what you've told me about these
map-pattern theories, geography – into his own private fantasy world."

"YOU DON'T EVEN KNOW HIM!" Stephen shouted back over his
shoulder just as he stepped up his pace, forcing Thompson again to try to
keep speed. However, the split tasks of running and shouting, coupled
with a now surging resentment that had been welling up all day from deep
within the academic's stomach, left him quite divided in his energies.

"You think I'm wrong?" he was now yelling back, his voice crackling
into a desperate gasp that belied the dispassionate approach he struggled
to espouse. "Well then just remember to ask your esteemed colleague if
he's really sure he wants to regress to the so-called wisdom of my ancestors. Remember to ask him about the slave trading. About buying and selling and killing our own – without a second thought. And don't forget
about the whale hunt. See if we'll all be so enlightened on this vibrant new
day that dawn will find us paddling around the Pacific in our dugouts trying to harpoon endangered mammals –!"

A parting in the distance revealed a sliver of grey-green water. Stephen
raced ahead to the top of a hill which overlooked the waves some hundred
yards past the point where the two men had come ashore. He stopped only
long enough to pinpoint the safest route down the steep incline before he
was off, half sprinting, half sliding for the bottom and the boat which lay
in wait for him, bouncing about on what was now a furious sea.

"Ask him if he knows why my grandparents and great-grandparents never fed squirrel to their young? ... See if he knows what I told you about propping the skeletal remains of our relatives up on those stilts. ASK HIM IF HE REALLY KNOWS ANYTHING ABOUT US AT ALL! AND WHILE YOU'RE AT IT ... ASK HIM WHERE THIS GODDAMN VIBRANT NEW DAY WAS FOR MY SISTER!! OR IS HE JUST TOO GODDAMN BUSY WITH THE GODDAMN BIG PICTURE!!! STEPHEN GET BACK HERE! WE'RE NOT THROUGH HERE!"

But even as he reached the hill overlooking the shore, his cries didn't come close to the retreating form of Stephen Gillis, now far below, chugging for the tug along the pebbled shore. Not nearly, given the roaring blow of the wind, the relentless pounding of water against rock ... and of course, the trees.

Chapter Five

"What the hell do you mean there's still one out there?!"

The outfitter was screaming before Kenton had even steered the tug close enough to toss his employer the mooring lines. This by way of greeting, despite the fact the young pilot had radioed ahead with the news over two hours earlier – just as soon as his lone returning passenger, having passed on the option of the outboard motor in favour of a very clumsy oaring technique, had finished wrestling the zodiac through the chop, then fumbled both it and himself back onto the charter. Since that call in, the outfitter had spent his energy pacing the dock, his concern escalating with every passing stride, for the day had turned positively black. The temperature had dipped well below freezing. The wind was whipping up crests even in the harbour and the sidelong spray of rain had now hardened into a stinging icy assault against his face. He knew there was no way his vessel could handle another trip out to fetch their stray. Not the way things were deteriorating. He had no choice. He would have to call the Coast Guard. And the RCMP.

"Sir, I need a word with you immediately," he announced, catching up to the one accounted-for client who had jumped spryly from boat to pier, then sprinted for the shelter of the dockside office and was madly punching numbers rapid-fire into the pay phone. "Mr. Gillis, I need to know whether Dr. Thompson gave you specific instructions to return to port without him."

"Boss, that's what I told you – "

"I'm not askin' you now Kenton!"

"But I'm tellin' you. The guy would not budge from the ridge. I tried yelling and gave him a bunch of arm signals to get his butt back down to the boat, but he just disappeared back into the woods. When Mr. Gillis here got back on board he told me Dr. Thompson had been tryin' to convince him to stay out there. I mean the guy did haul a ton of gear with him … and he's stayed out overnight both other times we chartered for him. I figured what's the difference."

"You know damn well the difference! It wasn't scheduled! He didn't set up an alternate return time."

"I know, I know! But shit, like I said … the guy wouldn't budge! I figured I'd make a run out in the morning like he had us do last time. Wasn't 'til later I got on the horn with you that I started hearing how bad it's comin' in from the north."

The owner shook his head vehemently. "Doesn't matter. Rain or shine, you know we have to get a client's stated intention to change his charter plans or we can be held liable … Mr. Gillis, I'm sorry but I really need to talk to you about this right away."

"What … oh, yeah sure," Stephen mumbled absently as he tried to punch through the jungle of retrieval codes for his office voicemail. There had been seven messages. All from Touchwater. All with the same theme as the first.

"Stephen … this is extremely urgent. I must talk with you as soon as possible. Call (818) 555-3163."

"Sir, please this is extremely important!" the charter owner repeated. "I need to know what Dr. Thompson said about –"

"Look I'm sorry," Stephen cut the man off as he quickly mouthed and pounded out on the keypad the number Touchwater had supplied. "But if you could just give me a minute, I'll tell you whatever you want to know … hello … yes … hello Robin? … Robin is that you?"

"*Stephen, where in God's name have you been?*"

"I know, I'm sorry. I was out of phone range. Where are you anyway? I don't recognise this area code."

"*I'll get to that in a moment Stephen. First I need to tell you that a rather deep-seated schism has cut into our ranks since we last spoke. And that split, my friend, revolves solely around you and Casey, and whether your experiences might not yet pertain to the pattern.*"

"Good. I knew it! I've spent the past day –"

"*Please, my friend. Let me get through this. Now, as you'll recall, our concern was that none of the radii projecting from Pasadena could accommodate either yours or Casey's experiences, and many – myself included as you know – had begun to distance our hopes from your particular story, especially given the progress we had been making elsewhere. You see, even since we last spoke, a significant number of new points have been revealed to further fill in the pattern. For example, four more points were found to fall on the Christchurch-to-Pasadena ley which was already rather impressive by its low deviation. And a nationalist uprising spilled over into a soccer match in the west of France to align with the anti-Redskin rallies in the Washington-Ukraine ley also with a very low degree of variance. In total, we have now discovered twelve separate spokes with points all aligning anywhere from three to eight episodes of sporting fervour that is in some way related to native spiritual reawakening. They've all occurred since that fateful Saturday in November. They all converge on Pasadena, California. Our findings have also been continually reinforced by Brother Amos and his steadfast visions of a terrible power wreaking havoc with the existing power structures of the day … 'smashing them like they were a construct no more sturdy than a house of cards' – his words, not mine. He has remained just as steadfast, however, in his belief that these visions surely include you and Casey. And in his latest correspondence, he spoke very eagerly of imminent events producing a day far brighter than any of the rest of us had ever yet dared imagine, suggesting the possibility that our spoke configuration may actually be organic. That is to say, a suspended pattern poised to evolve into something far greater when history finally converges. Stephen, it is the monk's fervent belief that you and Casey do not align into the present configuration because you two represent a point on this higher plane ... that is to say, you're already on the other side ... Stephen? ... Stephen are you still there?"*

~

The outfitter shook the remaining wet snow still stuck to the bill of his cap and the sleeves of his parka while he paced the floor waiting for his client to finish. Kenton stood by watching him, until his conscience bade him inch closer and offer some support.

"Look boss, I'm real sorry 'bout this. You think he'll be OK?"

"Christ, look at it out there!"

"I know. It was whippin' right up river 'bout thirty knots by the time we were pullin' in. But maybe he'll be alright. I mean the guy grew up around here, right? He should know what he's doin' out there. Soon as it blows over –"

"Blows over? Shit Kenton! Just how close were you listening to those radio reports? Prince Rupert's been stormed under since the middle of the night and Port Hardy's already had three trawlers broken up on rock. Two more missing."

"No shit –"

The outfitter paused to gaze out his office window.

"And that's not the half of it," he whispered softly, his face blank with worry. "I had the news on the tube at lunch. Stuff's happening up and down the whole damn coast. Washington's got power out from Bellingham down to Tacoma. The Interstates are closed down too. And down in Oregon, they got their eye on Mount St. Helens. They say she could go up again big time. Any moment."

"Mother of God. Imagine if that thing blew –"

"There's more, Kenton," the outfitter sighed, rubbing hard at the stubble on his cheeks. "Further down, in California. They're feeling tremors all along the San Andreas. Regular ones, and real deep at that."

~

"– Stephen?"

"Yeah ... I'm still here."

"Look I know I'm rambling but it's difficult not to get ahead of one's self. Now where was I?"

"Brother Amos including Casey and me."

"Yes, yes. I wouldn't have believed him Stephen. As God is my witness I swear I would never have come around had it not happened for me personally."

"If what hadn't happened?"

"Well, to know that you must first understand Brother Amos's effect. He tends to keep everyone else in The Watch quite busy trying to put a more manageable framework to the dream world he accesses. I am no exception. So when he shared his revelations of you and Casey with me, there I was, day and night for the past week trying any way I could think of to fit you both into the corpus of all our other events. Geographically ... etymologically ... anything. And when all else proved fruitless I embarked on one last desperate attempt by searching for some sort of commonality with the only other straggler from our pattern. You'll recall I mentioned it to you during one of our meetings. It was the episode of the ships that had been reporting eerie sightings around the ancient statues on Easter Island. Well, three days ago, around 5 in the morning, I had finally had enough. Screaming more than a few choice words, I grabbed a marker and a map of the Pacific, and carved a crude, jagged line from Estevan Point on Vancouver Island down and east to Pasadena, then zigzagged back so it connected with Easter Island. 'There!' I shouted at the top of my lungs, 'It's not straight, but it's as close as I'm going to get unless Pasadena decides to pack up and relocate 120 miles out into the goddamn Pacific Ocean!'"

~

"The newscast had an interview from the weather station where they monitor for stuff like that," the outfitter explained slowly as he peered out at the storm. "The woman kept going on about these huge seismic readings. Made it sound like there's a whole hell of a lot of pressure down there that's about to come to a head."

"Shit, you think it's the big one?"

The outfitter nodded. "They're talking about something called a *foreshock*. It's this rare thing. Pressure lets off these smaller quakes before a huge one gets set to blow."

"Well, hell … some of those fault lines run all the way right up here."

"Yes … yes they do," the outfitter replied and began to pace in front of the window, alternately checking his wrist-watch, the snow-sweeping winds outside and the pay phone over his shoulder. "You know it's funny. The wife and I were watching a TV show on earthquakes just last week."

"Yeah, I had that one on too. With all those geologist types talking about … what did they call 'em?"

"You mean the megathrusts?"

"Yeah, megathrusts, that's it. And did you see that one out-there guy? Goin' on about how one day some mother of all quakes will send southern California into the ocean; just break it away and split it from the rest of the continent."

"Yeah …" his boss sighed. "Let's hope some of those guys are just a bit strange with their theories. Talking about continents shifting over thousands of years is one thing. But it would take one hell of an earthquake to do it all at once."

Stephen's head bobbed up from the receiver with a start. "Earthquake?" he whispered.

~

"– I tell you Stephen, it was the most incredible thing! There in the very heart of my complete and utter exasperation, the very question that taunted me bore the seeds of my answer!"

~

"Yes Mr. Gillis, there have been reports of severe tremors down in California. But if you're through there on the phone, there are some other things we really need to talk about."

~

"– Stephen … Stephen … can you still hear me?"

~

"Mr. Gillis, do you understand?"

~

A droning buzz had suddenly insinuated itself upon Stephen's ears, rendering both Touchwater's exuberance and the outfitter's concern equally indecipherable.

"You're telling me California is getting earthquakes?" he repeated in a slow drawn-out sentence, as he squinted and cocked his head to combat the din, fast gaining in both pitch and intensity as it raced towards something of a screeching white noise. He could see the outfitter speaking something but couldn't make out any words. Just vague cognition of an angered expression. A stern stare. Hands thrown in the air. Impatient footsteps. Kenton too was saying something; something foreboding. And his face had paled. Paled as white as the wind-blown scene outside. He thought he would be sick to his stomach. He dropped his jaw and gasped for breath to calm his insides. This was it. After all the talk of greatness; after all the promises of great purpose that had dragged him from the simple precise scouting life he had known. ... first Willie speaking of a *Messiah* ... then Robin of the entire Cosmos opening up. But even at its most frustratingly elusive moments, at no time in the whole meandering journey had anyone ever suggested the outcome might be anything destructive. Sure Brother Amos had written of force and struggle, but these Stephen had taken as nothing more than the visionary's own poetic take on a college football game; mere fodder for that *something greater* Robin had promised. *Something* far more significant. *Something* ultimately for the *better.*

Stephen's mind flew back to the unconditional blackness of Touchwater's office, which he now suddenly remembered in the absence of a far different light. No longer was it the clear and focused haven he had craved but a few short hours ago, where a world of infinite possibilities could grow and breathe above the blare of modern life. Suddenly, it was a Watchtower – a space sanitised and cut off from the rest of the world, so that talk of destruction would carry no blood or strife; where the cries of a person, or beast, or bird or tree would scarce be heard. Where the eyes above the singular focus of a desk lamp shining on a pristine mahogany desktop could easily sacrifice the lives of thousands – tens of thousands, hundreds of thousands – so long as it promoted the goal.

The screech in his head was now a deafening roar, and, fight though he tried, the countering words that dribbled from his lips seemed so desperately weak as soon as they left his mouth.

"That's what this is about?" he stammered back into the telephone receiver. "An earthquake?"

"*Now Stephen I need to say something!*"

"My God ... we could be talking about millions of lives here! Children ... babies! For Christ sake, how long have you known?"

"*Stephen ...*"

"Jesus, don't you think you could have told somebody!? Instead of sitting up there in your little penthouse suite, all safe and secure, discussing the whole thing with your friends like it was just some kind of game!"

"*Stephen, I'm here. I'm in Pasadena.*"

"What?"

There was silence as the scout fought hard through the noise to be sure he had heard correctly.

"*It's the only way, my friend.*"

"But that's crazy, if you know what's about to happen –"

"*Stephen you're going to have to trust me on this, for I haven't the time to fully explain my motivations except to say that this is my only chance to see how this final chapter plays out. I know it sounds macabre, especially given most people's innate instincts for survival, but given how all of these revelations have manifested before me, there can be no more doubt. This is my destiny and whether it turns out I'm left standing amid the carnage or I'm immediately launched into a crevice and swallowed up by Mother Earth herself cannot be a factor. My life has been built to be a witness to this coming wonder and I must now fulfil that calling.*"

"Robin, if you're asking me to –"

"*I'm not asking anything of you Stephen. I just knew we needed to have this conversation. And I will conclude the way I did with the others.*"

"No wait, don't go yet. I haven't told you what I found out about Willie!"

"*Stephen, please.*"

"But you don't understand. I found him … or at least signs of him. And the scrapbook … the same one he had shown me the night we met."

"*Stephen, I'm sorry but there's no more time. If you've seen any news today you'll know it's near mass hysteria down here. All I can offer you is this. Our movement has been one predicated on the notion of convergence; convergence of time and space and energy. Revealed to us has been a massive convergence more vast than any of us could have imagined and I now truly believe Casey Bruford's rise to prominence has been a tapping of the same energies fuelling this imminent profound upheaval. But what I want to say is this: If there is contained anywhere in your soul even the slightest tug of resistance in a different direction … if you can truly pinpoint such a pull … then be satisfied that you have fulfilled your calling to help bring young Mr. Bruford forward, and let me urge you to go immediately and seek the point where this search that has so gloriously intersected with ours first came to be. And once you're there, keep good Watch. Beyond this, I have no more advice. I must go. Good luck, Stephen."*

~

Hearing the phone returned to its cradle, the outfitter immediately spun from his view out the window with a most commanding "there now." Sadly, before his next words were out of his mouth, the client bolted from phone to door, the violent jangling of the clapper bells serving both to mark his exit and warn of the ensuing whoosh of wind and snow that came howling into the outer office – easily out-competing the owner's calls to "come back and straighten this out" as well as his pilot's more succinct, "Hey buddy, where the hell do you think you're goin'?"

Where he was going – at least initially – was out of the parking lot and back out the town road, charging through a couple of small yet threatening drifts to do so. Then it was back on the highway, which at least looked to have seen a plough … to Campbell River, then south to Nanaimo and the ferry dock (the last run, he was told, before service was to be suspended due to the approaching storm). However, it wasn't until he was well back on the mainland, well east of Vancouver's endless stream of tail lights – slowed by the uncharacteristic volume of snow – before he became conscious that he indeed had a destination beyond the desperate panic-stricken need to chase the highway paint into the night. It had come with Robin's last words, his urging to find that personal point of convergence; for, not only had the idea resonated as true, it had quickly grown in his mind into an imperative, and the further he drove into the blinding squalls the clearer that point became. By the time he steered his car through the heavy streets of the town of Hope, there was no doubt. The turn north for the toll route was navigated without the slightest hint of self-questioning. He figured on 100 Mile House in five hours. Then north, up past Williams Lake, then Quesnel. Back to Prince George.

Chapter Six

To: sgillis@centennials.scout/west.ca

Dear Brother Gillis,

The hour has arrived. Be still, watch and abide the darkness for the night must surely weep before Mother Earth can recompose herself in splendour. Long have I seen the day approach. Two legions face to face, clad in armour, set to war. When from on high like circling winds foe and ally alike are put to the air, the very sod of the battle torn from beneath their feet, Mother Earth herself ripped open to bleed. Long too have I seen the fruit of your own vision rise forth from this mayhem. The Watch has almost ended. Do not fear, Brother Gillis. I am with you.

Brother Amos

~

He received his final correspondence in a motel office on the outskirts of Clinton, BC, where road closures had forced him from the highway.

There, for a hastily negotiated fee, he had convinced the day manager to let him borrow the services of a computer so he could download and print off any necessary e-mails.

There was, of course, another prophetic update from Brother Amos, as well as two letters. The first had been scanned into the computer system by a reluctant administrative assistant in the Toronto Centennials front office three days earlier, when Stephen had briefly spoken with her by telephone. Since it had been marked "Private & Confidential," it had taken a fair bit of cajoling by Stephen to persuade the young woman it would be alright for her to open it, scan it and forward it to him as an e-mail. Stephen now saw its contents for the first time.

Sabourin & Duff
14 Adelaide St.
Toronto ON
M1M 2G2

Stephen Gillis
c/o The Toronto Centennials Hockey Club
Suite 500
1st Ambassador's Place
6 Front Street
Toronto ON
M7D 2E4

December 26

Dear Mr. Gillis,

As agent for Casey Bruford, I have been instructed by my client to request that you have no further contact with his mother, one Liisa Bruford of Thunder Bay, Ontario – be it written, phone or personal. It has been brought to my client's attention that you and/or your associates have corresponded with Mrs. Bruford on at least two occasions and that much of the content of those correspondences has been of a personal and probing nature that has had a disruptive and unsettling effect upon both my client and his mother.

Please take note that, while nothing in your actions has overtly threatened Mrs. Bruford's safety, I believe your behaviour in this matter has called into account questions of professional conduct. Therefore, please be advised that I, in accordance with my client's wishes, have forwarded copies of both this letter and the body of correspondence with Mrs. Bruford to your employers with the expectation that the matter will be dealt with internally in an expeditious fashion.

Sincerely,
Barry Sabourin

∼

MEMO: (internal) December 29
FROM: Bruce Hellyer, General Manager

TO Stephen Gillis – Associate Scout, Western Canada

This note is to advise you, Stephen Gillis, that after discussion with your superiors and the board of directors of the Toronto Centennials Hockey Club, effective immediately, your contract with the scouting department of this organisation has been terminated on grounds of professional misconduct. It was decided by myself, with input from the Director of Player Personnel and Director of Public Relations, that your actions and your associations of recent weeks have not only reflected poorly, but have done grave damage to the health and the daily function of this organisation.

You will be contacted by our security office in the next few days to arrange an appointment to collect any personal effects and to vacate your office. You will also be required to surrender all Toronto Centennials accreditation at that time. Please note that in the meantime your building access card has been deactivated – as has your access to the Toronto Centennials' computer system, other than for inbound e-mails forwarded to your mailbox.

I thank you for your past years of service and wish you good fortune in all future endeavours.

Sincerely B. Hellyer

cc. Adam Benning, Director of Player Personnel
cc. Marilyn Atkins, Human Resources Manager

~

Once back inside the car he immediately began twisting the dials on the radio, his jittery hands at first mistaking the volume setting for the channel reset and sending a blast of white noise through the speakers to crash headlong into his already pounding migraine. After several panicky attempts he finally subdued the electronics, just in time to hear the dispassionate drone of a newscaster's voice coming over the air to announce that area highways would remain closed for at least another hour. Angrily he elbowed back the driver's seat to its full recline and threw himself backwards, kicking his feet through the sea of two dozen or more empty cups from coffee shops across the Canadian west. He pulled out the e-mails from his pocket to examine them again, his hands trembling quite uncontrollably, causing the lines to dance hopelessly in front of his face. His eyes squeezed further and further into a severe squint that threatened to close off completely and send the scout into one of his now all-too-familiar muscle-tense sleeps in hell. It was an urge he fought defiantly. Lying back in his seat and holding up the letters to the light of an ever-greying sky, with the constant chatter of the radio swimming in his ears as his free hand continued to spin the dial, he vainly tried to muster the fortitude to cry out against injustice … to cry out in anger … to cry out for any feeling at all.

~

… the time is 3 p.m. You're listening to CKAV. Topping the news this hour … Storm Watch! A massive winter storm has hit the Pacific Coast with a vengeance. Heavy accumulations, high winds and road closures are the order of the day throughout the Lower Mainland, Vancouver Island and the Caribou region.

State-side, all eyes are on Mt. St. Helens tonight as the volcano, dormant since 1980, shows signs of once again erupting … and in Southern California – where damaging earth tremors have been felt over the past thirty-six hours – fallen trees, overturned road signs and cracked foundations have been reported throughout central regions, from Palo Alto as far south as Santa Monica. While scientists continue to monitor the situation closely, many residents and vacationers have left the state, fearing the worst as some experts believe that the tremors are actually foreshocks, precursors to a full-scale earthquake of massive proportions. All freeways to and from the greater Los Angeles area are extremely busy and airlines are reporting heavy walk-up sales over the past day …

~

His last conscious image was a plaza parking lot across the street, and the hastened steps of those trying to wrap up their year-end chores early, scurrying inside the door of the bank for one last stash of cash to see them through the evening's festivities, or maybe one last trip to the grocer next door to cover one more contingency before the closed sign was flipped over to put a finish to the calendar. Then from off to the side, behind the far row of parked cars, was the vague awareness of a distant sound – one he couldn't be sure was part of the setting or merely an infiltration of the relentless dream world that lurked so close behind. It was the echo of clicking stick blades against a diligently cleared patch of asphalt. There, in the middle of all that cold … laughter. He fought momentarily from the fast-approaching sleep to squint through the slight crack he had left in his driver side window and see a dozen kids, twelve years old or so, stripped down from heavy parkas to a rainbow of replica jerseys, completely oblivious to the climate around them. And for one fraction of a second – that brief portal that hints of a glorious universe somewhere between everyday life and the world of sleep – Stephen became aware of his hands. He felt them flex; felt them reaching for the sensation of a sanded wooden shaft gilded at the end with carefully sculpted wads of tape. In that blink of an instant, he craved a stick again … craved for those kids' version of being twelve years old. But then, just as always … as had happened on the ferry ride from Nanaimo when he dared to doze, and just like all those times on his week-long drive out to the coast … in Medicine Hat, in Moosimin … and of course in Kenora … sleep slammed shut the portal and only the nightmare remained, reminding him how such a childhood could never have been.

∿

Gone is the plaza, the parking lot … the outline of tall craggy moun-tainsides – replaced instead by endless winter sky and flat prairie snow. Only the children remain, though their boots have now sprouted blades as the asphalt has frozen over solid. They play on. In and around the weeping form of a woman dressed in black … past the man in the weather-beaten parka clutching a scrapbook to his chest. "It's so dark. My God, you can't imagine how dark it is," he mumbles over and over again. Then comes the voice of his father … the screaming … the swearing … the raging. But from what direction? He can't pinpoint it. He can only hear it get louder …

∿

Stephen's head struck the steering wheel. He gasped and sputtered, and snapped back to attention to peer through the snowy dusk and regain some bearing on his surroundings. It had seemed like mere seconds. A flash of sleep. But the grocery store was now closed; the rows of parked vehicles were gone. The road hockey game was now no more than a skirmish of three or four stragglers, urgently racing against time to get in just one more rush; one more shot before darkness fell in earnest; perhaps the satisfaction of hitting the very top corner where the sweet-spot webbing just behind the weld between post and crossbar lets the puck catapult back with as much satisfying force as it had possessed on the way in. Clearly, it was next goal wins. Next goal was for the whole game and all the effort that had gone on before didn't matter one bit.

He was angry for having slept too long. For having put himself behind schedule to make Prince George by midnight. He cursed himself at length, then snapped the radio back on, giving the station dial a series of violent spins.

∽

… you're with CFDR, Kamloops' easy-listening alternative … current temperature is minus seventeen … winds out of the northwest gusting to 85 kilometres per hour …

∽

… Turning to weather, whiteout conditions persist throughout the Caribou region. Police are urging everyone to stay off the roads …

∽

… A UBC anthropology professor remains missing on the outer coast of Vancouver Island. RCMP are looking for a man driving a tan-coloured sedan with Ontario licence plates wanted for questioning in connection with the disappearance of Dr. David Thompson. Meanwhile rescue efforts for the missing 38-year-old man remain hampered by severe weather conditions …

∽

The car spun out of the parking lot and back to the highway, bullying its way first through a drift and then a few miles north, around the road closure barricade, before gunning onward through the plodding path of the under-ploughed road. The view of the street hockey boys – still mixed with the unshakable images of razor-sharp steel gliding across prairie ice – was now imprinted like a movie screen across his windshield no matter which way he turned, and with his gas pedal his only weapon he hurtled the car back into the blizzard in the hopes of outracing the nightmare … before the wind kicked up and the river turned its inevitable crimson … before the widow's stomach-wrenching wail. Diversion was what he needed; a counterpoint to the storm inside his head. Frantically he cranked down the car window to let the sharp bite of the gusting storm sting his face, then grabbed again for the radio, sliding it up to full volume, spinning the station select button further and further up the dial.

∿

… This is Chuck Jaworski with the evening news … In a press conference held earlier today, the mayor of Pasadena, California confirmed that tomorrow's Tournament Parade and football game will go on as planned despite the fear and unrest which has permeated Southern California for the past two days. While the chairman acknowledged that game attendance might be down somewhat due to backed-up airline schedules and many people's reluctance to stay in the region over the New Year, the teams themselves have been in town for a week and have both expressed a desire to see the marvellous and time-honoured tradition of this celebrated event go ahead as scheduled …

∿

… CFDR Action News has just learned that Stephen Gillis, 35, of Toronto, is wanted for questioning in the disappearance of UBC anthropology professor David Thompson, missing on Vancouver Island since yesterday

morning. Mr. Gillis is best known as an associate scout for the Toronto Centennials, and recently has also been implicated as a member of a quasi-religious group known as "The Watch." RCMP officials are canvassing all of Vancouver Island searching for a tan-coloured late model Chevrolet sedan, although officers also believe Mr. Gillis may have made his way onto the mainland just ahead of the stormy conditions that have plagued all of BC for the past two days …

~

He couldn't feel the road … couldn't feel the wheels track. And as he accelerated into each oncoming drift, their increasing size threw the car evermore sideways with each successive impact. He longed for the pure and simple focus of that clear, defined ribbon of paint to dissect the highway. He longed for it to clear his crowded movie screen.

"The hour has arrived. Be still, watch and abide the darkness for the night must surely weep."

For twenty kilometres, then forty … he chanted the monk's message over and over again. He screamed it overtop of the din from the radio. Shouted it in the ever-elusive direction of the visions superimposed on his windshield. Shouted it loudest at The Voice, now suctioned onto his conscience like a leech. The one that had chased him from his childhood, chased him from the grave and back … chased him, checked him, slashed him and hooked him day after day. It was The Voice he now realised he would never outrun, that its volume would only continue to grow through the remainder of his days while the rest of his existence – once such a careful and effective filter for these hauntings – now sat in a powerless shambles, a useless lump of flesh behind a steering wheel on a frozen treacherous highway.

He had but one remaining say in his fate. That was the choosing of when the history of Stephen Gillis would finally moult its skin, and leave exposed to the bone-chilling air the skinless sinew and cartilage that was his life; finally frozen free from its misery. When the dizzying wall of internal noise would finally subside. When the nightmarish movie screen that now shrouded the entire breadth of his imagination would finally fade. It felt like he was falling … falling right through the winter wind. Through a hole in the ground where gusts of snow just swirled and swirled, gathering speed in a spiralling free fall to oblivion.

◡

… This is the Resurrection Gospel Network, 89.4 FM in Spokane, 103.1 in the Idaho Panhandle. Our New Year's subject tonight: The day and the hour Unknown …

◡

They were all over the road. His father – a skull on slumping shoulders, sputtering blood from the cavity below two large and hollowed eye sockets. His mother, wailing. Willie, shaking his head. Then, out of nowhere, the young OPP constable … his hand reaching out and placed on the shoulder crest of a young boy's hockey jacket. He swerved instinctively and the car caught in a rut, careened off a guardrail, then back and forth across both lanes of the highway. The sound of a siren reached his ears, faintly at first then in a rapid crescendo, piercing through his anguish, working against the natural gravity and rhythm of his dive; back in favour of the painfully hopeless din of The Voice.

He had to run from it. He had to be free. But the road was like liquid beneath him and the car swerved violently as he fought to hold the wheel steady while he accelerated away from the sound. Suddenly there were children. He saw thousands upon thousands, innocently playing, completely unsuspecting of what would surely be fatal impact. He spun the wheel hard to throw the car from their path. Spun until only darkness filled the windshield. Until nothing but the dim outline of the trees was all that mattered before him. With a shriek of resolve, he accelerated toward the shadows. He could feel the heaviness of the undergrowth approach. Stone … metal … ice. He wanted it all to swallow him whole. The car hit the embankment hard, catapulting both car and driver into the black cold air. He threw his arms up in front of his face anticipating the blow of nothingness, and in that last split second sent one last blood-curdling cry skyward. A cry that, like a child's over-inflated balloon, would surely burst everything his life contained and all he had ever known into one final uninterrupted silence.

~

Chaos awakened with the crash. The sickening snaps of tree limbs obliterated by flying chrome and steel. The scrape of metal against rock face hiding in wait just below the snow-line. A blurred shadow moved across his face in slow motion while the rest of his senses drowned in the carnage. The salt of blood and sweat poured down his face and into his mouth. The smell of leaking gasoline, the sudden heat of fire. Sirens far closer now and still advancing. Then, the first wave of pain … the over-whelming throb of bone and skull. Then a second sensation, a sudden biting pain that stung deep into his shoulder. So too, his left arm, as though it were caught in a vice of knives. He thought he could hear clothes being torn. Swore he could feel his body forced roughly out of the folds of the wreckage. Swore he could feel the cool snow blowing over his wounds … moist heated breath hovering over him. A high-pitched whimper … the vague glow of two piercing steel-grey eyes, cold and steadfast … then nothing but wind.

~

The officer first on the scene knelt over the injured driver, holding his head as steady and motionless as possible. Vainly he tried to calm the victim's agitation, promising that help would soon be on its way. Telling him how for-

*tunate he was to be thrown clear of the wreckage now engulfed in flame …
to land in the forgiving snow. It was the same sentiment that would find its
way into the officer's report on the incident, as would his conclusion that
while severe weather conditions played a contributing role, excessive speed
and driver instability were the relevant circumstances. As evidence, the officer would cite three factors: the erratic steering observed by him and his partner just prior to the sedan losing control; the crumpled letters found in the
distraught driver's pocket – one informing the man he had been fired, the
other a threatening correspondence from another party's legal counsel. And
of course there were the inconsolable man's outbursts as he drifted in and out
of consciousness in the ambulance … screaming how he should be dead …
how he deserved to die … how he would have died had he not been dragged
from his vehicle …*

… by a wolf.

Part Four

I feel that ley-man, astronomer, priest, druid, bard, wizard, witch, palmer and hermit, were all more or less linked by one thread of ancient knowledge of power, however degenerate it became in the end

Grave marker of
William Joseph Skilliter

Chapter One

They called it a miracle. The meteorologists, the seismologists, on every radio broadcast and telecast, in every newspaper account ... no one seemed able to venture any further past the term by way of explanation. The storms beneath the Earth, the raging winds and churning oceans that swept across her surface with torrential downpours and smothering squalls, had all just suddenly and inexplicably stopped. Whereas only hours earlier the world had braced for the worst possible catastrophe, the population of the Pacific coastline awakened on New Year's Day to blue sky, calm waters and with nothing but firm and steadfast earth beneath its feet. The weather was crisp and cold in Canada and the northwest U.S., and it was warm and dry in Southern California, where, under cloudless skies and before a joyous, almost giddy sell-out crowd, the University of Arizona trotted out onto the football field, and with born-again conviction routed the upstart Central Michigan Chippewas 34–0.

~

PASADENA (AP) – Robin Touchwater, president and founder of Frontier Communications, died yesterday morning in his sleep while on vacation in California. The 83-year-old telecommunications magnate's passing was announced at a make-shift press conference in the hotel where he had been staying since shortly after Christmas. Frontier spokesperson Sharon Kyle would offer no further details, claiming only that Mr. Touchwater had been suffering under the burden of an unspecified illness of lengthy duration but had nevertheless been in Southern California to relax and take in the Arizona/Central Michigan football game. Mr. Touchwater's body will be flown back to Toronto where it will be interred on Friday.

~

The Frontier News Channel provided complete coverage, from the pallbearers' procession through the funeral service itself and on to the interment; the whole spectacle for all who cared to see, theatrically interspliced with an endless array of taped interviews from fellow entrepreneurs and magnates; businessmen and states people, each commenting upon the deceased's many exploits as they traced out vague mappings of the road that had taken him from one small radio broadcast in his boyhood home of Pembroke, Ontario to a massive 40-station empire, a stable of 27 television affiliates and five separate specialty cable networks. And yet for all the carefully choreographed laud and honour, the body of the late Robin Touchwater lay there beneath perfectly polished mahogany exactly as the man had lived. Hidden. Invisible. An enigma.

There was no knowledge of and therefore no mention of family. There was no commentary of loves or passions or hobbies beyond his work. No talk of his literary or philosophical interests, of his vast library or his pursuits in the field of Earth Mysteries. Certainly nothing was said that would remotely betray his confidential association with The Watch. Only the repetitive praises of work-obsessed telecommunication aficionados – anchors, reporters and pundits; interviewer and interviewee alike – all singing as one the virtues of a man whose image they had unwittingly honed to that of their own. Robin Touchwater, the single-minded. Robin Touchwater the determined. Robin Touchwater, the relentless winner who never rested on past victories; the driven perfectionist who surely accepted nothing less than complete success in any of his endeavours. Not even the curious epitaph chiselled on the man's grave marker in bold block letters and camera-ready for the interment broadcast could deter such a steadfast image; the presiding news anchor interpreting the words there inscribed as merely a fittingly modest quote from such a tireless and prolific empire-builder. They were, in fact, the words she chose to draw breathily through her lips and whisper to her viewers as she signed off, bending down to grave level for added poignancy as she read, "*I am, it turns out, but a weaver after all.*"

~

The patient spent his days in the common room. Mornings and evenings, always the same spot, slumped on his chair and leaning over the long table nearest the bay window and the bookshelves; as far from the nursing station and the daily traffic of patients, doctors and visitors as he could manage; where the remaining flat light of mid-winter's dull grey snow-scape hit the equally pallid tabletop – the faux oak veneer upon which he rested his right forearm while his left leafed through book after book. He chose a different title each day, the subject mattering little. He would begin in the middle and grow tired before the end, at best reading mere snippets at a time, pausing often and for long periods to peer out the window to the murky world beyond.

This was the spot where he had first been seated upon his arrival three days after the accident, still nursing several bruised ribs, a broken hand and the markings from a number of lacerations to the face and legs. This was where he had perched in uncomfortable silence in front of the admitting nurse while she shuffled through paper after paper, filling out the required documents for his entrance. Where he had stared blankly at the woman's co-workers as they busied themselves with the task of divesting the ward of any residual decorations from the holiday season; stripping the no-longer-appropriate paper cut-outs of elves and angels, trading in their bold reds, their warm rich greens and shining gold for a clearer view of the institutional puce which undercoated each and every wall in sight.

The television sat at a distance from the patient's favourite chair, up against one such wall, its screen dwarfed by the insipid colour, framed in the foreground by a number of upholstered recliners, a coffee table and a sofa. It was there – in between the lifeless heads and shoulders of the other screen-entranced bodies and the darting frames of hyper duty-filled orderlies and nurses scurrying back and forth – that the patient took in the funeral proceedings. Watching it in the same manner he now took in all his surroundings. Silent. Distant. Motionless. Staring through the room, seemingly unaffected by the faces and voices that stopped periodically to try to detach his gaze. Doctors with charts and files which they ticked with fine-tipped pens. Nurses chiming out meal times or medication schedules. Other patients leaning over to gawk into the patient's face or to slobber hello over and over again in their slow over-announced voices.

To one and all the patient steadfastly offered nothing in response. Not during the daily rounds by the doctors. Nor at any of the obligatory Friday afternoon group sessions. Nothing even for the once-frequent, then diminished attempts at light-hearted conversation whenever one of the custodial crew happened by. He had no need for chatter. No stake in hearing his own voice being accepted by any of theirs. He wanted none of the yearning that obsessed so many of the fellow sheep around him; sheep who followed the uniforms around, so eager to hear their names called out in greeting by someone on staff, prey to the façade of belonging, swayed by the misbelief that they were something more than caged animals, kept by the promises of calculated psycho-babble from a bunch of doctors. None of those doctors – the patient was certain – had ever once felt the wounds of screaming voices trapped inside their heads; nevertheless they demanded submission to their supposed authority, their clinical assessments, their pills, their talk of management skills and coping mechanisms … their coaching.

No, his sole refuge would be this spot beside the window. Where he could look out and view the laneway gradually sloping down through the dense screen of conifers and from there, he imagined, out to the highway. Once upon a time, long ago, he had kept a highway marker in such stead. But whereas that I-74 sign pointing out of the suburbs of Peoria had once tempted him with the promise of a sense of home, the grey shadows outside now only hinted of a silent never-ending road streaming out ahead of him into a cloudy meld of slush and sky, where the only achievable goal was to keep moving from horizon to horizon; grey to grey. To survive in the safety of being nowhere in particular.

There would be no more stops along the road to listen to fellow travellers, no matter how eloquently or persuasively they expressed their whims. There would be no attachment to their hopes or dreams or expectations. There would be no talk of chemistry or bonding. No discussion of visionaries or monks. He wanted no part of doctors or professors or Messiahs. No part of hope or healing or salvation. He would live his days as he had played the game … alone.

Chapter Two

BOSTON (AP) – The Toronto Centennials lost more than a hockey game, falling 4–0 to Boston last night. Rookie Centennials forward Casey Bruford is expected to miss several weeks with a separated shoulder courtesy of a vicious hit from fellow Western Junior League grad Bill Parkinson. Bruford has been mired in a lengthy slump of late with just one point in his last ten contests after collecting an astonishing 54 over his first 22 games. Nevertheless the Centennials can ill afford to lose his services. Last night the Blue and White could manage only 19 shots on net despite enjoying six power play opportunities. Toronto has just one win in their last eleven games dating back to the All-Star break and in that time have scored only 18 goals, having gone an abysmal 2 for 51 on the power play.

~

"Here he is … good luck," the orderly shrugged, passing his hand in front of the patient's eyes with sensitivity befitting the long drawn-out yawn that stretched across his face. When the figure did not move, the worker shrugged again, spun on his heel and loped back down the corri-

dor, leaving the visitor – a rather tall and gangly young man – to negotiate an introduction on his own.

"Mr. Gillis?" the boy began slowly, his lanky but slight frame looming
over the seated man. "Mr. Gillis, my name's Olan Krutzweiser. I play goal
for the junior team here in town. Casey Bruford and I used to billet
together when he was here."

Though he did not notice immediately, his head staying down as he
rather nervously wrung his hands together while he spoke his greeting, the
boy was rewarded where none other had been. His words were cause
enough for the man to shift his eyes, albeit slightly, from the view outside
the window.

"I called last week to see if it was OK to come out here. Shoulda done
it before. I mean it's back over a month since I first read about you in the
paper. Our team's not doin' much this year … again. We've lost five in a
row and we're back in last place. I don't know. Maybe I'd feel a bit better
about things if Casey was still around. He was one hell of an upbeat guy
eh."

Only then did the boy pause to glance up and gauge the reception to
his unsolicited visit. While nothing in the man's blank stare indicated any
interest, there were also no outward signs of disdain. The latter had been
the far greater fear for the lad, especially after the many cautionary tales of
the patient's anti-social behaviour he had received – first upon phoning to
inquire about visitation, and then from the orderly who had led him in.

Olan pulled out the chair opposite the man, youthfully oblivious to
the reactions his sudden movement caused. The clenched jawline. The
tightened grip round the edges of that day's unread book. The slow but
steady rotation of the head back towards the window.

"I mean I come from this completely messed-up home right? My folks
split up when I was eight. And then here's Casey … this guy who's never
even known who his real parents are at all. But he'd still let me go on as
long as I wanted about how I never got to see my dad. Just let me get it all
off my chest without bitchin' or complainin'. Crazy thing is, I could never
convince him to go out and look for his own mom and dad … I mean his

real mom and dad. And I don't get that 'cause if it were me, I sure as hell'd want to know. But not Casey. 'Think about it Ollie,' he'd say to me. 'Somebody was convinced they'd be better off without me, when they only knew me for a few days. I can't go chasin' them down now just in case they changed their minds.' Which sort of makes sense I guess, but … shit, a parent's a parent right? I mean deep down, they gotta care, don't they?"

The boy's head now rested comfortably on folded arms spread across the table. Like the patient across from him, his eyes had also found their way to the window and to the flat grey-white landscape of the grounds outside.

"Last year was great. I mean sure, the team sucked, but me and Casey, we had this way of keepin' each other going. See, he never stopped believin' our shot was out there somewhere. Imagine that, eh … a fourth-line centre and a back-up goalie dreamin' of makin' it big time. Hell some nights he'd just hang out in the rec room and imagine what it would all be like. Dreamin' what it would feel like to have the absolute game of his life. Visualising he called it. He said it was so he'd be ready when his chance finally came. 'A legit chance, Ollie. That's all I want,' he'd say. 'Cause if you knew for sure you had that, you could just go like hell and leave nothin' in the tank.' Turns out he was right."

"Turns out he was lucky."

The boy's head bobbed to attention. Instinctively he turned to scan the room for someone official. A nurse or doctor. Perhaps the orderly who had signed him in and had been so careful to limit his expectations. That urge, however, proved fleeting, curbed instantly by the patient's next words, likewise uttered barely above a whisper so that no one else apart from his guest would have any suspicion his silence had been broken.

"March 15 last year. Here against Kamloops."

"I knew it," the lad exclaimed, jumping up and slapping the table. He immediately scanned the room again, this time fearful lest his own exuberant tones had exceeded the institution's allowable level.

"I knew it had to be that game," he said with forced reserve as he seated himself once again. "I mean he was unconscious that night! First the collision with Parkinson. Four points in the third period. A come-from-behind win over the league leaders. But I mean … come on, you must have liked something about his game before that. I mean I know you took a lot of heat for drafting him, but a professional scout doesn't just pick a player based on one period of hockey, right?"

"Actually I didn't see any of it."

"What, you mean you weren't even there?"

"No, I was there. But I left after the second period."

The patient's voice faded even softer, barely audible as he bit his top teeth over his lower lip in the effort to quell a sudden wave of anger whose unanticipated force left him completely unprepared. It was that raw emotion that would bid the next words from his mouth, and those words once launched that would render his young guest an unsuspecting casualty of the struggle.

"But I don't get it," the goalie rambled on. "Casey barely got on the ice until the third period. I mean if that was really the game that clinched it for him why would you leave before he even got a chance –"

"I left because I was tired," the patient cut in hoarsely, an ill-willed grin cracking up from the corners of his mouth. "I was tired of seeing what scouts always see. A bunch of nervous players doing what nervous players do best. Skating the entire warm-up and spending the whole national anthem, and every single stoppage in play peering up into the stands trying to figure out which suit in the crowd they should be trying to impress that night … in the process getting themselves so worked up, they can't even, just for example say, make a simple glove save on the first fluttering wrist shot that comes their way."

The youngster was caught off-guard, as unprepared for the venom in the patient's voice as he had been for that forty-foot wrister that had eluded his glove hand a year ago.

"Look I'm sorry," he stammered weakly. "I just came by to see if you were OK. I mean I just figured since I was a friend of Casey's and you were the one who –"

"Casey and I aren't close."

"No ... I know ... I mean I knew you were let go by the Cents. Everybody knows that. Look I didn't mean to bug you. I just wanted to stop by and ... and ... ah shit I don't know why the hell I came."

~

It all should have ended right there – with the lad hastily retreating down the hall, the patient reverting to his tacit thousand-mile stare – had the young goalie not given into the urge so effectively bred into competitive hockey players. Upon a few seconds of reflection of how intentionally personal the man's attack had been, he momentarily abandoned all rules of decorum for the sake of retaliation.

None of the staff, not the doctors on call, nor the orderly who had led Olan in, nor anyone at the reception desk had noticed when the boy doubled back down the corridor and marched back into the common room. However, all were quite expedient in responding once he grabbed the patient by his shirt collar and the shouting began. Which was a shame as far as the young man was concerned. A shame in that his straightaway escort from the room, back down the corridor, and indeed right off the grounds, negated any opportunity for him to see the profound effect his visit had had. He would not have the opportunity to note the severely clamped facial muscles. Nor the white-knuckled hands clenched to the edge of the reading table in an effort not to move – not even the slightest curl of an eyebrow or flinch of a hand – until the patient was sure he had caught a glimpse of the boy's shadow passing by outside his window ... not until the parade of staff had finished coming by to ask if he was alright ... not until the last of the goddamn inhabitants had ceased with their gawking drop-jaw stares ... not until late that night, back in the solitary confines of his ten-by-ten puce-coloured room with the words of his young visitor still echoing fresh in his ears, when both muscle tissue and resolve would bend to the undeniable crescendo of sobs gathering from deep within. There, with his chest heaving uncontrollably against the front cross-straps of his bed restraint, he would break down.

The very next day, at his scheduled session, there began an irrepressible outflow of emotion from the patient's lips, spewed like an erupting mountain, before the startled psychiatrist – whose attendance by that time owed more to duty than expectation – could even finish posing her first question. It was an outpouring that began not with any talk of recurring nightmares or images of blood-soaked accident scenes, nor stories of wolves or ley lines or Earth Mysteries, but instead with a long-dormant memory of a woman's light feet tiptoeing into her child's bedroom … her warm arms sliding under her young one's neck to cradle and comfort him. Her calming voice whispering through the child's sobs, *"Close your eyes … close your eyes and imagine yourself as free as you ever wanted to be."*

He would speak of her depression. How she was never able to cope after the untimely death of her husband. How she had been bedridden in the end, consumed by grief and refusing to eat or get dressed. How in her own final days, with her weary voice tired so far ahead of its years, she would refer to herself as an anchor without a ship … left to drown alone on her own. Her life, her vitality, her gentleness all removed from her soul because for the sake of the Kenora Optimists Midget Tournament final, he had dared to do her will. Dared to be *free*. He spoke of his mother at great length, surprising himself at the ease with which the words flowed. Surprised by how closely it had all been lurking just below the surface of his soul. And all of it strangely, ironically … unwittingly brought on by the retaliatory words of a riled-up back-up goaltender and his steadfast faith in parenthood.

"MY DAD LEFT WHEN I WAS FUCKING EIGHT YEARS OLD!" the boy screamed upon his return to the room, his face crimson red, the pointed finger of his free hand jabbing at the patient's impassive face. "HE DRIVES TRUCK ALL OVER THE GODDAMN COUNTRY AND HE'S NEVER SEEN ME PLAY ONE GODDAMN GAME OF JUNIOR. NOT ONE GODDAMN GAME! BUT I GOT A CALL THAT MORNING SAYIN' HIS ROUTE MIGHT BRING HIM THROUGH. SO JUST FOR THE RECORD … I WASN'T STARIN' UP INTO THE STANDS LOOKING FOR SOME GODDAMN FUCKING HOCKEY SCOUT!!"

Chapter Three

TORONTO (CP) – Toronto Centennials' forward Casey Bruford, still recovering from a shoulder injury, will not be available for the rest of the regular season according to team doctors. Bruford, who participated in light practice for the first time yesterday, said the shoulder is responding more slowly than expected. The rookie, who had struggled since the all-star break, was still optimistic he would be healthy by playoff time, though he acknowledged the team would need a concerted push to the end of the schedule just to make the post-season, having fallen from third to ninth in the tight Eastern Conference over the past six weeks. The Centennials have only three wins in their last twenty games.

~

Over the next few weeks, when the sofas and the card tables emptied, when the presiding nurse checked her watch and dimmed the hallway lights to their more subdued after-nine-p.m. levels, when the room became his and his alone, the patient set to the task of finding a configuration more to his liking. He worked mostly with lighting, as that somehow seemed most key. He tried many combinations, starting with the option of extinguishing all the lamps altogether. Then everything save the table lamps located in each corner of the room. Then came further variations of alternating lights left on, drapes closed for more darkness, drapes left open to let the indirect glow from the parking lot's standards warm the shadows slightly. Finally, after two weeks of experimentation, he settled on the simple illumination of a tiny accent lamp on the nesting table beside one of the recliners; the one with the button-tufted leather upholstery that sat in front of the television; the one which the patient had slowly been working his way toward day by day. For there, more in the open yet still shadowed, he found he could now rest comfortably.

～

"I'm sorry. I should have come sooner."

The voice came from behind just as the television camera zoomed in for the start of the third period of a game between the Centennials and Vancouver. It arrived without warning of breath or footfall, but if that had been by design, the visitor's intent failed completely. The patient reacted with no greater movement than the slightest pivot of the head, his chin not even leaving the thumb and the forefinger upon which it was cradled as he watched the intruder shake the moisture from his coat and pant legs, then wring more yet from the smooth black locks of his tightly-bound ponytail.

"It's true. I've been calling for months now but your visitation restrictions were rather severe. Something about a screaming incident with some kid who came to see you."

Thompson stepped around the easy chair, sliding himself and a stacking chair between the nesting table and sofa and dropping it down in front of the patient's view of the TV.

"Hello Stephen," he said quietly, before pausing out of necessity to take in the difference in the man's appearance from what he remembered of their previous encounters. His face seemed older and tired. His weight appeared to be down, his musculature sagged and recessed around his midsection. He looked pale. And while the professor's initial instinct was to attribute it all to injuries incurred from the car accident, he could not deny the perception of deeper changes. Changes that he could not so directly pinpoint in shape or pallor, yet that were undeniably present somewhere behind those lifeless eyes, like the frayed and threadbare stitches where body has been ripped from soul. Then again, perhaps talk of one's soul owed more to how much he himself had changed since the two had last met.

"You shouldn't be here," the patient said flatly.

"It's alright. I negotiated an extension to the visiting hours."

"You shouldn't be here."

"Stephen, it's OK. They know I'm back here."

"That's not what I mean and you know it."

He shifted his weight, leaning out over the armrest on one elbow to relocate the television screen.

"I had to come. I need to talk to you about Touchwater."

"Touchwater's dead."

"I know that Stephen, but I need to ask you some questions about his convergence theory."

"That's dead too."

"Yes, I'm sure it is …" The academic drew up his breath slowly, and looking something like an Olympic diver teetering on his toes, blew out his cheeks and continued. "But perhaps … perhaps it died prematurely."

The patient's hand fell out from under his jaw, the professor's declaration succeeding at the task of surprise that his unannounced entrance had failed to do.

"Look I'm sorry. I know the last time we met all I did was shoot down everything you believed about Touchwater –"

"Sorry? Christ, don't apologise. You were right. Look around."

"I know. I know. But I believe there's a possibility that the road that led you to being institutionalised may not have been because Touchwater's theories were fiction."

"What the hell are you talking about?"

"I'm saying …" the professor sucked in breath again, "I'm saying he might not have been wrong. He may have just interpreted everything backwards. He might have been so intent on trying to make you and Casey a part of his agenda, he never bothered with the idea that his was merely a subset of yours."

The anthropologist took a break to study the anticipated look of disbelief in the hard stare that Stephen returned. He watched as the scout squirmed uncomfortably in his chair, watched his hands begin to tremble, his head shake from side to side as his eyes searched about for something safe to latch onto. Heard him as he began to whisper over and over again, "No, I don't need this … I don't need this …"

"Stephen, I'm sorry, the last thing I wanted to do is come here and disturb whatever progress you've made –"

"Christ, it's a little late for that."

"– maybe if you'd let me try to explain –"

"Explain? You sure as hell better explain. Walking in here and doing a complete one-eighty. Where the hell were you out there on goddamn Vancouver Island? You with all your talk about what's rational and what's real and what's scientific. How the hell can you just march in here now and –"

"Because something happened out there!" the professor interjected with a hiss, his eyes trying to hold the patient's angry gaze but soon defaulting to the faint blue-white light emanating from outside the bay window. His face was frozen in an expression that awakened in the patient a cognisance that was, at once, equal parts memory and premonition. A realisation that hearkened back to the image of a trembling figure sitting stiffly in an armchair, rocking back and forth in front of a large sliding glass door, shaking before the dancing lights of the St. Louis skyline.

"I was stranded out there for three days. Each day wondering if that one was going to be my last. A person just doesn't go through an ordeal like that without changing. Not when the wind starts howling and the snow is blowing in between the wall board. It strips you to the bone,

Stephen. It strips away everything and anything you thought was substantial about yourself. Makes it all seem like nothing more than window dressing … blown away with the first gust. And then the darkness settles in. And there's nowhere to turn to, except inward to your self. That deepest part of your self that you've always ignored. The part that knows just how fleeting all your theories and ideas and your degrees really are. The part that has always known, but has just bided its time until you're completely desperate and vulnerable. And you want to reach out and grab onto some sort of rope or lifeline. You want to maintain some sense of control. You want to feel something of yourself that's permanent and untouchable by the darkness. But try as you might, you can't come up with anything. All that's left is you. You and this undefined infinite nothingness. And then, just when you're finally drifting off to sleep … just when you'd think you might get a bit of a reprieve …"

His voice trailed off and his head reverted to the rhythmic shaking that the patient also remembered seeing when he first met the man. The image flashed before him. The once-proud academic standing there in his hotel suite, swaying like a helpless sapling in a windstorm, confiding to him – a stranger – the details of his sister's demise, of his cryptic dreamlife. And with that recollection came the epiphany. If this man was once again standing before him in need of his counsel, there was surely only one explanation for the visit. He reached forward and clicked off the television, and then the table lamp, leaving the room in darkness save for the indirect glow that filtered in from the window. At first his guest interpreted the actions as a pre-emptive rejection of all he still needed to share. But then he was given hope as he made out the hint of a silhouette, heading not for the hallway, but across the room toward the windowpanes, from deep shadow to faint moonlight, where it sat down again to rest beneath the moon's pale filtered beam.

"For what it's worth," the silhouette spoke softly with the rare confidence of complete understanding, "I still have nightmares too."

The patient heard his guest sigh deeply, heard his shoes scuffing against the floor, imagined the pacing – the hands scratching torturously through the hair, the sweat bubbling out on the forehead, the arms and shoulders trembling.

"They started again … out there," the professor began slowly. "But not like the others from last spring … at least not initially. I mean, in the end I always wind up stranded on a highway in the middle of a snowstorm. But this time … this time it was as if I were trapped inside a theatre watching everything unfold. Like a silent movie. I'm right there beside everyone involved, only I can't interact with any of them. I can't hear them or speak to them or warn them. I can only observe. The dreams begin the same way; with Jocelyn giving birth. Then she and James are sneaking out of my mother's house. Then the baby's sitting alone in his crib, his mother's body stretched out just beyond his reach through the bars. That's when the scene jumps back to me standing out on that highway in the middle of nowhere. And just like before, I can't move my feet. They're completely frozen into the pavement. But this time, Willie's there with me, standing off on the shoulder. And he's frantic. He's jumping up and down. Gesturing madly down the road. I can see that he's screaming but as I said I can't hear anything. Suddenly from around the bend, these headlights appear, swerving and weaving all over the highway. But for the life of me, I still can't move my goddamn feet to get out of the way. And it's always just as I get my first look at the car itself, the audio kicks in at full volume and I'm hit with this explosion of sound – the engine, the car horn blaring, the wind, and above it all, Willie's screams, *'No … No! Turn around!'* But I guess he doesn't realise I'm stuck there, so he shouts again, *'Turn around! Turn around! Look where the anger's coming from!'* And just as the words reach me, I get my first look at the driver. It's James, cradling a baby to his chest with one hand and ripping the steering wheel around to avoid hitting me with the other. With all the force I can muster, I manage to pull my boots from the road, spinning a full 180 degrees to brace myself for impact, just in time to see a brown car racing toward me from the opposite direction. I see the man behind the wheel. I see the rage on his face. I mean complete and utter rage –"

"My father's face," the silhouette whispered from the shadows.

"No Stephen … yours."

The faint but measured ticking of a wall clock somewhere in the room provided the only sound for quite some time, until eventually it was joined by the figure in the window, his voice quizzical as it whispered the words *my face* over and over again, each refrain growing softer than the last until the visitor was left again to wallow in what seemed an excruciating length of non-interpretable silence.

"You know Touchwater had this idea," the silhouette said finally, "… he had this theory that what made a specific sport popular was how well it mirrored some part of society that people thought was important. He had lots of examples … football was like war, baseball had to do with the industrial revolution, golf was all about manners and etiquette. The thing was, he could never really nail down hockey. The best he ever came up with was that the game represented winter."

"Winter?"

"That's right. Like it was this continuous battle for survival. From start to finish. Game to game. Year to year. Novice to Old-timers. For best results play angry, like there's this storm inside you. I remember thinking at the time that it didn't really apply. Not with kids today growing up skating on multi-alloyed blades with custom-fit moulded boots, wearing top-of-the-line pads and equipment, shooting with their brand new high-flex graphite sticks and playing their games in state-of-the-art arenas. But then I got watching that young winger Vancouver has on the right side this year. His name's Yvegeny Kaltzov and he's a 19-year-old Russian out of what remains of their national junior program. Did you know he spent the last two seasons in Moscow living in an unheated apartment with three other players? Two rooms between them, windowpanes cracked or missing, so the snow would pile up on the sill and on the floor below. I used to think guys like that played hard and angry because they were scared shitless of going back to conditions like that."

"And now?"

"Now …? Now I think they play the way they do because they still know winter."

The silhouette reached up and clicked on a floor lamp to reveal his position behind the honey oak veneers of the long bay-window table.

"Whatever it is you still need to tell me, can we do it over here?"

Thompson stepped gingerly into the beam of light. "Are you sure?"

Stephen nodded. "Just go slowly," he said. "I get tired easily."

"Yes! … I will … thank you!" Thompson exclaimed, and eagerly grabbed an overstuffed knapsack which had previously escaped Stephen's view. The professor dropped the sack's significant weight hard upon the table as he scrambled to pull out an old and tattered road atlas of North America.

"It's hard to find a good diversion when you're stranded in the wilderness," he stated by way of introduction. "And I really can't explain how I got started on the process any more clearly than to say I was desperate for something to keep me occupied. I found this in the cabin. So just as an exercise I began going over Touchwater's wheel theory of converging ley lines, not to mention the theories Willie had about you and Casey. My difficulty was that I only had the memory of your account from our boat trip to go by and, as I admitted earlier, I was not exactly the most receptive audience at the time."

Dubiously the patient watched the professor slide out, shuffle and rearrange a great many notes that had been pressed between the atlas's pages, then watched him open the large book itself to a map that depicted the entire breadth of Canada. Meticulously Thompson smoothed down the spine crease that fell somewhere in the vicinity of the Ontario-Manitoba border.

"First of all, I need to confirm some background information, seeing as it's the basis upon which this whole visit rests. So I want to just double-check something. Is it true that Willie was of the opinion that you and Casey weren't only connected because of the common name in your home towns, but also because they both happened to sit close to 49 degrees north latitude?"

Stephen nodded.

"Right … good. I thought that was correct. You see, I began playing around with this road map on that very basis – much like your friends from The Watch did, I would imagine. I started with a line through the two towns in question and then extended it all across the prairies and Rockies. Just to see what other towns intersected with yours. It was a completely blind exercise. I had no idea what I was looking for. But on my third night out there, despite the freezing temperatures, I swear I awoke from my dream drenched in sweat – all the images of James swerving to miss me and the other car bearing down still running through my head. I guess I must have nodded off looking at the atlas because when I lifted my head up I was staring right at this map here. And I can all but hear Willie's voice still echoing from the other side of my consciousness. *Turn around … turn around!* And for some reason I spun the book sideways so my nose is staring down the length of the prairies from west to east. And that's when the whole idea first hit me."

He slid the atlas across the table to demonstrate, running his index finger along a line he had drawn between Stephen's and Casey's birthplaces. The scout stared at the page a moment then looked up quizzically.

"You mean longitude?" the scout whispered.

The professor shrugged. "Well I wouldn't be sure until I was back at the university, but yes, that's what I started playing with, although I must say I was somewhat hampered by the fact that longitudinal markings aren't exactly a top priority on your standard Canadian road map. Nevertheless, as best I could, I measured the distance between Estevan Point, BC and Estevan, Saskatchewan, then extrapolated that same distance eastward along 49 degrees latitude from your home town over to the Quebec-Ontario border."

"And …?"

"And nothing. Unfortunately, according to the maps, at that latitude there's nothing but wilderness. It's north of any highway or settlement."

"So what's the big deal?"

"The deal is after I returned to school, a specimen came to us, shipped from an old logging camp in northeastern Ontario – a harpoon tip of stone and a couple of rattles. An old logger had brought it in to the museum in Toronto. One of their staff sent it on to us when they realised it looked like many artifacts they had seen from Vancouver Island. Now the old me … the me before those three days on the Island … would have started in on the articles, cataloguing them, comparing them to other pieces we had. That sort of thing. But I just had this overwhelming hunch. I had the Toronto museum people try to locate the man who found the items, but he had left no name or address. All they could tell me was he wore an old worn-out parka and toque, that he carried the items in an old shopping bag, and that he was absolutely adamant that they record the finding occurred in the bush 20 kilometres west of Val-Paradis, Quebec. Just inside the Quebec-Ontario border. Well, for some reason, and forgive me for being repetitive, but once again, I really can't explain why, I started playing around with the map some more, jumping the same distance eastward again. And this time … well, you'll see. I marked it there."

The professor slid the map over further so Stephen could read the highlighted town name on the facing page.

"Stephenville?"

Thompson nodded vigorously. "Now by that time I was sufficiently absorbed in the pursuit that I have to admit my first thought was of the linguistic commonality. *Stephenville, Newfoundland; Estevan Saskatchewan; Estevan Point*. And of course there's the connection with your own given name as well."

In the fuzzy light-starved reflection of the bay window, the professor caught a glimpse of the dumbfounded look on his friend's face, set motionless in the foreground juxtaposed against the frenzied gestures of his own arms and hands. Immediately he backtracked to defend himself against both images.

"Look I realise this must seem like such a radical departure from what you'd expect out of my mouth, but there comes a point where the shock of it all can't be helped. Every night for the past three months I've dreamed the sound of a baby crying in front of his dead mother. Every night I've jumped from my bed in a sweat trying to rip my feet from that frozen asphalt only to see my own demise racing toward me. This pursuit has been my only refuge, so I've kept up the chase. I've read and reread all of Alfred Watkins's writings on ley theory, as well as countless more modern texts on the subject. I've gone over dozens of Earth Mystery apologies including all the on-line materials left over from The Watch. I've used interlibrary loans to get a look at everything from local Stephenville histories to town maps and surveys. Hell I even sent away for copies of the region's phone books and yellow pages. And no, you don't have to remind me how crazy this all sounds, especially coming from my mouth. Trust me, the professor in me is looking over my shoulder every minute of the day reminding me just how ludicrous an exercise this whole thing is."

The professor slapped the sides of his jeans in a display of spent exasperation. "And like I said," he sighed, "I couldn't begin to tell you what it was I was looking for when I started. All I know is what I found."

"And what was that?"

"Willie."

The scout's head snapped up at the sound of the old man's name.

"It's true," Thompson sputtered. "I came across his listing in one of the phone books just last week. But as it turns out, it was an old edition from two years ago. He's passed away, Stephen."

"Willie's dead?" Stephen whispered.

The reply came by way of a pause, filled with uncertain trembling and irregular breath. And when the professor finally did gather himself to speak again he did so with a quiver and an edge to his voice that immediately suggested to Stephen that the most significant, perhaps the most incredible news was yet to come.

"I tried to make a few preliminary inquiries. Town records, church files, that sort of thing. But all I really know for sure is that Willie Skilliter was born on New Year's Day in 1936 and that he died on March 15 of last year."

"March 15? No wait. That's wrong. March 15 was the day I first met him. Right here in Prince George."

The professor dropped his head and severed his eyes from the scout's penetrating stare.

"Are you trying to tell me the guy I talked to … the guy I thought I talked to …" the scout hissed, a groundswell of raw bleeding emotion swirling and surging from somewhere deep in his abdomen, "… the guy I've been chasing around trying to find for a year … has been dead the whole time?"

There was the sound of another exasperated slap of denim. "I know, I know," Thompson grimaced, his eyes still averted to the floor, squinting below the beads of sweat which had imposed their way down his forehead. "And I'm sorry, I just don't know how to respond to that. But surely we can't just leave it all like this, can we? Don't we owe it to ourselves to see this journey through to a more satisfying conclusion? Don't we owe it to ourselves to go there and investigate –"

"GO THERE!?" the scout erupted, the force of his forearms thrust against the table apron causing his chair to recoil back against the wall as he sprang to his feet. "Christ, David, are we both insane here!? How the hell can you believe I should be anywhere but locked up in this goddamn place when it turns out the guy I've been trying to hunt down to make some goddamn sense of this fucking mess of a life, has been buried in some graveyard in bum-fuck Newfoundland the whole time!"

"Well … you see … that's just it," the professor mumbled from behind a hard swallow. "As it turns out, Stephenville doesn't quite align with 49 degrees north as accurately as the other places. In fact, it's much closer to the 48th. But there is a neighbouring town to the north and east that does. Quite closely in fact. It makes a jump of approximately 22 degrees longitude from the Ontario-Quebec border, practically the same distance as Estevan Point to Estevan; and from Estevan to this alleged logging camp. It also sits just off of 49 degrees latitude. But as fantastic as all this seems, I must confess I arrived at it all somewhat after the fact."

"After what fact?"

"After I discovered this is also the town that has, or at least had, a phone listing for one Willie J. Skilliter."

"So what are you saying? You just started going through all the towns in the Newfoundland phone book looking for the old man's name?"

"No Stephen, just this town."

Thompson grabbed the atlas and feverishly flipped past page after page until he landed on the template depicting western Newfoundland and Labrador in greater detail. He slid the text back under Stephen's gaze and pointed to the name of a town that had been circled and underlined in a variety of different inks, seemingly on a number of different occasions.

"There are regional flights," he continued quietly. "We can get from here to Calgary, then through Pearson in Toronto and land at Deer Lake. Then we're only about half an hour away. Of course the nurse at the desk here wouldn't divulge much about your progress, but when I phoned up here last week, they more or less hinted that you were close to being discharged. That's why I decided to see you. Because when that time finally comes … if you're up to it, that is –"

Though he could form no words and indeed would say little if anything for the remainder of his friend's visit that night, the emphasis of Stephen's reply was nevertheless indisputable – first just a slight bobbing of the head, then growing with such a surge of momentum, his arms had to cross in front of the chest to keep his entire torso from joining in. Yet all the while, the eyes remained steadfast, focused hard on the name of the little town printed clearly there on the inset map of western Newfoundland – the name that had been there all along, just waiting for those who knew where to look.

Pasadena.

Chapter Four

"This is Mark Loggins with a Frontier Sports thirty-second update …

… with two games remaining in their schedule, the Toronto Centennials will need to collect wins both at home against Calgary on Saturday and in Buffalo Sunday evening to entertain any hopes of advancing to the post-season. The Cents remained mathematically alive last night with a tie in Detroit while Buffalo, the team they are trying to catch for the eighth and final playoff spot in the Eastern Conference, lost 3–2 in New York. Buffalo now sits three points ahead of Toronto and should they win in Dallas on Thursday, the Centennials would be eliminated. Listen for a full report and interviews at the top of the hour …"

∼

The rather harried middle-aged man was a bundle of preoccupied hyper-activity as he wrestled with an unmanageably large stack of legal files, moving them, seemingly aimlessly, from desk to front counter and back to desk again, all the while trying to attend to the questions of the two unexpected strangers who had knocked on his door.

"I don't really know what I can tell ya ... Carol are these ready for me to take?" he called back over his shoulder towards a small windowless office where a woman, head down and focused, sat working far too busily to offer an expeditious reply. Still perplexed, the man scooped up the stack of documents and heaved them high atop a filing cabinet at the far end of the counter. His puzzled expression, his dishevelled white hair, the lop-sided glasses, the rumpled semi-tucked shirt-tail, and, most disconcertingly, the scattered glances around his office as if he were only then noticing details about the room for the first time, might have all conspired to convince both the scout and the professor they were not dealing with the contact whom they sought. But the man had introduced himself by the same name that adorned the brightly painted storefront window in green and gold lettering ... *Cecil McAllister: Barrister and Solicitor.*

"I'm sorry ... you caught us on a busy one, I'm afraid. Lucky to have caught us at all really. We're usually closed up Sundays, but we're trying to close on a real estate deal this afternoon. A clothing store down in Corner Brook. Now ... who was it you were asking about again?"

"A man named Willie Skill –"

"Old man Skilliter ... right, right. Well I don't know what I can tell ya," the man uttered again, seemingly unaware he was repeating himself. "Lived and died pretty much a loner. Why, he woulda ended up ... Carol where was old Willie Skilliter roomin' when he passed away?"

"I have an address for Third Street from an old phone book," Thompson offered.

"Wouldn'ta been Ruth Oglivie's place over on Third would it?"

"310 Third Avenue. Apartment 6."

"Geez you know I kinda think it was. What the blazes is the name of her place? Oakdale Residences? Oakwood? Geez I drive by that sign every day."

For the eager professor, the trickling flow of information following on the heels of a lengthy flight across country was unsatisfactory. This man whom he had traced to be Pasadena's only barrister, and therefore in all likelihood the legal officer responsible for executing William Skilliter's last will and testament, had comprised the extent of his leads before making the trip. So when the phone rang to further divert and impede the barrister's pedestrian train of thought, the anthropologist could abide his patience no longer. He betrayed his frustrations to the mat in front of the door, pacing back and forth in his patented quick and laboured strides; his shoulders hunched, suggesting the hands stuck in his pockets were not there to rest, but were curled into clamped fists and suspended halfway in by nothing more than tension.

Stephen, by way of contrast, stood waiting much in the manner he had undertaken the journey itself. Silent. Motionless. Strangely content to spend the passing hours reviewing the warmth that had greeted his face at the outset of their trip, when after four months of hibernation, he had finally stepped out the front doors of Evergreen Acres for good. To revisit and reflect upon the breeze that had lingered there on his cheeks, on the bridge of his nose, around his neck and the collar of his jacket. That, he had decided shortly after their initial takeoff, would be a far gentler fuel for his resolve, than engaging in Thompson's frequent and fervent bouts of strategising their so-called plan of attack. And indeed it had eased the travel effectively; from their departure at the Prince George airport, through connections in Calgary, Toronto and finally Deer Lake, Newfoundland; then the thirty-minute drive down to Pasadena itself. Down the main street, past a schoolyard full of squealing children, the Co-op, the Stedman's, a couple of small strip malls; past a good number of smaller residential streets radiating off in both directions, three or four church spires stretching over the rooftops of the houses. And, of course, the town's arena.

He had felt that breeze before. A great length of time before, he had concluded. Always the last game of the year – the end of the playoffs – when the bitter dregs of winter had been reduced to tired old mud-coated snow piles pushed to the far edges of the Estevan Coliseum, lying there on their deathbed beneath the strengthening sun. He remembered there was an initial weightlessness, walking out into that sun, free of heavy felt-lined snow boots, and all but bounding for his father's car. Sneakers loose. Coat open. No hood or gloves. He remembered that breeze had always been there … the last game of the year … win or lose … if ever so briefly. And from his perch in an aircraft at twenty-five thousand feet above the thawing countryside and thirty years removed from the memory, it suddenly no longer mattered that the feeling had faded as soon as his father's brown sedan wheeled out of its parking space – out around the team bus and out on the highway. It didn't matter that the feeling was long gone only two miles up the road when his dad's talk turned to the inevitable business of summer hockey camp registration and a better off-ice conditioning program. It didn't matter. It had still been there, present for the senses, unanswerable to any burdens or limitations. For there comes a moment, even for an orphan of winter, when Spring finally arrives. And her relieving breeze reawakens in the recipient an unanticipated hope for redemption that he – cold for so long – had forgotten he had ever possessed.

"I'm sorry," McAllister returned as he hung up the phone. "That was Corner Brook. We're just real busy in here today … trying to close on a real estate deal down there. A clothing store that the buyer –"

"Mr. McAllister," Thompson broke in with a sigh, "I appreciate how hectic you are sir, but we've come a long way and if there's anything you can tell us, anything at all –"

"Well what can I say? He died alone. No family as I recall. Pretty much penniless too. Now … at one time, his family ran a grocery store here in town, but that woulda been quite a ways back … Carol when would the Skilliter store have been up and running? … Geez I think it was his dad who packed it in. Moved everybody out west as I recall."

"To become a preacher." The voice had chimed in quietly from over Thompson's shoulder where Stephen stood leaning against the door, hands in his pockets, staring blankly back out the lawyer's front window.

"Is that so? Well you're one up on me then. All I really did was execute the man's will and if memory serves all that amounted to was a few dollars to take care of a modest little grave mark –"

A small glow crossed the lawyer's face. He snapped his fingers, turned on a heel, and retreated to the back office where he and his assistant conversed in low indistinguishable tones, consulted a file, then conversed further, before he emerged again triumphant, wagging a victorious finger in the air.

"I had a hunch … I had a hunch," he announced, throwing his coat over his shoulders and patting the pockets while he scanned his office's work surfaces to find and snatch up a set of car keys. "I knew there was somethin' about that name. Carol, keep an ear out for Corner Brook would ya," he shouted back to his clerk. "I'm gonna lead these fellahs out to old Willie's gravesite."

~

"With the last remaining playoff spot up for grabs, tonight's tilt promises to be a spirited affair. Buffalo's loss on Thursday, coupled with the Toronto Centennials' come-from-behind squeaker against Calgary last night, leaves the Cents one point back of eighth place. And Toronto will have a full complement of players healthy for the first time in weeks, including rookie centreman Casey Bruford. Bruford will dress for the game tonight, despite a still very tender shoulder, as the Centennials coaching staff hopes to inject their team with some of the magic the young forward displayed when he first dressed for the Blue and White last November. From Buffalo, I'm Mark Loggins reporting for Frontier Network Sports."

~

The radio cut off as Thompson suddenly steered to the curb, following the unexpected stop by McAllister in the car ahead. The lawyer motioned the two to follow him out of their vehicle and up the walk of a large plain-looking three-storey home.

"Mrs. Oglivie!? Mrs. Oglivie!?" the lawyer called out, having already pounded three rounds of knuckle-wraps on the front door, as well as a few more on the pale blue vinyl siding, by the time the pair joined him on the stoop.

"Mrs. Oglivie?!"

"We're full up!" came an abrupt voice from inside.

"Mrs. Oglivie? … It's Cecil McAllister from down at the law office. I got a couple of lads from out west here askin' about old Willie Skilliter. I was gonna take 'em on down and show 'em the cemetery but I saw the drapes open so I thought I'd stop and show 'em where he was living."

The door creaked open slightly, and one eye framed by wrinkled skin peered out into the daylight at the three visitors gathered before her door.

"We're busy as the deuce down at the office, but maybe the lads here could just have a moment of your time … step inside and ask you a few things –"

"Whatever talkin's to be done, we can do right here," the voice inside snapped, while the single eye continued to dart from face to face, pausing with added suspicion to inspect the long straight locks of black hair that framed the darkened complexion of the man to her right. "William Skilliter never hurt nobody. He spent his life serving God just like his father before him … and maybe things just didn't work out for him as he planned, but he's up there in heaven now. So don't expect me to believe you're another one of his so-called long-lost friends. My Lord, where were all of you when he was here all alone?"

"Wait ma'am, what do you mean another friend?" the professor pressed, squinting into the shadow behind the door jamb. "Are you saying someone else was by, asking about him?"

"The other one!"

"Other one?" McAllister repeated.

"Like that one there!" the eye inside replied bluntly, sending the tip of a gnarled and weathered forefinger out into the daylight to gesture in Thompson's direction. "And whatever you've come to get your hands on, you can forget it, 'cause he beat yas to most all of it!"

The professor drew a long breath to bide his patience before returning quietly but firmly, "You would be referring to another native man then?"

"Yer darn right I am … last fall back in November. Looked about yer height I guess. Same hair too. But a whole lot stockier. And what do I do but fall hook, line and sinker for some sob story about how he's lookin' for a man named Skilliter. Tells me the man used to teach his father back out in BC at one of them schools for Indians. So what do I do but let him have a look at Willie's room for old time's sake, and when I check on him, he's up there defacin' the property. Scratchin' away at the desktop with a jack-knife. I give him a scream and next thing I know, he grabs a bag full of poor Willie's personal effects and makes a break for the front door!"

"But Mrs. Oglivie," McAllister broke in, "I don't think you need to worry about these two gentlemen. Why, Mr. Thompson here says he's a professor back at the University in Vancouver, and as for Mr. Gillis here, why I'm sure he means no disrespect."

"Ma'am," the professor stepped forward. "This man … this Indian … did he mention his name or maybe –"

But before he could finish his question, the woman slammed the door shut in his face, leaving him and the rest of the trio to interpret the proper amount of time they should remain upon her step. Thompson was first to move, bolting back for the car, leaving in his path a litany of language muttered faintly out from under his breath. McAllister and Stephen glanced at one another briefly before they too stepped back toward the street. But before they had taken more than a few steps, the front door opened again, this time flung to the widest angle of its hinges to reveal the short and stout figure of an elderly woman in a bright yellow-and-orange-check housedress. She clutched a door key in her hand.

"No doubt strung out on drugs or sniffin' God knows what!" the landlady ranted on. "Why else would anyone bother with a poor man's bag full of memories? Here, go take a look at what he did to my desktop. You think I'm over-reacting, go see for yourself!"

The professor took a step forward to accept the key but the woman snatched it back into her palm.

"Not you … you," she instructed, pointing past Thompson to the scout. "It's my house and I'll trust who I see fit!"

"Now Mrs Oglivie," the lawyer cut in again.

"Now nothing. It's one thing for the likes of these to go to such lengths to steal a poor man's belongings … why, William had no more to show than a few scrapbooks and keepsakes to his name. But you know as well as I do, Counsellor, the real atrocity that befell the man. You know it. I know it. By Lord I'll bet these two know it as well."

Thompson turned to face McAllister, unable to abide the accumulated frustrations of his day a moment longer. "What in Christ's name is she talking about?" he blurted out.

The lawyer hemmed and shuffled his feet in reply, mumbling something about how this was what he had remembered back in his office but had wanted to tread softly because firstly, he wanted to be sure the incident that had popped into his head was indeed poor Willie, and secondly … well, you know how stories like this have a way of getting over-embellished by small-town coffee-shop gossip.

"Enough stallin', Counsellor. You tell 'em or I will!" the landlady threatened, both arms now folded protectively over the key.

"Well let me just begin by saying that it was an isolated occurrence," McAllister stalled. "Certainly nothing Pasadena is proud of, but by the same token, certainly nothing we've had any other trouble with over the years."

"Yer not runnin' for mayor … get to it!"

"But you see, we're not even sure how it happened," the lawyer continued, glancing up to find Thompson staring back stone-faced, suddenly suspicious of the scattered foggy account of Willie the lawyer had maintained back in his office. "So I wanted to get you two out to the cemetery itself before I started in on you with the whole story. And truth be told … it's got my curiosity up a bit, 'cause to tell you the truth I've never got around to stopping out there and having a look for myself."

"Mr. McAllister, please!" Thompson broke in, his impatience measuring out each syllable of the name in an even monotone.

"Willie's grave was dug up and robbed," the woman snapped. "The very day after that Indian pays me his visit. I tell ya, nobody deserves that kind of fate. Especially not a good Christian like William. Why, he was clergy. Heard the call just like his father and chose to serve the gospel by teachin' the likes of that fellah in them schools. And for all his troubles, how did he get to live his days? Cooped up in a boarding house with nobody to talk to. Oh sure, he'd put on a brave face for me and he'd have a smile for everybody out on the street or down at the arena. Loved ta watch the boys skate, he did. Only joy he had by the end, I suppose."

She dangled the key out in front of the scout's face. "Up the stairs, third door. Come on ... I don't got all day!"

So off Stephen went, cautiously at first, though he could not place what was making him so hesitant as he climbed the staircase and left the three voices receding behind him.

"Mrs. Oglivie if you'd just let me accompany him upstairs, I promise you I have no intention of –"

"Promise all ya like, you're stayin' down here where I can keep an eye on you. And don't bother with some story about how well you knew poor William. That one's only gonna work once on me."

"The other fellow said that?"

"Course he did. And let me tell ya, even if it were true of any of yas, it don't make you a friend of mine. Geez, where the hell were ya all those times I used to hear him up in his room, cursing himself up and down a blue streak ... and this was still a man of the cloth remember. Sometimes I'd go up and sneak a peek when things seemed to be gettin' too loud. There he'd be, always the same. Hunched over his desk starin' at that old photograph of his. Just shakin' with grief, he was ..."

Stephen closed the door behind him.

～

Did something happen up there in that dingy little boarding room? Though he thought he heard something, thought he saw a flash of something, Stephen never knew for sure and therefore, for the rest of his days, never said a word to anyone. Not in the many subsequent visits he and Thompson would have, pouring over the many details of the converging life voyages that brought them together as friends. Nor to James Richard, when the two finally met fifteen years later, both showing up to pay homage at the professor's funeral. No, he kept the accounts to what he was certain he had taken in, for surely there was meat enough in those renditions to satisfy all.

The room was small. A square, save for the long narrow extension that reached out through the underside of the roof to a gable window, in front of which sat a small desk table wedged between the walls of the narrow passageway. There was a single bed, made up long ago judging by the mothball odours of the blankets folded at its foot. There was one chest of drawers, all empty, Stephen discovered upon conducting a cursory search, although the scout did so with trepidation, not completely certain if Mrs. Oglivie's invitation included such liberties.

He walked out to the window, hunched over, as the ceiling, even at the roof's peak, did not accommodate his full upright height. Bent forward, he could see Thompson, McAllister and the landlady still on the stoop, she gesturing wildly with pointed jabbing fingers aimed towards the professor's face. The lawyer, palms out and upward, appearing to play the role of mediator. And though he could not hear the exchanges from behind the double storm glass, he still felt compelled to lose the view, pulling out the chair and plopping his weight down behind the desk. From there the view was only of sky, bright and full through the branches of a maple tree waiting to bud her leaves, gradually bluing with the break of the rain clouds that had dominated the early day. The arriving sun beamed obliquely across the tabletop in front of him and illuminated the detailed knife work of two carvings in the wooden surface – one an oblong-shaped human skull, the other a figure of a wolf. Stephen stared at the images at length until his attention was diverted by the dance of a shadow across the glass front of a portrait-sized photo leaning against the windowsill. The picture was of a man dressed in the garb of clergy, his arm hooked affectionately around the shoulder of a small smiling native boy, his hair cropped short like a freshly-mown lawn, his plaid cotton shirt buttoned stiffly right up to the neckline. Slung over the boy's shoulders was a pair of skates and in his hand he held a hockey stick. Pencilled below the two, in faded script were the words *"With Harold Richard – Father of James"*.

Stephen grabbed the photo to bring it into closer focus and in doing so discovered the reason it had been left to lean against the wall. The hinged support of the frame was missing, the backing having been replaced by what at first appeared to be a rather crude cover, fashioned haphazardly out of a bulky piece of cardboard, too thick and bent to fit into the back of the frame's edging. By his mere lifting of the frame, Stephen caused one of the corners to pop loose, revealing the true culprits of the picture's overstuffed appearance. Inside, between the cardboard and the photo, were two items. The first was a small paperback which Stephen recognised immediately, for he too owned a copy – *The Old Straight Track Revisited: Understanding the Theory of Ley Lines*.

He leafed through a few of the opening pages, past the inside cover where Willie's name was inscribed, then on to the introduction – the same words he had tried to conquer five months earlier in a hotel room in St. John's. This time though, he stopped short at the dedication – the caution-ary words of the ley line founder himself, offered up as a humble starting-point for the book's further inquiry. "I feel that ley-man, astronomer, priest, druid, bard, wizard, witch, palmer and hermit, were all more or less linked by one thread of ancient knowledge of power, however degenerate it became in the end." His eye could not keep from dwelling on the passage. It had been circled repeatedly in bright red ink, the same colour as the angry jagged letters scratched out below on the page. *So why should Reverend Fathead deserve any rest?*

The second item took more effort to extricate. It felt like another book, or an old magazine perhaps, something of sufficient width that its edges were curled up and caught in the housing of the frame. When Stephen finally managed to manipulate its pages away from the catching traps of screws and wire – his first more robust pulls having produced nothing more than the sound of tearing paper – the treasure revealed itself in the form of a very old school notebook, its orange cover adorned with spaces for a student to write down his or her name, grade and subject. The spaces were not filled in.

General notes on Mowachaht people read the heading on the first lined page, followed by a number of statements gathered and written, it seemed, at various times as the colour and brightness of the ink – in some cases just pencil lead – differed from one to the next.

1) *Feasts and dinners were the best times to teach or speak or persuade others of your opinions as it was believed a person absorbed more knowledge while swallowing food.*

2) *Potlatches could last up to two weeks and the solemn ceremonies usually commenced around ten days in.*

3) *Participants received black paint and coloured paint on their face at such ceremonies … two fingers dabbed across the cheek.*

Stephen counted sixteen pages of snippets before they abruptly stopped, with no more writing of any sort until well near the back of the book. Disjointed thoughts and paragraphs – one to a page – scribbled like a rushed and desperate diary.

Educating myself does nothing. I am and will always be conflicted. It was I who started the cycle. I accepted the boy's version of events. How he came in possession of the stick and the skates. Accepted it out of a weakness for the game, for wanting my passion to be his; just as I had insisted his faith and that of all the children be exactly as mine. But with religion as with sport, I'm afraid such insistence owes not to good judgement.

There was just something so inherently gifted in the boy's athleticism. The way he ran the schoolyard. The way he thought his way around a game of shinny with the others. So very gifted. But there is blood on my hands. This game I prayed would free him was his falling. There is blood on my hands.

~

I am not my father's keeper. I am not the offspring of his smugness, his pompousness. The assumed superiority that granted him license to kill tradition and culture and language with his so-called civility; his so-called Christian virtue.

The Reverend Edward Vincent Skilliter!! Founder of the Gold River Residential School … defender of Protestant prudence against the onslaught of the Papist dogma that defiled the Indian education system of Vancouver Island. I succeeded him as headmaster. I did not succeed his zeal!

~

There is blood on my hands. I accepted the boy's version of events, how he simply found the skates lying there, found the stick leaning against the wood pile … accepted it out of weakness for the game … accepted it because I was the one who put them there for him to find.

Resisting arrest was the report. But I was there. I saw the blood seep from his nose and ears, heard the thud of boots against ribs and chest and head. One constable, then two, then two more. And I was the one who put him there.

~

The dreams continue. My father stands over me in judgement each and every night. My faith has expired. I see darkness for generations ahead. I see the folly of my own convictions as fuel for the night. Fuel for the separation … the pain … How we must make our mothers cry. We who play out the roles to perpetuate this cycle. Father to son to father … approval to confusion … to disgrace.

How we must make our mothers cry!

~

Reverend Fathead will not make his students speak English.
Reverend Fathead will not make his students speak English.
Reverend Fathead will not make his students speak English.
Reverend Fathead will not make his students speak.
Reverend Fathead will not make his students speak.
Reverend Fathead will not speak of being forgiven.
Reverend Fathead will not speak of being forgiven.
Reverend Fathead will not speak …
Reverend Fathead will not speak …
I will not speak …
I will not speak …

Forgive me Harold.

Then, scribbled in the bottom corner, the words that clinched it all. There in the furthest recesses of the scout's search, the last pages of a lost diary found in a rooming house more than three thousand miles from where the journey began for all concerned … there sketched roughly in handwriting much smaller and uncertain than Willie's. James's amendment. "Forgive me too Jocelyn."

~

Did something happen up there in that dingy little boarding room? Not a day goes by in Stephen's life when he doesn't replay the few moments that followed. Those couple of minutes at the most between his discovery of James's words in Willie's secret notebook and when he bolted from the room and bounded down the staircase two at a time, back to the street where David and the lawyer stood silently leaning against their cars, past the vague awareness of Mrs. Oglivie standing at the bottom of the banister with a steady stream of warnings how if she found anything more missing or defaced, she had the licence plates of both cars in her driveway and she wouldn't think twice about calling the police.

He would remember how his eyes had fallen from the book back into the gentle rays of sunlight, back to the carving of the wolf head and the skull. He would recall how he rubbed his hands over the deep indentations that defined the figures' features, all the while mulling over the name Fathead. Trying to guess whether this had been some sort of self-damning moniker that Willie had concocted himself in the face of his disillusionment. Or whether – his fingertips played with the cuts in the wood that depicted the eye sockets and the mouth cavity – perhaps this was a name he had heard as a teacher. A derisive nickname he learned of when he heard the whispers of teenaged boys who thought they were out of earshot; powerless kids left to retaliate against the wrath of a strict residential headmaster the only way they dared. The best some angered adolescent kid could come up with on short notice. Perhaps they had just been reprimanded. Maybe punished or even humiliated in front of classmates by this cold, unfeeling, insensitive fathead.

The scout's head bobbed back to the picture. Then back to the skull. Then the picture again this time, focusing much more intently on Willie's face. He wanted to bridge the years that would have passed between the young teacher shown in the photo and the far more greyed and aged version of the man whom he had encountered personally. He wanted to fling back his memory to that night in those near-deserted bleachers and remember how those same eyes in the photo had peered into his very soul, bore through him as that enigmatic playful voice wove its compelling tales of ley lines, of spirituality … of *Messiah*. Yet now, sitting there alone, his fingertips playing against the indented outlines of the desk carvings, the scout's powers of recollection seemed incapable of returning there. Incapable, in fact, of finding a path back beyond anything prior to the stormy events of Estevan Point, the long shadows of old-growth trees, the swirling sounds of ocean and rainforest. And then – suddenly – the surprising memory of Thompson's voice trying to reassure him. *"Yes Stephen, it's a skull with a very wide head … that is all."* A sudden wave of recognition cascaded over the scout. Warm as a chinook. As real as spring, yet nevertheless producing a chill down the scout's spine solely by its speed and unexpectedness. Then came the realisation. That which explained why the landlady had been so deeply disgusted. That which had attacked her sensibilities so severely; had reinforced her prejudices so profoundly; had desecrated the life of her tenant so irrevocably. For suddenly in that sun-streaked moment Stephen Gillis *realised* he had indeed come face to face with Willie on one other occasion. Realised he had stared into those pale persuasive lively eyes … or at the very least, the sockets that had held them.

Did something happen up there in that dingy little boarding room? In retrospect he would never know for sure. Would never know if the shadow that panned across the wall over his shoulder was actually nothing more than the work of lingering clouds dancing in front of the afternoon sun. Would never know if the second cold chill that panned simultaneously down his spine was but the product of his imagination running with the revelations just bestowed upon him. Would never know for certain if the whispering voice that sent him scrambling for the stairwell – forgetting completely about the documents that had facilitated those revelations – had been nothing more than wind whistling around the barren tree branches and through the cracks of the window frame. Whistling in a manner that sounded for all the world like the voice of an old man.

"*Thank you.*"

~

"Stephen what is it?"

Thompson jumped to attention and came bounding up the walk only to be surprised when his friend bounded right past him and straight for McAllister still leaning against the front fender of his vehicle.

"Take us to his gravesite."

"Well I'd like to but we're awful busy in the office trying to –"

"Take us to Willie's grave."

"Stephen what is it? What did you find?"

"I found an old picture of Willie with one of his students. Harold Richard."

"James's father?"

"They called him Reverend Fathead."

"Oh hell ya, he was one funny lookin' fellah," the lawyer cut in. "Oh don't get me wrong. I don't mean any disrespect. I just meant whenever I laid eyes on him the first thing I noticed was –"

"An unusually large head," Stephen completed the thought, his eyes focused dead straight upon his *Mowachaht* friend's gaze.

"Mr. McAllister," the scout continued slowly and deliberately, "forgive us for prying further into what you and Mrs. Oglivie here seem to think is none of our business … but hypothetically speaking, if my friend here and I were to find out where he was buried all on our own, and if we got the crazy idea to just start digging up poor Willie's remains, what would we find?" His eyes remained fixed and steadfast on his friend. "I mean, I'm not right up on the ins and outs of grave robbing, but if we were to go down there and just start unearthing the poor guy's body, would we find anything missing … like, say, the guy's skull?"

Chapter Five

There is a curious thing about Interstate 74, as Stephen Gillis discovered that morning he finally called it a career and steered his car out of Peoria. As you drive out of the city, you find that the freeway actually dips south – and for a considerable distance – before it eventually bends back around and finds the I-55 North … for the long trip home.

~

"There it is," McAllister announced, gesturing with his hands through the pockets of his overcoat towards a plain stone grave marker that appeared out of place in the context of the rows of polished granite lined around it. It looked grey and prematurely weathered, as if someone had built the rest of the cemetery around a block of limestone that happened to jut out of the earth and into the air. It was, however, of a decent size which was not only fortunate but necessary – as every bit of its length was needed to house the lengthy inscription carved into the face.

The lawyer paused what seemed a sensitive amount of time, letting the visitors kneel down before the marker, seemingly oblivious to the spongy give of the waterlogged ground. There was very little movement from either. The professor was staring intently into the inscription, as if he were as interested in the font used as he was the actual words themselves. As for the other … the quiet one, well McAllister couldn't be certain, but he thought he could hear him reciting the quotation on the grave marker, something attributed to a man named Alfred Watkins, so the headstone said, though the name meant nothing to the barrister. It all seemed a bit of a curiosity, given the man's head was not even pointed at the gravestone at all, but appeared to be raised toward the sky; his eyes closed. As if he already knew the passage.

"Well … we're pretty busy back at the office," the barrister finally spoke up, unable to deduce any further role for his assistance. "I'll leave you two be."

～

Stephen was the first to move, rising to meet a gathering gust of wind at full height as he gazed down the sloping side hill of the graveyard, past the slightly curved laneway, to the pebbly shoreline of a small lake that sat on the far side of the road back to town.

"Feel that?"

"All I feel is frustration." The professor sighed, as he reached up to grab onto the top of the grave marker and pull himself up from the ground.

"Why?"

"Why? Because I still have no idea why the hell we've been sucked into this whole misadventure."

"Maybe this is why," the scout offered, his gaze scanning the entire breadth of the tree-line that spiked the horizon beyond the far shoreline. "Maybe what we're supposed to find is right here … or at least here as much as anywhere else."

"And what in hell do you mean by that?"

Stephen raised his eyes and squinted into the skyline as if the answer was faintly written in the white cloudy sky.

"What do I mean by that? Let's see, well … I guess I'm talking about a change. I mean how long can we keep this up? Sure we can chase this mystery all over the country … but where will it lead us? It's not going to bring back your sister or my father, or James's father for that matter."

With a strange and, to the professor's way of thinking, unwarranted sense of calm, the scout drank in once again the air just above his forehead, tilting his face back to receive the wind against his skin.

"I've come to a conclusion," he continued softly. "I think I must have heard Willie wrong. I don't think he ever meant Casey was going to be The Messiah. I think he just meant *our* Messiah. I mean after spending the better part of the year reading up on ley lines and religion … falling for Touchwater and his 'new dawn of civilisation' talk … all those universal questions and cosmic theories have gone by the boards. But you and I, my friend, we are still here … you, me and James I should really say."

"James?"

"He was up in that room, David. There's no doubt. And from what I saw, there's no doubt he went there to forgive the old guy."

"What? Are you crazy?"

"No that was before, remember?" Stephen sighed. "Look, you told me that James's father died young, right? Well, Willie Skilliter was the teacher for a boy named Harold Richard, and from what I saw and read up there, it looks like he blamed himself for the boy's death."

"But that makes no sense. Harold Richard died when the RCMP cornered him outside the Port Alberni arena. That was common knowledge."

"According to his diary Willie blamed himself because he introduced Harold to the game in the first place. Who knows? Maybe he had an idea that Harold's unborn son James was destined to grow up to be some fatherless bad-ass. Or maybe he just became this tortured spirit beyond the grave looking back to all our life stories weaving in and out of this one big cycle of suffering. Your sister's death. Casey being abandoned. My dad's crash. Maybe this is what happens to tortured spirits or ghosts or whatever the hell Willie was when he came and talked to me. Maybe they need to close off that cycle. And maybe James digging up the skull was his way of trying to make things right."

The professor could hear no more. "James Richard does not try to make things right!" he exploded. "James Richard does not seek forgiveness. James Richard is a goddamn thug!"

He stormed from his spot in front of the grave marker, marching angrily down the walkway to the front gate. Once there and still dissatisfied that he hadn't exhausted his position fully, he continued the barrage with an intensity that more than made up for the distance between the two. "That sick twisted son of a bitch stole my sister's life. And you might be comfortable pulling out some excuse about a fatherless upbringing to apologise for his actions, but not without sacrificing Jocelyn in the process. So just so we're clear, even if you could get me to overlook the matter of an eighth-grade drop-out possessing the wherewithal to hunt down the gravesite of his father's former headmaster clear across the goddamn country ... there is no way in hell you would convince me he was motivated by anything other than revenge!"

"But remember the skull back in the Watch House, David?" the scout called back calmly. "Set up high on those stilts. You told me that was only done as a sign of respect."

"For someone who follows the traditions of ancient *Mowachaht* shamans and whalers, sure! Not an illiterate career criminal who's been drunk every day from the age of ten, off sniffing glue since he was eleven and luring girls down to the beach since he was thirteen. You tell me, does that sound like the traditional life of a proud and conscientious *Mowachaht* to you?"

"No ..." the scout paused to choose his words carefully. "But maybe it did to Willie. Don't you see, David? If that old man could suddenly appear and get an uptight hockey scout like me to select an unknown like Casey Bruford ... and if he had the power to persuade you, a professor of anthropology – a scientist – to make decisions based on what he dreamed the night before? Well then, why the hell shouldn't we believe he could change James Richard's life too? I know she was your sister and that has to hurt. But think about it. This guy came home and found his girlfriend dead. Maybe he grabbed the baby and ran because he was just scared … or because he wanted to hold onto him as long as he could. Like I said, I know she was your sister, but … maybe he's lived in hell because of all this too."

Thompson sat down on a patch of snow beside the drive, drew his knees up tight to his chest and rocked. "Have you ever heard a mother's wail? Not just cry or sob. I mean wail. Just pure unmitigated grief?" He scooped a handful of pebbles from the pathway beside him and began lobbing them into a nearby puddle. "It starts like this low guttural drone …"

He lost his words in the circular patterns of gentle ripples and in their mesmerising effect, failed to notice that his friend was nodding in complete and profound agreement. And he failed to recognise that the same single tear that was irresistibly drawing a line down his own cheek, was also tracing a path down the scout's. But whereas he remained seated – low to the ground and balled up against the last remnants of winter – his friend was standing at full height, as if to ask if the faint mild breeze that had just emerged might dry his eyes.

"I'm trying to remember a word," the scout spoke up, clearing his throat to do so. "Something either Willie said or something I heard from Touchwater, I just can't remember which. What do you call it when someone – a religious person I guess – uses some little saying or prayer and just repeats it over and over?"

"You mean a mantra?"

"Yeah that's it … mantra. That's the word," the scout replied, granting the term a few repetitions of his own, as he took a moment to deliberate over the sound of it. "I was just thinking back to college. We had mandatory weight training every night we weren't playing a game and the weight room was right beside one of the gyms. Every time I'd go in or out I'd see this older guy – one of the basketball coaches it turned out – shooting free throws night after night. He'd be there before the start of the workout and still there when I was done, taking one shot after another all by himself. So after the better part of two years, my curiosity finally got the better of me and I walked up and asked him why he does it … you know, expecting some stock answer about work ethic or setting an example for the kids, or staying sharp for practice. But instead, without even breaking his shooting rhythm, he says to me, 'Because it feels so good'. Said he just liked the way the swoosh of the netting caught the spin of the ball. Said it was this real satisfying thing for him. And you know what? I knew what he meant. Because it was the same on the ice, when you finally got the rink to yourself. When you found yourself shooting puck after puck just to hear the echo off the side boards. Like it was this little ritual you just had to *do*."

"Stephen, I'm sorry, it's been a very long day. Where exactly is this going?"

"I think I need to find something like that again, you know?" the scout continued, and began slowly walking towards the direction from which the breeze met him, his eyes staring right through the arched iron gate of the cemetery, transfixed on the vista of the lake and the treetops beyond.

"What? Wait … where are you going?" The professor scrambled to his feet to peer in the direction his friend was heading.

"Tell me David, if I had been a young *Mowachaht* whaler, I bet I would have had no end of rituals, right?" he called back over his shoulder, his strides picking up in length and speed with the downward grade of the laneway. "What would I have had to do?"

"What?"

"What would I have had to do! Maybe run out into that lake and stand there till I couldn't feel my feet any more? Something like that?"

"Well, yes … that might have been part of it," the professor shouted forward and began trotting down the lane himself, trying to close the distance from his friend. "But even to get the privilege, you would've had to be offspring of a chief … Stephen where are you going!?"

"What else?" the scout called back eagerly.

"Stephen, the car's the other way."

"WHAT ELSE!?"

He was now half-way across the shore road. Thompson threw up his arms, sighed and broke into a full run.

"Well all sorts of things," he panted. "First you'd be granted permission by the shaman. Then you might be sent into the forest by yourself for a certain number of days to fast and pray. And you'd be made to promise to abstain from sexual relations."

"Not a problem for old Newt Gillis ... what else?"

"Jesus, will you just hold up a minute!"

"WHAT ELSE?"

"OK, OK. It was all designed to purify the whaler's soul. There were rituals of rubbing stone into the skin and rubbing nettles against your sides and stomach. It's a ritual of self-denial that anthropologists have found to be pan-native amongst the traditional hunting-and-gathering societies. The *Blackfoot,* for example, would send young boys out into the Badlands to endure the climate and the wildlife ... STEPHEN WHAT THE HELL ARE YOU DOING!?"

He only flinched momentarily – when the first bit of dampness seeped through the toes of his boots and into the fabric of his socks. But then, buoyed by the late-day sun he carried on, wading further into the lake so that by the time the professor had reached the water's edge, he was already knee-deep some thirty feet from shore.

"So then," he called back over his shoulder. "You're saying I would have taken a bunch of jagged stones and scraped them across my ribs till I bled because I would have believed it was the only way I could be worthy in the eyes of my father?"

"Stephen for Christ's sake, that water's freezing!"

"Maybe ... but you know, old Coach Hayes back at my college would never have had his mantra if he hadn't decided one day to pick up a basketball and try his very first shot."

"I have no idea what that's supposed to mean," the professor sighed.

"Flesh and blood, David!" the scout called back just as the cold wet seeped through the thighs and crotch of his jeans, and sent an accompanying albeit far deeper involuntary sound echoing across the water and back up the cemetery hill. "I mean for all your lifelong devotion to digging up other people's past, it doesn't look like it has any effect on you. You just spew it out automatically. And it seems to me, somebody who studies things like people's rituals and beliefs would need to remember that once upon a time, somebody, somewhere, started each and every one of them all by himself. I mean, whether some ritual's five years old or five thousand, shouldn't matter, should it? Because before some prayer or hike into the woods or swim could become a ritual and be repeated over and over again, it had to be somebody's cry in the dark. Somebody who was struggling and needed to shake things up in a big way. Somebody like you and me David!"

"So you're going to stand out there and risk hypothermia just so you can play the part of a *Mowachaht* whaler from 300 years ago?"

Stephen, now waist-high and seemingly unaffected by the temperature of the current, turned and faced his friend with a smile. "No … I'm playing the part of an ex-hockey scout and ex-hockey player who got those roles because of an impossibly demanding father. No wait … in spite of an impossibly demanding father. Ah what the hell, I still don't know which, but here's what I believe. I believe I'm going to stand out here and freeze my balls off until it's all fucking OK! As for the *Mowachaht* part …" his smile broadened. "I'm just borrowing that from a friend."

And with that he bent over to yank off his shoes, pulled his windbreaker and turtleneck up over his head, flung all the articles back towards shore and with a high-pitched *"yeeaargh"* dipped his entire body below the otherwise still surface of the lake.

He fought the initial heart-pausing shock as the water slid in and around his undershirt, then took three bold strokes completely submerged, glided along the lake bed before angling back up towards daylight. Once surfaced, he rolled onto his back to float with his eyes skyward, kicked his own frothy wake up into the newborn sun, where the dance between water and light bubbled with flashes of rainbow colours in the churning drops spouting up and then fountaining back to the surface all around his knees and chest. And then he began to laugh. First a chuckle, then suddenly a deep full-bellied heaving so unanticipated, he heard its unfamiliar tone first in his ears before realising that he himself was generating the waves of convulsive joy now surging through his lungs and throat.

He was free. And it was a freedom he had only dared approach on one other occasion. But whereas that freedom had come at such high mortal cost, this feeling seemed completely unencumbered. And whereas that first liberation had been a mere fleeting twenty minutes cut from the Kenora Coliseum ice by the sharpened edges of a fifteen-year-old boy's skates, this was infinitely more exhilarating. Touchwater was wrong. Hockey was never *winter*. Not for Stephen Gillis. Hockey was merely stops and starts. It was wind sprints. It was weight rooms and treadmills, books and programs that preached mental toughness and skill development. It was try-out camps and power skating school. But for all its window dressing – for the attempts to mythologise itself as something more than a pastime, and for its attempts at self-exaltation as a teacher of values and a dispensary of life lessons – the reality was that skaters like himself, from peewee to pro, played the game under the ruling auspices of the humourless discerning eyes that watched from their perch in the arena rafters; cheering the game with stone-faced nods and lording over the skaters the sport's real prize. A prize not fashioned of rings of silver and brass, not carved nor smithed from gold or bronze, nor even measured with a tallying of the score, but formed from nothing more than the elusive word and gesture of approval from somewhere behind those serious, lifeless eyes. No, hockey wasn't *winter*. Not for Stephen Gillis. Hockey was but fathers and sons. And Stephen Gillis, now floating and as weightless as a fourth-line orphan, was finally free … gliding across his river of melted ice.

~

Lured by what he observed in his rear-view mirror, the very busy lawyer had doubled back in his car to watch the curious behaviour of the two visitors from an inconspicuous spot on the road high atop the hill. He had watched in amazement, unable to conceive how the quiet one could just wade right out into the water undeterred by its still-frigid April temperature. And he found himself nodding in silent solidarity with the other one – the professor's voice of reason – who called from shore imploring his friend to abandon such a foolhardy endeavour and come back to dry land. But as the academic's jumping and shouting gradually tired out, the barrister soon became lulled almost to a trance by the gentle lines of the swimmer's wake, mesmerised by the lines traced straight and true back and forth across the water's glassy surface. But then to both his and the swimmer's surprise, the serenity of the moment was suddenly shattered – pierced by a hell-bent scream and the sudden crash of lanky legs churning through water; then the sight of a second form stripped to the waist and russet-brown against the setting sun chugging hard to meet the first before the realisation of the ice-cold lake took hold. Then the cart-roll into a cannonball splash that sent a curtain of spray exploding into the air.

And so with rashness winning out over better judgement, the lawyer resolved to keep his vigil a while longer, though he did so with the smile and even the occasional chuckle of one entertained as he took in the subsequent splashing fights, the somersaults, the childlike echoes of laughter floating across the water, bouncing from the distant hillside and back up to his parking spot above the lake. Finally with dusk settling, both men made for shore, the trailing figure calling out something as he went. Something that sounded like, "Hey Stephen … you don't mind if we skip the bit with the nettles!" – which, while eliciting much laughter from his friend, could only cause the barrister further pause.

The two scrambled to recover their shed clothing, then sprinted for the shelter of their vehicle and soon the voices grew faint. One of the last things he made out for sure was the quiet one calling back to his friend, "Your phone. Quick, I need your phone." The lawyer watched intently as the man dialled, waited, then engaged in some urgent debate which seemed to raise both his ire and his voice. He heard him clearly call out, "I know … I know. Of course he won't talk to me. Just give him a message!" which was the last thing he would make out with complete certainty. The caller's mannerisms, however, continued to intrigue. He seemed at once eager and cautious, as if he had but a moment to get the wording of some critical sentiment exactly right. He couldn't be sure, but he thought he could hear him pass on wishes of good luck … and then some sort of advice. *"Tell him to imagine himself free … as free as he's ever wanted to be …"* Or so it sounded, at least. It was hard to be sure. The voice had fallen calmer now. Fainter. Barely distinguishable from the gentle breeze whistling through the car window and, of course with game time so near, the commentary from his car radio.

∿

"From the Auditorium in downtown Buffalo New York, welcome to Frontier Sports Radio and tonight's do-or-die battle for the last playoff spot in the Eastern Conference. The Toronto Centennials have pulled out all the stops, even dressing injured rookie sensation Casey Bruford in the hopes he can supply that same scoring punch that sparked the team to a ten-game winning streak back in November.

"Good evening ladies and gentlemen, I'm Mark Loggins coming to you from rink-side and the noise and the excitement down here is simply electric … sheer bedlam …"

∿

A thousand miles away, the two men sat in their car overlooking the lake. And while the figure in the driver's seat was taking great pains to adjust the heater to its full power so as to ease the chill from his still damp and quivering body, as soon as the puck dropped, the passenger door was flung open and his compatriot swung from the seat to prop himself against the open frame.

"If you don't mind," he explained, "I prefer to stand." Then he leaned forward and with his gaze set upon the water, rested his chin to his forearm to let the commentator's voice be his guide around the rink.

Soon the lake was but a faint mirror, shimmering beneath the clear night sky, alit by stars and moon, smooth and glassy, like untouched ice. Soon all sound had subsided save for the gentle drone of play-by-play set against the music of the distant woodlands; the gentle clacking of wind-lulled tree branches; the patient hoot of an owl; the whisper of the lapping shoreline … and in the distance – far beyond – the faint but unmistakable cry of a wolf.

Rob Ritchie is a born storyteller fluent in many genres. He is a gifted musician and lyricist as well as an incisive author. In the early 90s, he wrote, produced and toured three musical dramas throughout Ontario's schools. From 1996–2002 Rob served as piano player and contributing songwriter for the Canadian folk/roots group *Tanglefoot* (Borealis Records). He marked his return to performing with the release of his debut solo CD *Five O'clock Shadow* in 2004.

Rob resides in Wiarton, Ontario with his wife Ande and two boys, Josh and Toby. *Orphans of Winter* is Rob's first novel.